# WEST

## OF

# DODGE

***Also by Louis L'Amour
in Large Print:***

The Broken Gun
Crossfire Trail
Down the Long Hills
Education of a Wandering Man
Hondo
Lando
Law of the Desert Born
The Man Called Noon
The Outlaws of Mesquite
The Rustlers of West Fork
The Sky-Liners
Son of a Wanted Man
The Trail to Seven Pines
Valley of the Sun

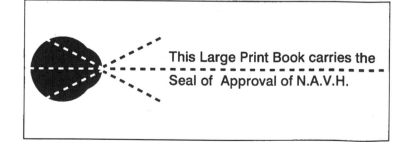

This Large Print Book carries the
Seal of Approval of N.A.V.H.

# WEST
# OF
# DODGE

Frontier Stories by

## LOUIS L'AMOUR

**Thorndike Press · Thorndike, Maine**

Published in 1996 by arrangement with Bantam Books,
a division of Bantam Doubleday Dell Publishing Group, Inc.

Thorndike Large Print ® Western Series.

The tree indicium is a trademark of Thorndike Press.

The text of this Large Print edition is unabridged.
Other aspects of the book may vary from the original edition.

Set in 16 pt. Plantin.

Printed in the United States on permanent paper.

**Library of Congress Cataloging in Publication Data**

L'Amour, Louis, 1908–
West of Dodge : frontier stories / by Louis L'Amour.
p.cm.
ISBN 0-7862-0803-1 (lg. print : hc)
1. Large type books. 2. Frontier and pioneer life — West
(U.S.) — Fiction. 3. West (U.S.) — Social life and customs
— Fiction. I. Title.
[PS3523.A446W47 1996b]
813'.52—dc20
96-20872

# CONTENTS

# INTRODUCTION

For the past couple of years I have been working on a biography of my father. It is a long and complicated process; he left behind no single document that explains the where or when of his life, let alone the reasons why he did many of the amazing things that he did. What little correspondence he was able to save over the years paints one picture. His personal journals, many of which were lost or not kept up on a regular basis, fill in some other areas. The writing he did in *Yondering* and *Education of a Wandering Man* I have found to be very useful but slightly slanted in the direction of whatever message he was trying to deliver at the moment.

I have tried to get as close to the story that I will be telling as is feasible. I have also tried to remain objective: Dad was fifty-three when I was born; when he was in his twenties he was a different — sometimes almost unrecognizable — character. The world that he lived in, the world that formed

7

him, was a different — almost unrecognizable — world.

So far, I have traveled the trail that he followed when he was forced to walk out of the Mojave Desert. I've searched out the houses, hotel rooms, boardinghouses, auto courts, lumber piles, and hobo jungles where Louis slept as a youth. I've talked my way through the security gates that now seal the waterfronts and rail yards. I've turned off the interstate and driven miles on the forgotten dirt roads that our nation had instead of highways seventy years ago. I have followed the winding route that my grandparents, my father, and his adopted brother traveled between 1923 and 1931, when they packed their last possessions in an old touring car and set out across the American West on a fruitless search for a better life.

One of the first steps in getting a handle on this project was going through every single thing my father left behind and examining each one carefully for clues. After he died I had spent quite a few weeks sorting out all of the stuff he left behind. That process had simply amounted to packing everything away in boxes labeled with one of five or six different categories, like "Fan Mail," "Pieces of Manuscripts," "Film and TV Treatments." Now I had to go back to those boxes and sort through everything page by page. It was sort of like being an archeologist digging a hole in the ground with a spoon and a toothbrush.

I found a tiny yellowed date book from 1924 that briefly documented the period when he became separated from his parents and walked and hitchhiked across New Mexico and Arizona trying to find them. Stuffed in the back of one of his 1960s-vintage journals were six pages that covered a different time period, about two weeks in June and July of 1936 when he was working as a mercenary fighting bandits and the Japanese in Shansi Province, China.

To find treasures such as these and many others, I have gone through Louis's papers carefully, examining everything I have in my possession. I've made it a point to read through every manuscript, notebook, letter, and file that he left behind, no matter how far afield the subject seemed to be. That is how I happened to find this collection of stories.

I'd finished months of checking old documents page by page and was starting to go through his other belongings, long disused briefcases, camping gear, anything that might give me a clue — like the name of a bookstore in Portland, Oregon, stamped on the inside cover of a book along with, miracle of miracles, the date. In one closet in Dad's office I found a treasure trove of artifacts that I myself had stashed there years earlier when cleaning up the office after he died. A ceremonial shield from New Guinea, a marvelous machete in a sheath of carved wood that Louis had taken from an Indonesian pirate, and several boxes of old carbon paper. The writing on the boxes was in German, and I now know through examining his journals from the World War II period that he "liberated" this carbon paper from an office in a German aluminum factory where he was quartered near the end of the war. I was methodically going through everything, so I opened the first box to find it still half full of disintegrating fifty-year-old carbons. The second box, however, seemed to contain blank typing paper. I was about to put it down when I saw the rusty outline of a paperclip on the top sheet. It wasn't old unused paper. . . . The box was full of short stories that had been dropped in facedown. And as I looked through them I realized that they weren't like the stories in most of the other L'Amour collections, old stories that had been published in the pulp magazines at one time or another — these were stories I didn't recognize, they were stories that had never been published before!

As I read them over carefully I began to put together the mystery of how they had come to be there. I'm guessing, but the story makes the most sense if it unfolds thus: In the 1950s the fiction magazine business was dying out, replaced by paperback books and television. Luckily for Louis, he was able to break into writing paperback originals in the mid-fifties, but there was a period of transition, a time when, although he was beginning to have some luck with the novels, he was still trying to sell short stories in a dying market. The majority of these newly discovered stories are a little less violent (several make it a point to avoid the typical kill-all-the-bad-guys-in-a-final-shootout ending), more character oriented, and have less lurid titles. This suggests to me that he was aiming more toward the slick-magazine market (like *The Saturday Evening Post*) than the rapidly failing pulps. He'd had some success in this area ("The Burning Hills" was first seen as a *Post* serial), but the slick market was becoming more and more crowded with ex–pulp authors and was publishing a good deal less fiction itself, and so my theory is these stories were never sold.

What all this means to you is that what

we have here is a collection of Louis L'Amour's western short stories that have never before been published. They are stories of higher quality than we have been able to release in quite a few years both because they were aimed at the more literary slicks and because they were written at the end of Louis's career in short stories and so were created by a writer at the top of his form.

I found enough new stories for two or three collections. Following *West of Dodge*, the next book or books (due out in spring 1997) will contain a group of fine western short stories and novellas that were the genesis of some of Dad's novels, like *Tucker* and *Kiowa Trail*. These are not stories like the ones that we published in the previous collections, *The Rider of the Ruby Hills* and *Trail to Crazy Man*, where the novel version was an almost identical story, only longer. These new stories are obviously experiments with the plots and themes that later became novels, but the story lines are quite different — in some cases better than the later novels.

The other group of stories that I found in that dusty box was the most exciting group for me. It was several adventure stories, but not in the comic book style of "Night over the Solomons" or "West of

Singapore." Some of these stories are more or less dramatized accounts of adventures from Louis's life, like the stories in *Yondering*, or they are pure fiction but are drawn from places he'd been or people he'd known. Not only did I find these to be interesting reading, but occasionally they contained clues to Louis's life and the people he knew.

That leads me to the last subject for this foreword. I have been traveling around interviewing various people for Louis's biography. I have been fortunate enough to have talked to several members of his family, people he knew in Oregon in the 1920s, Oklahoma in the 1930s, and Paris, France, and outlying areas in the 1940s. All have been most warm and gracious, very helpful and generous with their time. All have also been blessed with extraordinary memories, a true miracle, as I am asking them to remember back fifty, sixty, sometimes seventy years. Finding these people has been difficult, and now as I have been slowly working through all the easy ones, I am having to get more and more inventive about seeking these people out.

I am hoping that you, Louis's faithful readers, can help me out. In the back of this book I am going to place a list of names.

These are people who were an important part of Louis's life at one time or another, but now all I know are their names and where and when he knew them. If you know any of these people, please ask them if they would write to me at the address in back.

Many of the people on this list may be deceased, but if there is a family member or acquaintance who knew the person well I would also like to hear from them. I would be very grateful for any help anyone could give me. If you are one of these people on the list, please don't be shy or feel like you don't really know enough about Louis. I am very good at asking questions and I am only interested in the time period in which you knew him, nothing more.

So check out the names in back if you want to help and drop me a card at the address at the end of the list. I'll enjoy hearing from you. I hope you all enjoy this collection of stories — it surely was a find and we are proud to present it to you.

Until we meet again . . .

— BEAU L'AMOUR

# BEYOND THE CHAPARRAL

Jim Rossiter looked up as the boy came into the room. He smiled, a half-nostalgic smile, for this boy reminded him of himself . . . fifteen, no . . . twenty years ago.

"What is it, Mike?"

The boy's eyes were worried. He hesitated, not wanting to tell what he had to tell, yet knowing with his boyish wisdom that it was better for Rossiter to hear it from him, now.

"Lonnie Parker's back from prison."

Jim Rossiter did not move for a long, long minute. "I see," he said. "Thanks, Mike."

When the boy had gone he got to his feet and walked to the window, watching Mike cross the street. It was not easy to grow up in a western town when one wanted the things Mike Hamlin wanted.

Mike Hamlin did not want to punch cows, to drive a freight wagon or a stage. He did not want to own a ranch or even be the town marshal. Mike was a dreamer, a thinker, a reader. He might be a young

15

Shelley, a potential Calhoun. He was a boy born to thought, and that in a community where all the premiums were paid to action.

Jim Rossiter knew how it was with Mike, for Jim had been through it, too. He had fought this same battle, and had, after a fashion, won.

He had punched cows, all right. And for awhile he had driven a freight wagon. For a time he had been marshal of a trail town, but always with a book in his pocket. First it had been Plutarch — how many times had he read it? Then Plato, Thucydides, Shakespeare, and Shelley. The books had been given to him by a drunken remittance man, and he had passed them along to Mike. A drunken Englishman and Jim Rossiter, bearers of the torch. He smiled wryly at the thought.

But he had won. . . . He had gone east, had become a lawyer, had practiced there. However, memories of the land he left behind were always with him, the wide vistas, the battlements of the mesas, the vast towers of lonely cloud, the fringing pines . . . and the desert that gave so richly of its colors and its spaces.

So he had come back.

A scholar and a thinker in a land of action. A dreamer in a place of violence. He had returned because he loved the land. He stayed because he loved Magda Lane. That love, he had found, was one of the few things that gave his life any meaning.

And now Lonnie Parker was back.

Lonnie, who had given so much to Magda when she needed it, so much of gaiety and laughter. Lonnie Parker, who rode like a devil and fought like a madman. Lonnie, who could dance and laugh and be gay, and who was weak — that was Magda's word.

Rossiter, who was wise in the ways of women, knew that weakness had its appeal. There was a penalty for seeming strong, for those whose pride made it necessary to carry on as best they could although often lonely or unhappy. No one realized — few would take the time to look closely enough. The weak needed help . . . the strong? They needed nothing.

Sometimes it seemed the price of strength was loneliness and unhappiness . . . and the rewards for weakness were love, tenderness, and compassion.

Now Jim Rossiter stared down the dusty street, saw the bleak faces of the old buildings, lined with the wind etchings of years, saw the far plains and hills beyond, and knew the depths of all that loneliness.

Now that Lonnie was back it would spell the end of everything for him. Yet in a sense it would be a relief. Now the threat was over, the suspense would be gone.

He had never known Lonnie Parker. But he had heard of him. "Lonnie?" they would say, smiling a little. "There's no harm in him. Careless, maybe, but he doesn't mean anything by it."

Rossiter looked around the bare country law office. Three years, and he had come to love it, this quiet place, often too quiet, where he practiced law. He walked back to his desk and sat down. He was supposed to call tonight . . . should he?

Lonnie was back, and Magda had once told him herself, "I'm not sure, Jim. Perhaps I love him. I . . . I don't know. I was so alone then, and he understood and he needed me. Maybe that was all it was, but I just don't know."

Jim Rossiter was a tall, quiet man with wide shoulders and narrow hips. He liked people, and he made friends. Returning to the West he had come to this town where he was not known, and had brought a new kind of law with him.

In the past, the law had been an instrument of the big cattleman. The small men could not afford to hire the sort of lawyers

18

who could fight their cases against the big money. Jim Rossiter had taken their cases, and they had paid him, sometimes with cash, sometimes with cattle, sometimes with promises. Occasionally, he lost. More often, he won.

Soon he had cattle of his own, and he ran them on Tom Frisby's place, Frisby being one of the men for whom he had won a case.

Rossiter made enemies, but he also made friends. He rode miles to talk to newcomers; he even took cases out of the county. He was a good listener and his replies were always honest. There had been a mention of him for the legislature when the territory became a state.

He had seen Magda Lane the morning he arrived, and the sight of her had stopped him in the middle of the street.

She had been crossing toward him, a quiet, lovely girl with dark hair and gray-green eyes. She had looked up and seen him there, a tall, young man in a gray suit and black hat. Their eyes met, and Jim Rossiter looked quickly away, then walked on, his mouth dry, his heart pounding.

Even in that small town it was three weeks before they met. Rossiter saw her box handed to a younger girl to smuggle in to the box supper, and had detected the colors of the wrappings. He spent his last four dollars bidding on it, but he won.

They had talked then, and somehow he had found himself telling her of his boyhood, his ambitions, and why he had returned to the West.

Almost a month passed before she told him of Lonnie. It came about easily, a passing mention. Yet he had heard the story before. According to some, Lonnie had held up a stage in a moment of boyish excitement.

"But he didn't mean anything by it," she told him. "He isn't a bad boy."

Later, he was shocked when he discovered that Lonnie had been twenty-seven when he was sent to prison.

But others seemed to agree. Wild, yes . . . but not bad. Not Lonnie. Had a few drinks, maybe, they said. He'd spent most of the money in a poker game.

Only Frisby added a dissenting note. "Maybe he ain't bad," he said testily, "but I had money on that stage. Cost me a season's work so's he could set in that game with George Sprague."

The stolen money, Rossiter learned, had been taken in charge by the stage driver to buy dress goods, household items, and other odds and ends for a dozen of the squatters around Gentry. A boyish prank, some said, but it had cost the losers the few little things they needed most, the things they had saved many nickels and dimes to buy.

Yet, on the evenings when he visited Magda, he thought not at all of Lonnie. He was far away and Magda was here right now. They walked together, rode together. She was a widow — her husband had been killed by Indians after a marriage of only weeks. At a trying time in her life, Lonnie had come along and he had been helpful, considerate.

Now Lonnie was back, and he, Jim Rossiter was to visit Magda that evening.

It was not quite dark when he opened the gate in the white picket fence and started up the walk to the porch. He heard a low murmur of voices, then laughter. He felt his cheeks flush, and for an instant debated turning about. Yet he went on, and his foot was lifted for the first step up the porch when he saw them.

Lonnie was there and Magda was in his arms.

He turned abruptly and started back down the walk. He heard the door open behind, then Magda called, "Jim! Oh, Jim, no!"

He paused at the gate, his face stiff. "Sorry. I didn't mean to interrupt." He heard Lonnie's low chuckle.

She called again but he did not stop. He walked down the street and out of town, clear to the edge of the mesa. He stood there a long time in the darkness.

Leaving the restaurant at noon the next day, he saw Lonnie Parker, George Sprague, and Ed Blick sitting on the bench near the door. They looked up as he passed, and he had his first good look at Lonnie Parker.

He was tall and pink-cheeked, and had an easy smile. His eyes were bland, too innocent, and when he saw Rossiter he grinned insultingly. Lonnie wore two guns, and wore them tied down.

Sprague was a cold, silent man who rarely smiled. Ed Blick boasted of a local reputation as a gunman.

"That's him," Blick said. "That's the gent who's been takin' care of your girl for you, Lon."

"Much obliged," Lonnie called out. He turned to Ed Blick. "I seen him last night. He was just leavin'."

His face burning, Rossiter walked on. Mike Hamlin was waiting for him when he reached the office.

"Jim." He got up quickly. "You said

when I was fourteen you'd give me a job. I'm fourteen next week and I'd sure like to earn some money."

Rossiter sat down. This had been his idea, and he had talked to Mike's mother about it. If Mike was going to college he would have to begin to save. "All right, Mike," he said, "get on your horse and ride out to Frisby's. Tell him I sent you. Starting to-morrow morning, you're on the payroll at thirty a month."

Thirty a month was more than any boy in Spring Valley was making. A top hand only drew forty! Mike jumped up, full of excitement. "You'll earn it," Jim told him dryly, "and when you show you can handle it, I'll go up to forty." He grinned suddenly. "Now get at it . . . and save your money!"

During the week that followed he made no effort to see Magda, and carefully stayed clear of the places where she was most likely to be. He avoided mail time at the post office and began to eat more and more at home. Yet he could not close his ears nor his eyes, and there was talk around.

Lonnie was to marry Magda, he heard that twice. He saw them on the street to-gether, heard them laughing. Work was piling up for him and he lost himself in it. And there was trouble around the country.

23

Ed Blick had returned to town from Durango, where he had killed a man.

Lonnie spent most of his time with Sprague and Blick. He had made no effort to rustle a job, but he seemed to have money. Once Jim saw him buying drinks in Kelly's, and he stripped the bills from a large roll.

Rossiter was working late over a brief when Frisby came to his office. He was a solid, hardworking man, but he looked tired now, and he was unshaven.

"Jim," he came to the point at once, "we're losin' cows. Some of yours, some of mine, a few other brands."

During the night Mike Hamlin had heard the sound of hooves. He had gotten out of bed in the bunkhouse and had caught up a horse. There was a smell of dust when he hit the grass country, and at daybreak the boy had found the tracks. At least thirty head had been driven off by four men.

"They drove into the brush east of my place. When we tried to follow, somebody shot at us."

East of the Frisby place was a dense thicket of the black chaparral, a thicket that covered twenty square miles, a thorny, ugly growth of brush through which there were few trails, and none of them used except by wild game or strays. A rider could see no more than a few yards at any time. It was no place to ride with a rifleman waiting for you.

"I'd better get Mike out of there," he said. "I don't want him hurt."

"Don't do it, Jim," Frisby advised. "You'd break his heart. He's a might set on provin' himself to you. He sets up night after night with them books, but he figures he's got to earn his money, too. He's makin' a hand, Jim."

Frisby was right, of course. To take the boy off the job would hurt his pride and deprive him of the money he would need if he were going to college. As for the cattle . . . Rossiter walked across the street to the sheriff's office.

George Sprague was standing in front of Kelly's smoking a cigar, and Jim was conscious of the man's sudden attention.

He had never liked Sprague, and never had known him. The man always had money, and he gambled, although he never seemed to win big . . . but he always had cash. He disappeared at intervals and would be gone for several days, sometimes a couple of weeks. His companion on these rides was usually Ed Blick. Now it was also Lonnie Parker.

Sheriff Mulcahy was a solid, serious man. A hard worker, intent on his job. "Third complaint this week," he said. "Folks gettin' hit mighty hard. Got any ideas?"

Rossiter hesitated the merest instant. "No," he said, "not yet."

Stepping out of the sheriff's office, he came face to face with Magda Lane.

"Jim!" Her eyes were serious. "What's happened? You haven't been to see me."

"The last time I called," he said quietly, "you seemed rather preoccupied."

"Jim." She caught his sleeve. "I've wanted to talk to you about that. You made a mistake. You — "

"I think I made my mistake," he said, his voice tightening, "at a box supper. Some time ago." Abruptly he stepped around her and walked on.

A moment later, he was furious with himself. He could have listened . . . maybe there was an explanation. So many things seemed what they were not. Still, what explanation could there be? And it was all over town that she was to marry Lonnie Parker.

Saddling his horse, he rode out of town. The turmoil aroused by seeing her demanded action, and he rode swiftly. He was crossing the plains toward Frisby's when, far and away to the east, beyond the chaparral, he saw a smoke column. He drew up, watching.

The smoke was high and straight. As he watched, the column broke, puffed, then became straight again.

Smoke signals . . . but the days of the Indian outbreaks were over. He turned in his saddle, and from the ridge back of Gentry he saw another signal. Even as he looked, it died out and was gone. Somebody from town was signaling to somebody out there beyond the chaparral.

Taking a sight on that first signal, he started toward it, passing Frisby's road without turning in.

There was only one reason of which he could think for a smoke signal now. Somebody in town would be sending word to their rustlers that the sheriff had been notified, or that he was riding. Probably the former. He, Rossiter reflected, was only a cow town lawyer, and not a man to be feared.

He rode into Yucca Canyon and followed it north, then climbed the steel dust out of it, skirted the mesa, and headed east again. He was high in the chaparral now, where it thinned out and merged with a scattered growth of juniper. Weaving his way through, he was almost to the other side when he came upon the tracks of cattle.

It was a good-sized herd, and it had come out of the chaparral not long before. From droppings he spotted, he judged the herd had been moved not more than four or five hours before.

The country grew increasingly rugged. It was an area into which he had never ventured before, a wild, broken country of canyons and mesas with rare water holes. By sundown he was too far out to turn back. And he had no bedroll with him, no coffee, and worst of all . . . no gun.

Yet to turn back now would be worse than foolish. This was, without doubt, a rustled herd. Time enough to return when he discovered their destination. As there were still some minutes of daylight, he pushed on. On his right was a long tongue of a lava flow, to the left a broken, serrated ridge of rusty rock. Before him, at some distance, lifted the wall of the mountain range, and it seemed the cattle were being driven into a dead end.

Coolness touched his face and the trail dipped down. The desert was gone, and there was a sparse growth of buffalo grass that thickened and grew rich as he moved ahead. The lava flow now towered above his head and the trail dipped down, and rounded a shoulder of the lava. He found himself in a long, shallow valley between the flow and the pine-clad range. And along the bottom grazed more than a hundred head of cattle.

He swung the steel dust quickly right to get the background of the lava for concealment. Then he walked his mount forward until he could see the thin trail of smoke from a starting fire. Concealing his horse, he walked down the slope through the trees.

When he reached a spot near the camp the smoke had ceased, but the fire was blazing cheerfully. A stocky man with a tough, easy manner about him worked around the fire. He wore chaps, a faded red flannel shirt, a battered hat . . . and a gun.

Rossiter turned and started back through the trees. If he cut across country he could have Mulcahy and a posse here shortly after daybreak.

A pound of hooves stopped him and he merged his body with a pine tree and waited, alert for trouble. Through an opening between trees he saw three riders. Two men and a boy.

A boy . . .

With a tight feeling in his chest he turned abruptly about and carefully worked his way back toward the camp. Ed Blick, George Sprague — and Mike Hamlin.

Mike's face was white, but he was game. His hands were lashed to the pommel of his saddle.

The red-shirted man looked up. "What goes on?" He glanced from the boy to Sprague.

"Found him workin' our trail like an Injun."

The man with the red shirt straightened and dropped the skillet. "I don't like this, George. I don't like it a bit."

"What else can we do?"

"We can leave the country."

"For a kid?" Sprague began to build a smoke. "Don't be a fool."

"Lonnie said Frisby went to Rossiter, then Rossiter to the sheriff." Blick was talking. "I don't like it, George."

"You afraid of Rossiter?"

"That lawyer?" Blick's contempt was obvious. "Mulcahy's the one who worries me. He's a bulldog."

"Leave him to me."

Their conclusion had been obvious. Mike Hamlin had found their trail, and now he had seen them. They must leave the country or kill him. And they had just said they would not leave the country.

The red-shirted man had not moved, and Rossiter could see the indecision in his face. Whatever else this man might be, Rossiter could see that he was no murderer. The man did not like any part of it, but apparently could not decide on a course of action.

Rossiter had no gun. . . . He had been a fool to go unarmed, but he had intended only to ride to Frisby's to talk to Mike and look over the situation on the spot. He had never considered hunting the thieves himself, but there came a time when a man had to fork his own broncs.

Whatever they would do would be done at once. There was no time to ride for help. Blick lifted Hamlin from the saddle and put the boy on the ground some distance away. The red-shirted man watched him, his face stiff. Then Blick and Sprague slid the saddles from their horses and led them out to picket. Jim worked his way through the brush until he was close to the fire.

Rossiter knew there was little time and he had to gamble. "You going to let them kill that boy?" he asked quietly.

The man's head came up sharply. "Who's that?"

"I asked if you were going to let them kill that boy?"

He saw Rossiter now. His eyes measured him coolly. "You want them stopped," he said, "you stop them."

"I wasn't expecting trouble. I'm not packing a gun."

It was his life he was chancing as well as Mike's. Yet he believed he knew men, and in this one there was a basic manhood, a remnant of personal pride and integrity. Each man has his code, no matter how far down the scale.

The fellow got to his feet and strolled over to his war bag. From it he took a battered Colt. "Catch," he said, and walked back to the fire.

Jim Rossiter stepped back into the shadows, gun in hand. He had seen Mike's eyes on him, and in Mike's eyes there had been doubt. Rossiter was a reader of books, a thinker . . . and this was time for violence.

Sprague and Blick came back to the fire and Sprague looked sharply around. "Did I hear you talkin'?"

"To the kid. I asked if he was hungry."

Sprague studied the man for a long minute, suspicion thick upon him. "Don't waste the grub." He started to sit down, then saw the gap in the open war bag. With a quick stride he stepped to the boy and rolled him over, glanced at the rawhide that bound him, then looked around on the ground.

Blick was puzzled but alert. The man in the red shirt stood very still, pale to the lips.

The gambler straightened up and turned slowly. "Bill, where's that other gun of yours?"

"I ain't seen it."

Rossiter smelled the acrid smell of wood smoke. There was the coolness of a low place and damp grass around him. Out on the meadow a quail called.

"You shoved it down in your pack last night. It ain't there now."

"Ain't it?"

Bill knew he was in a corner, but he was not a frightened man. It was two to one, and he did not know whether the man in the shadows would stand by him — or even if he was still present.

"I'm not fooling, Bill. I won't stand for a double-cross."

"And I won't stand for killin' the kid."

Sprague's mind was made up. Ed Blick knew it, and Ed moved left a little. Bill saw that move and knew what it meant. His tongue touched his lips, and his eyes flickered toward the pines.

Rossiter took an easy step forward, bringing him into the half-light. "If you're looking for the gun, Sprague, here it is."

The gun was easy in hand . . . Blick saw something then, and it bothered him. No lawyer ever held a gun like that. He tried to speak, to warn Sprague, but Rossiter was speaking.

"Bill," he said, "untie that boy."

Sprague's lips had thinned down against his teeth. The corners of his mouth pulled down, and the skin on his face looked tight and hard. "Leave him be. I'm not backing up for no cow town lawyer."

"Watch it, George," Blick said. "I don't like this."

"He doesn't dare shoot. One of us will get him."

"Untie the kid, Bill." Rossiter's eyes were on Sprague, a corner of attention for Blick. He sensed that Blick was wiser at this sort of thing than Sprague. Blick was dangerous but he would start nothing. It would be Sprague who would move first.

Bill walked across to Mike and, dropping on his knees, began to untie him.

"Back off, Bill," Sprague warned, "or I'll kill you, too." He crouched a bit, bending his knees ever so slightly. "Get ready, Ed."

"George!" There was sudden panic in Blick's voice. "Don't try — !"

Sprague threw himself left and grabbed for his gun. It was swinging up when Rossiter shot him. Rossiter fired once, the bullet smashing Sprague in the half-parted teeth, and then he swung the gun. He felt Blick's shot burn him, then steadied and fired. Blick backed up two steps and sat down. Then he clasped his stomach as if with cramp and rolled over on his side and lay there, unmoving.

Bill touched his lips with his tongue. "For a lawyer," he said sincerely, "you can shoot."

Rossiter lowered the gun. Mike was sitting up, rubbing his arms. He walked over to where the other man's kit lay on the ground and dropped the pistol onto a blanket. "Much obliged, Bill. Now you'd better saddle up and ride."

"Sure."

Bill turned to go, then stopped. "That gun there. I got it secondhand." He rubbed his palms down his chaps. "I'll need a road stake. You figure it's worth twenty bucks to you?"

Rossiter drew a coin from his pocket and tossed it to Bill. It gleamed gold in the firelight. "It's a bargain, Bill. A good buy."

Bill hesitated, then said quietly, "I never killed no kids, mister."

Nobody was in the street when they rode

in at daybreak. There was a rooster crowing and somewhere a water bucket rattled, then a pump squeaked. Rossiter walked his horse up the street, leading two others, the bodies of Sprague and Blick across them.

Mike started to turn his horse toward home, then said, "You never said you could shoot like that, Jim."

"In a lifetime, Mike, a man does many things."

Mulcahy came from the door of his house, hair freshly combed. "Ain't a nice sight before breakfast, Jim." Mulcahy glanced at the two dead men. "You want me to put out a warrant for this Bill character?"

"No evidence," Rossiter replied. "Let him be. The last of them is Lonnie Parker. I want you to let me come along."

"Tomorrow," the sheriff said.

It was noon when he got out of bed. He bathed, shaved, and dressed carefully, not thinking of what was to come. He left Bill's gun on the dresser and went to a chest in the corner and got out a belt, holster, and gun. The gun was a .44 Russian, a Smith & Wesson six-shooter. He checked the loads and the balance, then walked out into the street.

Magda was just leaving her gate. She hesitated, waiting for him. She looked from the gun to his eyes, surprised. "Jim . . . what are you doing?"

He told her quietly of what happened, and of Bill riding away.

"But," she protested, "if they are dead and Bill is gone — "

"There were four rustlers, Magda," he said gently. "I don't know what the other one will do."

She got it then and he saw her face go white. One hand caught the gate and she stared at him. "Jim!" Her voice was a whisper. "Oh, Jim!"

He turned away. "I don't want trouble, Mag. I'm going to try to take care of him for you. After all," he said with grim humor, "he may need a lawyer."

Sheriff Mulcahy was waiting up the street in front of his office. The time had come.

He was gone three steps before she cried out, and then she ran to him, caught his arm.

"Jim Rossiter, you listen to me. You take care of yourself! No matter what happens, Jim! Jim, believe me, there was never anybody else — nobody at all — not after I met you. The night he came to town I . . .

I was just so glad to see him, and then you saw us and you wouldn't talk to me. He took too much for granted, but so did you."

His eyes held hers for a long, long minute. Up the street a door slammed, and there were boots on the boardwalk. He smiled, and squeezed her arm. "All right, Mag. I believe you."

He turned then, and felt the sun's heat on his shoulders and felt the dust puff under his boot soles, and he walked away up the street, seeing Lonnie Parker standing there in the open, waiting for them. And he was not worried. He was not worried at all.

# A HUSBAND FOR JANEY

H e had been walking since an hour before sun-up, but now the air had grown warm and he could hear the sound of running water. Sunlight fell through the leaves and dappled the trail with light and shadow, and when he rounded the bend of the path he saw the girl dipping a bucket into a mountain stream.

He was a tall boy, just turned eighteen, and four months from his home on a woods farm in East Texas. He looked at the girl and he swallowed, his Adam's apple bobbing in a throat that seemed unusually long, rising as it did from the wide, too-loose collar of his homespun shirt.

He swallowed again and cleared his throat. The girl looked up, suddenly wide-eyed, and then she straightened, her lips drawing together and one quick hand brushing a strand of dark hair back from her flushed cheek. "Howdy, ma'am," he said, his accent soft with East Texas music. "Sure didn't aim to scare you none."

39

"It . . . it's all right." Her alarm was fading with her curiosity. "Are you goin' to the goldfields?"

A measure of pride and manly assurance came into his voice. "I reckon. I aim to git me money to go back home to Texas an' buy a farm."

They faced each other across the stream. The boy swallowed, nervous with the silence. "You . . . your pa washin' gold about here?"

"Yes . . . Well, he was . . . He's gone to the settlement. He's been gone three weeks."

The boy nodded gravely. It had taken him two days to walk up from Angel's Camp, and with that awareness that comes to those who walk the trails he knew her father was not coming back. It was a bad time to be traveling with gold in one's poke.

"You doin' all right?" he asked. "You an' your ma?"

Janey hesitated, rubbing her palms on her apron. She was shy but she didn't want him to go off on his way, for it was lonely with no one about of her own age, and without even neighbors except for Richter. "Ma — she's just back here. Would you like some coffee? We've some fresh."

He crossed the stream on the rounded

stones and took her wooden bucket. "Lemme fetch it for you," he said. "It's a big bucket for such a little girl."

She flashed her eyes at him. "I ain't . . . I mean, I'm not so young! I'm sixteen!"

He grinned at her. "You're nigh to it."

Mrs. Peters looked up from the fire she was tending. She saw the two coming down the trail and her heart seemed to catch with quick realization. And yes, with relief. She carefully noted the boy's serious expression, and when he put the bucket down on the flat rock she saw how his eyes went to Janey's and her quick, flirting glance. This was a strong young man with sloping shoulders and an open, honest look about him.

"Howdy, ma'am." He felt more sure of himself with the older woman. She reminded him of his aunt. "My name is Meadows. Folks back home call me Tandy."

"Glad to know you, Tandy. I'm Mrs. Peters. Jane, get this young man a cup. The coffee's hot." She looked at the boy, liking his clean, boyish face and handsome smile. "Goin' far?"

"To the head of the crick." He slid the pack from his back and placed it on the

41

ground, and beside it his Roper four-shot revolving shotgun. "I figure to stake me a claim."

It was cool and pleasant under the great, arching limbs of the trees. There had been some work done on the bench where the stream curved wide, and the cabin was back under the trees out of the heat. A line had been strung for the washing from its corner to the nearest tree.

He stole a glance at the girl and caught her looking at him. She smiled quickly and looked away, flushing a little. His own face colored and he swallowed.

Em Peters filled the cup Jane brought, and he accepted it gratefully. He had started without breakfast, not liking to take the time to fix a decent meal. Em Peters looked at him thoughtfully. He was a well-mannered boy, and she suddenly knew, desperately, that he must not leave. She must keep him here, for Janey.

It wasn't like back home, where there were lots of boys, nice boys from families one had grown up with, and who would work at honest, respectable work. Out here one never knew what sort of people would be coming around. Dave had been small protection, but where there was a man around — well, it was a good feeling.

Dave should never have come west, of course. It was Roy Bacon who talked him into it, and they had sold their place and started out. The wagon and team used up most of the money, and by the time they arrived in California there was almost nothing left. Dave had been a quiet, serious man who needed a steady job or business in a small town. She knew that now, although she had not tried to dissuade him when he talked of going to California. It was the one big thing in Dave's life, and fit for it or not, she knew he had loved it. Crossing the plains, he had been happy. Only at the end, when they arrived, had he been frightened.

Em Peters knew with deep sadness that Dave was not coming back. When he had been two days overdue she knew it, for Dave always had been precise about things. Nor was he a man to drink or gamble. The first rush of the gold hunting was over and some of the tougher men who had been unable to find a good claim, or had lacked the energy or persistence to work one, had taken to the trails. Murders were the order of the day even along the creeks, and in the towns it was worse, much worse.

It was not herself for whom she was

worried. She would manage — she always had. It was Janey.

Em Peters had seen the speculative eyes of more than one man who came along the trail or paused for a few minutes. Worst of all, there was Richter. She had been afraid of him from the first. Had warned Dave he was not to be trusted, but Dave had waved off her objections because Richter had showed him how to build a rocker, actually helping with the work.

Only two days before, he had come to her. "Ma'am," he said, "I hate to say this here, but I figure somethin' happened to Dave."

"I'm afraid so."

"You two," Richter said, "it ain't safe for you. I figured maybe it'd be better if I moved over here."

Her throat had grown tight, for she could see his eyes following Janey. "We'll be all right," she had said.

He cocked his head. "Maybe," he said, "but that there girl o' yourn, she sets a man's blood to boilin'. If I was you, I'd find her a husband mighty quick."

"Janey has plenty of time." She forced herself to be calm, and not to answer him as sharply as she felt like doing. "And we'll be all right." Her voice stiffened a little.

"Men in the goldfields won't allow good women to be molested. I've heard of men being hung just for speaking the wrong thing to a woman."

Richter had heard of it, too, and he did not like the thought. It irritated him that she should mention it. "Oh, sure!" he said. "But you never can tell. Fact is," he said, rubbing his unshaven jaw, "I might marry her myself."

Em Peters had her limits, and this was it. "Why, I'd never hear of such a thing!" she exclaimed. "I would rather see Janey dead than married to you, Carl Richter! You're no man for a girl like Janey!"

Angry blood darkened his cheeks and his eyes grew ugly. "You ain't so high-falutin'," he said angrily. "Gettin' 'long by yourselves ain't goin' to be so easy. You try it, an' see!" He had stomped off angrily, but Em had said nothing to Janey, beyond the suggestion that she avoid him. Janey needed no urging. Richter was nearing fifty, a big, dirty man whose cabin was a boar's nest of unwashed clothing and stale smells.

Tandy liked his coffee. He nursed the cup in his hands, taking his time and not wanting to leave. Janey was suddenly very busy, stirring the fire, looking into pots, taking clothes from the line.

Em Peters looked down at Tandy, and then her eyes went down the creek to where it emerged from the shadowing trees into sunshine. The thought that Dave was not coming back waited in the back of her consciousness, waited for the night when she could lie alone and hold her grief tightly to her. There was not time for grief now, and she could not let Janey know that hope was gone. Janey was too young for that. She had no experience with grief, none of the hard-found knowledge that all things change, that nothing remains the same. In time Janey would know, but there was time.

"You . . . you'll be goin' on?" she asked gently. "You have something in mind?"

"Not really, ma'am. Just aimed to find me a bench somewhere an' start workin'. I'm a good worker," he said, looking up at her. "My aunt Esther always did say I was the strongest boy she knew. For my age, that is," he added modestly.

Em Peters knew no way of approaching it with care. She looked now for the words, hoping they could come, knowing that somehow they had to come. This was a good boy, a boy from a good, simple, hard-working family. He — whatever it was, she

46

forgot, seeing Richter coming up the path.

Richter did not notice Tandy Meadows. He was full of his own thoughts. It was stupid, he decided, to let the woman put him off. Why, there wasn't another man in twenty miles!

"You there!" he said to Em. "Changed your mind about me marryin' Janey? If you ain't, you better! I done made up my mind! No use this here claim standin' idle! No use that there girl runnin' around loose, botherin' men, worryin' me."

They all froze, looking at the big man in astonishment. "Carl Richter." Em Peters's voice was level. "You get out of here! You may go away and don't come back, or the first time the men from the mines come by, I'll set them on you!"

Richter laughed. "Why, that's . . ." His voice broke and trailed off, for the tall young boy was standing there, looking at him calmly. "Who the hell are you?" Richter demanded.

"You-all," Tandy Meadows said, in his soft East Texas voice, "heard what the lady said. She said you should go."

Richter's eyes went cruel. He had been startled, but then he saw this was only a boy, and a country boy at that. "Shut your trap, pup!" he said. "Beat it. I'll give you what's coming to you 'less you git yourself down the road."

"Ain't figurin' on it," Tandy said quietly. He moved over to stand between Carl Richter and the women.

Richter hesitated. This youngster was bigger than he had thought. He had big hands, and in the lean, youthful body there was a studied negligence that warned him whatever else this boy might be, he had probably done enough fighting around school and the farms to take care of himself. All the boyish shyness was gone now, and Tandy was sure of himself.

"You got no business here," Richter growled. "You git out while the gittin's good. I'm coming back an' you better be out of here. If you ain't," he added, "there'll be a shootin'."

He turned abruptly and walked away, and Tandy looked after him, faint worry in his eyes. But Janey rushed to him at once. "Thank you!" she exclaimed. "I — I can't imagine what got into him." She blushed with embarrassment. "He's talking like a crazy man."

"I reckon." He swallowed, his eyes going to Em. And Em Peters was frightened. What had she drawn this poor boy into? Richter had killed men. She knew that. A man down in town had told Dave about it. Richter had killed several men with a gun. One man he had beaten to death with a neck yoke. He was a bitter, revengeful man.

Tandy picked up his cup. "Any more o' that there coffee, ma'am?" he asked gently.

She gave it to him, then held the pot. "Tandy," she said, "you'd better go. We'll manage all right. I don't want any trouble."

He was still a boy, but there was steel in him. The eyes into which she looked now were cool, but they were eyes strangely mature. "I reckon I'll stay, ma'am. Down where I come from, we don't back water for no man.

"I figure," he added, "I'd better stick aroun' until your own man fetches back with the supplies. Meanwhilst, I can work some on that rocker. Never worked one o' them an' the practice won't do me harm."

He had been working for two hours when Janey came down the path with a pot of coffee and two big sandwiches. She had changed her dress and the one she wore now was freshly smoothed and clean. She looked at him, longing to be pretty in his eyes, and finding that the quick wonder in them was even more than she had hoped.

"Are you getting any color?" she asked.

"Pa said this was one of the best claims along the creek."

"Seems good," he agreed, accepting the coffee and sandwiches. Between bites he looked at her. "You sparkin' anybody?" he asked.

Her chin lifted. "Who wants to know?" He said nothing to that and she glanced at him. "Don't you suppose I know any boys? Don't you suppose they would like me?"

There was not another boy within miles, and Janey Peters had not seen a boy even close to her own age for four months, but he was not going to know *that*.

"Sure. I figure so."

"Well, then. Don't you be sayin' I don't know any boys! I do so!"

He looked at her in complete astonishment. "Why . . ." He was utterly flabbergasted. "I didn't say that — !"

"You did so, Tandy Meadows! You did so!" Tears welled into her eyes and panic tightened in his throat.

"No, ma'am!" he protested desperately. "I never done it! I mean — well, I sure didn't aim to!"

"You needn't think you can come along here an' . . . an' . . . don't call me *ma'am!* "

He got up. "Guess I better get back to

work," he said lamely. Women! He thought, who could ever figure them out? No matter what a man said, he was always in the wrong. There was no logic in them.

Janey pouted, occasionally stealing a careful look at Tandy to be sure he was feeling sufficiently miserable. Soon she began to feel miserable herself. She turned a little bit toward him, but he avoided her eyes. She moved her feet on the gravel, and he stole a look at her shoes and ankles. Suddenly aware of her scuffed shoes, she hastily drew her feet under her skirt, flushing with embarrassment.

Tandy had not noticed. He dipped up water with a wooden bucket and let some run into the rocker. Then, holding the bucket with one hand, he began to rock vigorously, letting water trickle over the edge of the bucket. The water and the rocking washed the smaller sizes of gravel through the screen into the apron. The abrupt stops at the end of each stroke jarred the gravel against the sides of the rocker.

Putting down the bucket, he mashed up some chunks of clay and mixed them in water, agitating the rocker as he did so. When no more particles came through the screen, he searched the heavier gravel for any nuggets of a size too large to pass through the mesh. Then he dumped the tailings and filled the rocker once more. Sweat darkened his shirt and trickled down his cheeks. Acutely conscious of Janey's presence, he said nothing. He was sure he had grossly offended her, but suddenly she was bending over the apron. "Oh, you've got some color!" she exclaimed. "A lot!"

He swept the particles together and then blew out the lighter grains of sand. It was not, he decided, a bad bit of work.

Several times Em Peters came to the edge of the bank and looked down toward the bench. There was no more talking now. Tandy was working hard and without any breaks. Janey hovered about him excitedly. Once they found a nugget the size of the end of his finger and she danced with excitement.

When he cleaned the riffles and the apron after two hours of work, he had nearly an ounce and a half of gold to put in the leather sack.

It *was* a good claim. No wonder that Richter was bothering around. Trust him to be thinking of the claim as well as Janey. Although, he decided, beginning to show some intelligence about girls, it would be better not to suggest that to her. At sundown, when he walked wearily back up the path to the cabin, he had two ounces of gold.

Em smiled at him. "My! You've worked hard! How did it go? Did Janey bother you?"

"Naw!" he said. "I didn't even know she was there."

Janey flared. "Oh — Oh, you didn't?" She flounced away angrily and began rattling pans.

Tandy stared after her, deeply puzzled. Em put her hand on his shoulder. "That's all right, Tandy," she said. "Girls are like that."

"That's right!" Janey called out angrily. "Take his side!" She burst into tears and walked away toward the edge of the woods.

Tandy stared after her helplessly, and then dried his hands and followed. "Look," he protested. "I didn't — "

"Oh, go away!" She turned half around, not looking at him. "Don't talk to me!"

He looked at the back of her neck where little whorls of hair curled against a whiteness the sun had not reached. He hesitated, tempted to kiss her neck, but the thought made him flush guiltily. Instead, he lifted a tentative hand to her shoulder.

She let it rest there a minute, then jerked her shoulder away. "Don't *touch* me!" she said.

He looked at her, then slowly turned and walked back to the fire where Em smiled kindly and handed him a plate and a cup. He sat down, suddenly conscious of his hunger, and began to eat. He was enjoying the food hugely when he saw Janey come up to the fire, her face streaked with tears. She glared at him. "That's it — *eat!* All you ever think about is *eating!* "

Tandy looked at her in astonishment, his mind filled with protest. Words rose to his lips but were stifled there. He looked at his food, and suddenly his appetite was gone. Disgustedly, he got to his feet. Whoever could figure a girl out, anyway? What was she mad about?

He turned back to Em. "Ma'am," he said, his eyes showing his misery, "I reckon I'm makin' trouble here. Janey, she's some aggravated with me, so I figure you'd best take this here gold. I'll be walkin' along."

"She's not really angry," Em said. "Girls are that way. I expect they always will be. A girl has to fuss a certain amount or she doesn't feel right."

"I don't know about that," he said doubtfully. "Sally, she — "

Janey had turned on him. "So that's it! You've got a — a — " Tears rose to her eyes. "You've got a sweetheart!"

"No such thing!" he protested.

"Well." Her head came up and her eyes flared. "I don't *care!*"

Janey turned away from him, her chin high. He pushed the gold sack into Em Peters's hand and picked up his pack and shotgun and turned away. Em stared after him helplessly, and Janey, hearing his retreating footsteps, turned sharply, pure agony in her eyes. She took an involuntary step after him, then stopped. Tandy Meadows walked into the brush, and they heard him moving away toward the main trail.

Wearily, Em Peters began to scrape the food from the dishes. Neither of them saw Richter until he was close alongside them. "Pulled out, did he? I figured he would."

Em Peters faced him. "You go away, Carl Richter! I don't want you around here, nor any of your kind!"

Richter laughed. "Don't be a fool!" he said. "I'm stayin'. You'll get used to me." He looked around. "Janey, you pour me some of that coffee."

"I'll do no such thing!"

Richter's face turned ugly. With a quick step, he grabbed for her.

"I'd not be doin' that."

All eyes turned toward Tandy Meadows,

who had come silently back through the trees.

Carl Richter stood very still, choking with fury. He had thought the boy was gone. By the — ! He'd show him. He wheeled and started for his rifle.

"Go ahead." Tandy was calm. "You pick that rifle up. That's what I want."

"I'll kill you!" Richter shouted.

"I reckon not." Tandy Meadows eared back the Roper's hammer.

Not over fifteen yards separated them. Richter considered that and four loads of buckshot in the cylinder of the boy's shotgun and felt a little sick. He backed off warily from the rifle. "I ain't huntin' no trouble!" he said hoarsely.

"Then you start travelin', mister. I see you along this crick again, an' I'll fill your measly hide with buckshot. You head for Hangtown, you hear me?"

"I got a claim!" Richter protested.

"You get you another one." Tandy Meadows had come from a country where there were few girls but lots of fights. What he lacked in knowledge of the one he more than made up with the other. "You don't get no second chance. Next time I just start a-shootin'."

He stood there, watching Richter start

down the trail. He felt a hand rest lightly on his sleeve. Janey said nothing at all, watching the dark figure on the evening trail.

"Did," the voice was low, "did you like Sally . . . very much?"

"Uh-huh."

"Did . . . do you like her better than me?"

"Not near so much," he said.

She moved against him, her head close to his shoulder. Sally was his sister, but he wasn't going to tell Janey that.

He was beginning to learn about women.

# WEST OF
# DODGE

Lance Kilkenny looked across the counter at the man with the narrow face and the scar on his jaw. "Watch yourself," Hillman said. "This is Tom Stroud's town. He's marshal here, and he's poison for gunfighters."

"I'll be all right." Kilkenny paid for his shells and walked to the door, a tall, spare man looking much less than his two hundred pounds. His was a narrow, Hamletlike face with high cheekbones and green eyes.

His walk was that of a woodsman rather than a rider, but Hillman had known at once that he wore the two Colts for use rather than for show.

It disturbed Kilkenny to find himself known here, as a gunfighter if not by name. Here he had planned to rest, to hunt a job, to stay out of trouble.

Of Marshal Tom Stroud he knew nothing beyond the bare fact that some two months before Stroud had killed Jim Denton in a Main Street gun battle.

Yet Kilkenny needed no introduction to

reputation-hunting marshals. There had been Old John Selman and others who fattened their records on killing gunfighters — and were rarely particular about an even break.

At the hitch rail Kilkenny studied his gaunt, long-legged buckskin. The horse needed the rest, and badly. Torn between dislike for trouble and consideration for his horse, the needs of the horse won.

He headed for the livery. Glancing back at the store, he saw a slope-shouldered man with dark hair and eyes step awkwardly into the doorway to watch him ride away. Something about the way the man stood, one hand braced against the wall, made Kilkenny think that he was a cripple.

Hillman had not guessed his name. That was fortunate. A man of his sort might guess if given time . . . of his sort . . . now where had that thought come from? Rubbing down the buckskin, Kilkenny gave consideration to the idea. What was Hillman's sort?

Something about the storekeeper had marked him in Kilkenny's mind, and it left him uneasy that he could not make a proper estimate of his instinct about the man, yet something disturbed him, left him wary and uncertain.

Hillman was a man in his thirties, as tall

as Kilkenny, and only a little bulkier, but probably no heavier. He had a careful, measuring eye.

From the door of the livery stable Kilkenny studied the street, still thinking of Hillman and Stroud. Usually, a storekeeper would want to avoid trouble in a town. Maybe he believed a warning would cause Kilkenny to move on. Building a smoke, he considered that.

Like many western towns, this one was divided into two sections. One was a rough collection of saloons, shanties, and bawdy houses along the railroad and backed by a maze of corrals and feed sheds where cattlemen put up their herds while waiting for shipment east. This was the old town, the town that had been built by the hard-drinking track crews and cattle buyers in the wild days before the town had ever thought to build a church or a schoolhouse.

Running at right angles to the tracks was the newer Main Street. Away from the smell and the flies of the holding pens, it had been built by the merchants who came as the town grew. There were carefully built buildings made of whitewashed planks or brick, with boardwalks connecting one to the next so that the shopper or businessman only occasionally had to brave the rutted mud of the street. There was only one saloon in this part of town, and it was a pretentious affair situated on the ground floor of the new two-story hotel. Behind the stores of the street were grids of one- to five-acre lots where the townspeople lived. Most of the houses had vegetable gardens growing corn and tomatoes, and each had a carriage house, stable, or barn. At the bottom of Main Street was the livery, where Kilkenny now stood, and opposite him, the marshal's office . . . a bridge, or a barrier, separating one world from the other.

Kilkenny crushed out his cigarette. He wore black chaps and a black, flat-crowned, flat-brimmed hat. Under his black Spanish-style jacket he wore a gray flannel shirt. They were colors that lost themselves in any shadow.

He was weary now, every muscle heavy with the fatigue of long hours of riding. His throat was dry, his stomach empty. His mind was sluggish because of the weariness of his body, and he felt short-tempered and irritable because of it.

Normally, he was a quiet, tolerant man with a dry humor and a liking for people, but in his present mood he was wary of himself, knowing the sudden angers that could spring up within him at such times.

Darkness gathered in the hollows of the hills and crept down into the silent alleys, crouching there to wait their hour for creeping into the empty streets. Kilkenny rolled another smoke, trying to relax. He was hungry, but he wanted to calm himself before walking into the company of strangers.

A stray dog trotted up the street . . . a door slammed. The town was settling down after supper, and he had not yet eaten. He dropped his cigarette, pushing it into the dust.

There was a grate of boot soles on gravel. A low sentence reached his ears from the bench outside the door. "Reckon Stroud knows?"

"Who can tell what he knows? But he was hired to keep the peace, an' he's done it."

"In his own way."

"Maybe there ain't no other."

"There was once. Stroud shut down the gambling and thievin', but he stopped the Vigilance Committee, too. They'd have strung the worst of them and burnt the old town to the ground. There's some say we'd be better off."

As he crossed the street Kilkenny did not turn to look at the men who had spoken behind him. He could feel the rising tensions. Something here was still poised for trouble. Alive to such things, currents that could mean death if unwatched, he was uneasy at remaining, yet he disliked the idea of going on. Towns were scarce in this country.

It was no common frontier-style boardinghouse he entered, but a large, well-appointed dining room, a place suited to a larger city, a place that would have a reputation in any city.

There was linen on the tables and there was silver and glass, not the usual rough wood and crockery. A young woman came toward him with a menu in her hand. She had a quiet face and dark, lovely eyes.

He noticed the way her eyes had seemed to gather in his dusty clothes and rest momentarily on the low-hung guns. She led him to a corner table and placed the menu before a place where he could sit with his back in the corner, facing the room.

His eyes crinkled at the corners and he smiled a little. "Does it show that much?"

Her own eyes were frank, not unfriendly. "I'm afraid it does."

"This," he indicated the room, "is a surprise."

"It is a way of making a living."

"A gracious way." She looked at him more directly as he spoke. "It is a way one misses."

A small frown gathered between her eyes. "I wonder — why is it that most gunfighters are gentlemen?"

"Some were born to it," he said, "and some grow into it. Men are rude only when they are insecure."

He was eating his dessert when the door opened and a man came in. It was, Kilkenny guessed at once, Tom Stroud.

He was a square-faced man with the wide shoulders and deep chest of mountain ancestry. He was plainly dressed and walked without swagger, yet there was something solid and indomitable about him. His eyes were blue, a darker blue than that usually seen, and his mustache was shading from brown to gray.

Stroud seated himself, glanced at the menu, and then his eyes lifted and met those of Kilkenny. Instant recognition was there . . . not of him as a name, but as a gunfighter. There was also something else, a narrow, measuring gaze.

The slope-shouldered, limping man that he had seen at Hillman's earlier entered the room and crossed to Stroud's table. Stroud's face indicated no welcome, but the man sat down and leaned confidentially across the table. The man talked, low-voiced. Once, Stroud's eyes flickered to Kilkenny. Deliberately, Kilkenny prolonged his coffee.

The woman, Laurie Archer, walked over to him. "Will you be with us long?"

"A day . . . perhaps two."

"You would be wise to move on — tonight."

"No."

"Perhaps you would take a job outside of town? I have cattle, and I need a fore-man."

"How many hands?"

"Two . . . now."

In reply to his unspoken question she added quietly, "I had a foreman — Jim Denton."

Neither spoke for several minutes and then, knowing he needed the job, he said, "I would only hire to handle cows. Denton was none of my affair."

"I want it no other way."

"My name's Lance. By the way, what about him?" He indicated Stroud. "What will he think about you hiring me?"

She shrugged. "I have no idea."

At the ranch two men awaited him, a

capable, tough-looking man of past fifty named Pike Taylor, and a gawky youngster of seventeen, Corey Hatch. There was a small cabin where Laurie Archer stayed when on the ranch, a bunkhouse, a stable, and corrals. There was a good bit of stacked hay, and several thousand acres of unrestricted grazing, much of it bottom land.

For a solid week, Kilkenny worked hard. He rode the fence, repaired broken stretches, put in new posts. He fenced off some loco weed, cleaned several water holes, dug out a fresh one where the green grass indicated water near the surface. He found some fifty head of mavericks and branded them, moving all the cattle to lower ground for the best grass. And he thought about Laurie Archer.

Corey Hatch liked to talk. "Some folks don't take much to Stroud," he said. "Hillman an' them, they hired him to clean up the town, but some figure he done too good a job. The gamblers an' them, they'd like to get a shot at him."

When he rode into town he stabled his horse and then dropped in at the store. Hillman filled his order, then said, low-voiced, "Watch yourself. There's been talk."

"Talk?"

"That you're takin' up for Denton.

Stroud will be watchin' his chance."

The warning made him angry. Why couldn't people let well enough alone? No doubt Stroud was getting the same sort of talk . . . was it planned that way? Deliberately, to build it into trouble?

But Hillman had been the man who hired Stroud, so that made no sense. He himself did not want trouble. He had a good job on the ranch, and was earning sorely needed money. He wanted no trouble. He considered going to Tom Stroud, having it out.

Yet that might precipitate that very trouble he was attempting to avoid. He crossed to the restaurant and was scarcely seated before Stroud came in. Two men at an intervening table got up and left without finishing their meals.

After dinner he walked down the street and across the tracks to a saloon. He sat at a table, apparently lost in thought but keeping an ear on the conversations around him. "Used to be a live town," a man said, "before they hired Stroud."

"Whyn't they fire him?"

"Them across the way hired him. Hillman, an' them shopkeepers. They want to keep him."

Restless, and disturbed by the feeling

in town, he walked outside. From up the street there was a sudden shot, then a wild yell and pounding hoofs. A rider came down the street and slid from his horse. He was swaying and drunk, waving a drawn pistol. It was Pike Taylor, from the ranch.

"Where's that murderin' son? I'll kill — !"

Tom Stroud materialized from a dark alley beside the saloon. Pike's side was toward the marshal. Pike had fired a gun, still held it gripped in his fist, had threatened to kill. Stroud had only to speak and shoot.

It would be murder, cold-blooded, ruthless, efficient. Kilkenny stepped out on the street, waiting. His mouth was dry, his hands loose and ready.

Stroud did not see him, yet he knew that if Stroud moved to kill the old man, he would kill Stroud.

Stroud had hesitated an instant only, then he walked through the soft dust toward Pike. Taylor started to turn but the marshal was swift, incredibly so. His left hand dropped to the old man's wrist with a grasp of iron, while his right hand came up under the barrel and broke the gun back against Pike Taylor's thumb.

Death had stalked the street, and then Pike stood disarmed and helpless. Seizing the old man's arm, Stroud started him toward the jail. And as he turned he saw Kilkenny.

Thirty yards apart their eyes met. Stroud's gun hand gripped the old man's arm.

Kilkenny heard a sharp intake of breath, then from the shadows a voice. "Now's your chance — *take him!*"

Kilkenny walked slowly forward. "Havin' trouble, Marshal?"

Stroud's eyes, wary but faintly curious, met his in the light from the windows. "Careless shootin'. Are you going to take him back to the ranch, or does he sleep it off in jail?"

"In jail — it will keep him out of trouble."

Stroud nodded, started to turn away. Kilkenny said, "You could have killed him, Marshal."

Stroud turned sharply. "I never kill men," his voice was utterly cold, "unless it has to be done."

Kilkenny walked back to the saloon and ordered a drink. The bartender came leisurely down the bar and slammed a glass before Kilkenny. He slopped whiskey into it. His eyes were insolent when he looked up.

Kilkenny did not change expression. "Drink that yourself. Then get a fresh glass and pour it without spilling."

The bartender hesitated, not liking it, but not liking what might follow. Suddenly, he tossed off the whiskey and followed instructions.

The man with the sloping shoulder and the limp edged along the bar, faint contempt in his eyes. "Had him dead to rights. He got you buffaloed?"

"Why should I shoot him? He means nothing to me."

"He's gunnin' for you."

"Is he?"

"Everybody knows that. Sure he is."

"I've seen no signs of it." Kilkenny lifted his eyes. "And I can read sign. If you ask me there's a lot of skunk tracks around here."

Kilkenny gave him time to reply, but the man stood silent, his face tight and worried. Events had taken a turn the limping man did not like. After a moment he shrugged, then shuffled back across the room and sat down at a table covered with papers. He took up a pencil and began adding what looked like a column of figures. Again, Kilkenny had that strange feeling that he'd met this man before, and that the man had just done something that by all rights should have told Kilkenny where that memory came from.

"I never knew Jim Denton," Kilkenny said then. "His troubles were his own. Anybody who hopes to promote a battle is wastin' time. I fight my own wars . . . this one ain't mine."

Irritably, Kilkenny walked to the hotel, got a room, and turned in. He had slept scarcely an hour when, restless, he awakened. He sat on the edge of the bed and lit a cigarette.

Obviously, he had been elected to kill Tom Stroud, but who had done the electing? Whoever, they would not cease planning because of his statement in the saloon. What they seemed to need was a scapegoat, for evidently the powers in town were evenly balanced, and the Hillman crowd — What was it about him that never ceased to worry Kilkenny?

What about Laurie? Where did she stand? Despite her comment that he was not to take up Denton's quarrel, Kilkenny was not at all sure. She was poised, intelligent. Her interests would seem to be aligned with those of the storekeepers, but was she not a little ruthless? Yet, he had seemed to detect something in her manner to Stroud that was different.

Was he becoming too suspicious? Maybe, but if he killed Stroud or they killed each other, it could be set down as a gunman's quarrel. Perhaps a certain group would then find a marshal more susceptible to corruption.

What would they do now? Still considering that, he fell asleep.

He awakened for the second time with a faint scratching outside his window. He swung his feet to the floor and moved swiftly to where he could see. The alley was empty.

The moon was behind a cloud, but as he flattened against the wall he suddenly caught a faint flicker of movement. Somebody was at the end of the alley, standing in the shadows. It was a woman. It was Laurie Archer. He could see the arm of her gray coat . . . she gestured to him.

He held his watch to the faint light — it was past three o'clock. What would she be doing up and around at this hour?

Hurriedly, he dressed. Belting on his guns, he stepped from the window into the alley. Swiftly and silently he moved to the end of the alley where Laurie had disappeared, and then he saw her, some distance off. He hurried after her, and then she vanished.

He crouched at the base of a huge old cottonwood, debating this. Suddenly, he heard a horse stamp. Turning his head, he beheld the animal standing not a dozen yards away, bridle reins trailing . . . and that meant the horse had been ridden lately and would be ridden soon again. He went to the horse . . . its flanks were damp. He touched the brand — a Lazy A, Laurie Archer's brand!

There had been no time for her to get to the ranch and return. Therefore, Corey Hatch must be in town.

Why?

A kid . . . proud, defiant, loyal . . . a kid riding for the brand, and Pike Taylor arrested. Remembering his own youthful feelings, Kilkenny knew how Corey must feel. He would believe Pike must be freed — but how had he known about Pike?

Somehow, someone had gotten word to him. That meant the man behind the scenes was setting up a situation that could only lead to violence, and somehow, in the confusion, Stroud would be killed.

Only Stroud?

Very likely he, Kilkenny, was to be killed, too. That meant they had to get him on the scene of the fight, and that meant Laurie was part of it somehow. But she had led him nowhere, she — he stared around him, suddenly.

A half dozen cottonwoods and some

willows behind a building . . . a blacksmith shop. And next door? Suddenly he came to his feet, tense and ready.

They had succeeded, they had led him into a trap. They had gotten him close to Stroud, and when they killed both it could be signed off as a gun battle. Didn't everybody know they were hunting each other?

For the building next door to the blacksmith shop was the jail — and Tom Stroud lived in the front of the jail.

Time was short, only seconds must remain, for they could not hope to keep him here long. . . .

A crash from the jail started him running. He ducked around the blacksmith shop, and was just in time to see the marshal step into the door. The moon had come from under a cloud and he caught a fleeting glimpse of Stroud in the doorway. At the corner of the building was Corey Hatch, gun in hand!

Kilkenny opened his mouth to shout a warning, and then the night was ripped apart by a crashing volley. Tom Stroud took one step forward and then fell headlong, sprawled across the steps.

Kilkenny triggered his gun into the darkness from which the shots had come, then ducked and ran to the fallen man. Corey stood where he had been, his mouth opened wide, then, the surprise wearing off, he dropped to the ground.

Stroud was hit several times, but alive. Kilkenny looked up. "Corey! Over here!"

Startled, yet knowing the voice, the boy slipped onto the porch. Together they got the marshal inside and stretched on a bed. Taking a sawed-off shotgun from the wall, Kilkenny handed it to the boy. "Take that and guard the door. Let nobody in! Understand? *Nobody!*"

Kilkenny stripped the shirt from Stroud's body. He had been hit once high in the chest, once in the leg. His side had been grazed by another bullet, his shirt torn in several other places.

Swiftly, Kilkenny went to work. From of old, he knew bullet wounds and what to do about them. A half hour later, he joined the boy near the front of the jail.

"Nobody stirrin'," Corey said. "What happened, boss? I don't get it."

"I'll explain later. Let's get Pike."

Taylor was on his feet and at the door of his cell. He had, he explained, received a note. When he read the note he got loaded and started for town.

The note? He took it from his shirt

pocket. It was printed on a coarse bit of wrapping paper:

*Jim Denton was bringing this bottle to you when he was murdered by Stroud. Figured you should have it. He's going to get your new boss the same way.*

*A Friend*

The very simplicity of it angered Kilkenny. The writer must have known the old man would have a drink, and then another, and he would think about Denton dead, and this new boss, Lance, about to be killed. So he got a gun and started for town.

"How about you?" Kilkenny asked Corey.

Corey took a note from his jeans. It was the same coarse paper, the same pencil style:

*Stroud's got Pike in jail. Pull the bars off the window while I handle Stroud.*

*Lance*

Kilkenny explained the situation. Obviously, whoever led the element opposed to Stroud hoped to get him killed, and to kill Kilkenny or one of the men from the ranch in the fight. That tied it to a grudge battle over Denton, and would arouse no controversy with the townspeople, nor would they be likely to suspect a plot.

Kilkenny walked back to the door. The blinds were drawn and tightened down. Nobody outside could see what happened inside. They might know Kilkenny was there, and if they did they would act, and soon.

Stroud was awake and breathing heavily when Kilkenny stepped to the bed. The marshal looked up at him. Kneeling beside the bed, Kilkenny began to talk. He told what had happened as he saw it clearly, concisely.

"Now," he said, "you make me your deputy."

Stroud's brow puckered. "What — ?"

"Don't worry. I'll carry on while you're down. Just make me your deputy."

Speaking in a hoarse whisper, Stroud swore him in before Pike Taylor and Corey Hatch.

Leaving the two to guard the wounded man, Kilkenny let himself out the back door. It would soon be daylight. He had little hope of finding anything that would lead him to the ambushers, but it was a chance.

From somewhere, they might be watching. On the other hand, as it was nearing day, they might return home and stay quiet, waiting for the news of the morning. For whatever had happened would be known to everyone shortly after daybreak.

Circling around, Kilkenny examined the ground where the ambushers had been concealed. They had hidden behind a water trough that stood near the mouth of an alley. No brass shells remained. The tracks were confusion.

Kilkenny went down the street and crossed, in the first graying of the eastern sky, to the house where Laurie Archer slept. He was starting up the walk when he stopped, frowning.

The yard had been watered the evening before with a hand sprinkler, and water had run across the sand path to the doorway. So much water had been used that the sand had been left quite damp, and it was smooth, unbroken by any tracks!

Circling the house, he found there was no back door. The windows were high, too high to be used with comfort. He was standing, staring around, when she spoke to him from the window.

"Just what exactly are you looking for?"

He walked toward the window. "I'd like to talk to you. It's important."

She wore a wrapper, and her hair was

rumpled, but she looked even more lovely and exciting. "All right. I'll open the door."

When he was inside, he looked around. It was a pleasant sitting room, not so cluttered with bric-a-brac as most such rooms of the period, but done in the Spanish style, with Indian blankets and only a couple of pictures. It was somehow like her; it had charm and simplicity.

"Where's your gray jacket?" he asked abruptly. "And that gray hat?"

She waited an instant, studying him. "Why . . . why, I left them at the restaurant. Is it important?"

"Yes . . . Did you leave this house last night? Or very early this morning?"

She shook her head. "I had a headache. I came home early and went to bed. I had just gotten up when you came."

He glanced around him again. Everything was neat, perfect. Had it been someone else wearing her clothes last night, one of the girls from down on the tracks, perhaps?

She noticed the star on his chest, and she frowned. "Where did you get that?" Her voice was a little sharp. "Where's Tom Stroud?"

Briefly, he explained. He was startled to see her face turn deathly pale. She put a hand on the table at her side. "He . . . he'll live? I mean . . . ?"

"I think so."

"I must go to him."

"No."

The harshness of his reply startled her. She looked up quickly, but before she could speak he said abruptly, almost brutally, "Nobody will see him but myself and my two men until this is cleared up. He's being cared for."

"But — "

"No," he said firmly and definitely. "Too many people want him dead."

Leaving her house, he walked swiftly down the street. The limping man . . . Pike had said his name was Turner, and told him where to find him. He went up the walk to the house and, without knocking, shoved the door open and stepped in.

Two men were sitting at a table cleaning rifles. They took one look, glimpsed the badge, and the nearest one grabbed for his gun. Kilkenny shot him in the throat, his Colt swinging to cover the other man who slowly lifted his hands, gray-faced.

"Fast," the man said. "You're fast, Lance."

"I've had to be." Lance looked at him and said, "The other name is Kilkenny."

The man jumped as if stabbed. "Kilkenny," he said, "the Neuces gunfighter!"

"Who hired you?" Kilkenny's voice was low. "Just tell me that, and you can ride out of here."

"Nobody." He started to continue, but Kilkenny's gun muzzle tilted and he stopped. "Look, I — "

"You've got one minute," Kilkenny said, "then you get a hole in your ear. I don't reckon I'll miss. Howsoever, I might notch it a little close."

The man swallowed. "All right. It was Turner."

He saw the man into a saddle, and then walked back to the house and sat down. The body of the dead man had been removed to the barn. He looked around the bare room and saw on the wall a picture. It was a faded tintype of the main street of Dodge.

Kilkenny stood up for a closer look, and suddenly, it hit him like a flash. He started to turn, and then stopped. The limping man stood in the open door, and he held a gun in his hand. "Howdy, Lance." His eyes were faintly amused, yet wary. "Like that picture?"

Kilkenny lifted a hand slowly to his cigarette and dusted the ash from it, then returned it to his lips. "I went up the trail a couple of times," he drawled conversationally. "She was quite a town, wasn't she?"

Obviously, the two men he had surprised in the cabin had been two of those who ambushed Stroud. Turner would be another. The three could have done it, but there had probably been at least one more.

"Where's the boys?" Turner moved into the room, keeping Kilkenny covered.

"One's lyin' out in the barn." Kilkenny's voice did not change. "He's pretty dead. The other one got a chance to take out, and he pulled his freight."

Turner studied him. He was puzzled. Kilkenny was so obviously in complete possession of himself. This man who called himself Lance was a mystery in many ways. He —

"When you were in Dodge," Kilkenny said, "did you ever hang out at the Kansas House?"

Turner's face seemed to tighten and his eyes went blank. "Remember the place," he said.

"So do I."

Kilkenny drew deep on his cigarette. "Better put that gun down, Turner. You're through here. Stroud isn't dead. I'm the deputy marshal." He jerked his head toward the town. "The folks over there know it.

You try anything now, and they'll all come down here and burn you out. I might say they've been considerin' it."

Turner hesitated, not liking it. He hitched around, looking quickly out the door. Kilkenny made no attempt to grab for his gun. He just waited. "You're through, Turner." Kilkenny's words repeatedly went through his head. He had a deep-seated fear of the people across the tracks. He knew many of them disliked the saloons and gambling houses, and lived only for the day when the town could be cleaned up.

"You fellows should know when you're well off," Kilkenny continued. He was remembering bloody Kansas and a cold rage was settling over him. "If you'd only known, Stroud was keepin' you alive. With him down, there ain't a thing to prevent them comin' across here and makin' a cleanup. As long as he kept the peace, they kept their hands off. But you were greedy. Those trail town days are over. You can't turn the clock back."

Turner suddenly looked up. "All right," he said, "give me a chance and I'll ride."

"No," Kilkenny said, and drew. His Colt came out fast and Kilkenny stepped in close to Turner and had the muzzle pressed against his ear before the crippled man could bring his gun to bear. He snatched Turner's pistol away with his left hand and pushed Turner back into one of the chairs.

"That picture got me thinking. I remember you from Kansas . . . a long time ago. You were using the name Barney Houseman back then. You and your family skinned a lot of good people out of their money. Killed a few, too." Kilkenny moved to one side and gestured with his free hand. "Get up."

"Lance." The man turned in the chair. "You let me ride out of here. I know I can make it worth your while."

"You're wrong. Stroud made me take an oath when I pinned on this badge. If I hadn't, you'd be dead right now." Barney Houseman looked at him blankly. "We've never met, but I've heard of you. I'm Kilkenny."

Houseman's eyes narrowed, and his knuckles stood out white where he gripped the chair. "All right," he croaked. He struggled to get his lame foot under him as he stood. Awkwardly, he reached down to steady himself against the chair — and pulled a short-barreled Colt Lightning from a hideout holster!

Kilkenny stepped back and Houseman's gun roared, the slug catching him across the front of the shoulder. He shot, but he was already falling and the bullet went wild. Houseman frantically pulled the trigger three more times as Kilkenny scrambled for cover behind the table, hot lead catching him again, this time in the thigh. His gun was gone, the room full of powder smoke.

Houseman slammed out the door and half fell into the road. He headed for Main Street, reloading. Kilkenny was wounded, maybe dying. They had to move quickly but, he consoled himself, they had done it before and it was time. This had been a good bet, but he knew when his time was up. He had always known. The others had stayed behind at Bannock and at Dodge and other places. He pulled stakes before the Vigilance Committees and United States Marshals got wind of him. He had always moved when the time was ripe. It was ripe now.

Hillman had just opened his store when Houseman limped across Main Street and followed him inside. "Open the safe, Hill," Turner said, "we're getting out. I've just had a shoot-up with Kilkenny."

Hillman looked incredulous, and the limping man shrugged. "I'm not crazy. That gunfighter Lance — he was Kilkenny.

85

I should have remembered. He's used the name before.

"We've got to move! Get the safe. He's in no shape, but people heard the shots and he'll get help."

The look in Hillman's eyes stopped him. Hillman was looking in back of him, over his shoulder.

Houseman turned and stared, his hands hanging. Kilkenny stood in the doorway, his chest covered with blood from the still-oozing cut across collarbone and shoulder. Standing silent in the doorway he was a grim, dangerous figure, a looming figure of vengeance.

Hillman drew back. "Not me, Kilkenny. I'm out of it. He's made life hell for all of us, Barney has. He's made us all do his dirty jobs. And I won't move on to rob another town."

Kilkenny did not speak. He was squinting his eyes against the pain. He could feel the blood trickling down his stomach. He was losing a lot of blood, and he had little time.

Barney Houseman was a murderer many times over. He was a thief and a card cheat, but always he had let his brother and uncle carry the burden of suspicion while he handled the reins. In Dodge they had believed it was he who left Kilkenny's saddle partner dead in an alley with a knife in his back.

Kilkenny had long given up the chase, but his memory was good.

The limping man . . . Barney Houseman.

"I beat you just now," Barney said, "I'll do it again." His hand went down for the gun and grasped the butt, and then Kilkenny took a step forward, his gun sprang to his fist, and something slapped at Barney's pocket. He was angry that anything should disturb him now. He started to lift his gun, and something else slapped him and he suddenly felt very weak and he went down, sinking away, and saw the edge of the table go by his eyes. Then he was on his back, and all he could see was a crack in the ceiling, and then the crack was gone and he was dead.

Hillman twisted his big-knuckled hands. "He was my nephew," he said, "but he was a devil. I was bad, but he was worse."

Kilkenny asked him then, "Who is Laurie Archer?"

"My daughter."

Kilkenny walked back through the street and people stared at him, turned when he passed, and stared after. He walked up to the jail, and Laurie stood on the steps. Her face was drawn and pale. "Can I see him now?"

"Yes," he said. Then he added, "Barney's dead."

She turned fiercely, her eyes blazing. "I'm glad! *Glad!*"

"All right." He was tired and his head ached. He wanted to go back to the hotel and wash up and then sleep for a week, and then get a horse, and —

He indicated the man on the bed inside. "You're in love with Stroud?"

"Yes."

"Then go to him. He's a good man."

Kilkenny turned around and started back up the street, and the morning sun was hot on his shoulder blades and there were chickens coming out into the street, and from a meadow near the creek, a smell of new-mown hay. He was tired, very tired . . . rest . . . and then a horse.

# THE PASSING OF
# ROPE NOSE

To err is human, and Bill McClary was all too human, which accounted for the fact that the six-shooter pride of the Big Bend lay flat on his face in the bottom of a sandy draw with a hole in his head.

McClary was a reckless and ambitious young man known from Mescal to Muleshoe as fast on the draw, and finding that punching cows failed to support him in a style to which he wanted to become accustomed, he acquired a proclivity for cashing in his six-shooter at various cow country banks. To say that this practice was frowned upon by the hardworking sons of the sagebrush was putting it mildly, and Ranger Johnny Sutton had been called upon to correct McClary's impression that the country owed him a living.

Now the Big Bend of the Rio Grande has spawned some tough characters, and during his brief hour in the sun Bill McClary had been accounted by all, including himself, as one of the toughest. For a long time

McClary had been hearing of Sutton, and had memorized descriptions of him until he knew he would recognize the Ranger at once. He had long entertained the idea that Johnny Sutton was an overrated four-flusher, an impression he was determined to substantiate.

He had dismounted in that draw south of Nine Point Mesa and waited, smoking a cigarette in cheerful anticipation of the early demise of one Texas Ranger.

Sutton appeared, riding a zebra dun that had an eye full of hell and alkali, and McClary duly informed him that he was going to blow his head off, and would he dismount and take it on the ground?

Johnny, being in an agreeable mood and aware that a fool must follow his natural bent, dismounted. Bill McClary dropped his cigarette, pushed it into the sand with a boot toe, and then with the cheerful smile for which he had been noted, reached for his gun.

The debate was brief, definite, and decisive. Johnny Sutton's Peacemaker put a period to the discussion, and Bill McClary paid for his mistake, cashing in his chips with a memory engraved on his mind of a Colt that appeared from nowhere and the realization, too late, that being the fastest man in the Big Bend did not make him the fastest in Texas.

As a result of the affair in the draw, Ranger Sutton found himself in possession of two saddlebags stuffed with gold coin and bills to the tune of seven thousand dollars, which is a nice tune on any sort of instrument. It is also a sum for one hundredth of which a man could be murdered in any yard of the miles between the Rio Grande and the Davis Mountains.

Moreover, there were in the vicinity several hard customers who knew what McClary had been packing, and would guess what Sutton was bringing back in those extra-heavy saddlebags. Due north of him, and awaiting with keen anticipation any well-heeled passing stranger, was the outlaw town of Paisano. In the choice between a hot meal in Paisano to a cold night among the cat claw and prickly pear, Paisano won hands down, and late in the day Johnny Sutton rode into the dusty main street.

To Rope Nose George, proprietor of the Mustang Saloon, the arrival of Johnny Sutton posed a problem of the first order. Rope Nose was unofficial boss of Paisano, the official boss being Pink Lucas, but Lucas was below the border on a raid. Rope

Nose was disturbed, for he recognized Sutton the moment the dun stopped in front of the saloon, and he guessed what he carried. Now the guns of a Ranger are feared, yet seven thousand dollars has been known to turn many a yellow streak into the deep red of battle lust. This Rope Nose realized, and with misgivings.

He was aware that the town of Paisano existed solely because the Rangers had ignored it, being busy with immediate problems, but he was quite sure that if a Ranger were killed in Paisano the town would instantly be awarded first place on the list of Ranger business. In fact, even those not given to superstition in any form were willing to testify that killing a Ranger was bad luck.

Johnny Sutton carried his saddlebags when he came through the doors. With scarcely a glance at the hangers-on, he stepped to the bar. "Howdy, George! Mine will be rye, a meal, and a bed. How about it?"

"Sure thing! Surest thing you know, Mr. *Sutton*." George spoke that name loud enough so anyone in the room would know who had arrived and be hesitant to start anything. Seven thousand or no seven thousand, Rope Nose wanted nothing so much as to get the Ranger out of town.

Hurriedly, he put the glass on the bar, and a bottle beside it. "There's a good room right at the head of the stairs," he whispered confidentially. "You'll like it there." He hesitated, his curiosity struggling with his better judgment, and the better judgment lost in one fall. "You . . . you run into Bill McClary?"

John Sutton's black, steady eyes centered on Rope Nose and the saloonkeeper felt a little chill go up his spine. He'd heard about the feeling those eyes inspired, and now he was a believer. "Yeah," Johnny said. "I saw him."

"He . . . he rode on south?" Rope Nose asked hopefully. Personally, he had liked McClary, the most cheerful of a bad lot of bad men, most of them a humorless crowd. "He was goin' on?"

"When I last saw him," Johnny replied, "he didn't give the impression that he was goin' anywhere. Fact is," he added, "I suspect he's right where I left him."

Perk Johnson edged along the bar. "You must be some slick with that gun," he said admiringly. "Bill always said he aimed to try you on."

Sutton's gaze was frosty. "Bill McClary," he said, "was a mighty good man with damn bad judgment. I hope bad judgment ain't contagious around here."

The swinging doors smashed open and a little brown bobcat in the shape of a girl rushed through the door. Her eyes were flashing and gray, startling against the deep brown of her face. Her dress was torn and she held a shawl about her shoulders. "Are you the Ranger?" she demanded of Sutton. "If you are, come an' help me! Some thieves got my pa in the place next door, skinnin' him in a card game, an' I found another goin' through my wagon!"

There was no maidenly shyness about her. "Well, come on!" she said angrily. "Don't just stand there!"

"If your father's in a poker game he went into it of his own free will, and," Johnny added, "if he's your father I figure he's man enough to take care of himself. No coyote spawned a wildcat."

Her eyes flashed. "Are you another of these no-good, loafin' cowhands, or are you a Ranger? They've got my pa drunk an' he can't see to hold his cards. I went to get him an' they nearly tore my dress off. You come help me or I'm goin' back in there with a horsewhip!"

Sutton tossed off his drink. "Hold that grub, George," he advised, "an' open your safe an' put these saddlebags in it." As Rope

Nose George's eyes bulged, Sutton added, "And don't get any ideas. I know just how much there is in there an' you're personally accountable for every dime of it!" George's heart pounded. Seven thousand dollars was the stuff outlaw dreams were made of. He was a notorious coward who lived in fear of both the law and the other men in Pink Lucas's gang, but this was sorely tempting.

Sutton watched him stow the bags carefully into the safe, and when the door was closed he turned and followed the girl outside. She said nothing more but walked toward the light from the next door with a free swinging stride.

She pushed open the door and instantly there was a yell of enthusiasm and a rush. "She's back, boys! She's back! Let's teach that filly a — !"

The rush stopped so suddenly that one man almost fell down, for Johnny Sutton had stepped through the door after the girl. "Go back an' sit down!" he ordered. "An' damn you for a lot of mangy coyotes!"

Four men sat at a card table. The girl's father was obvious enough. He was not only so drunk he couldn't see, but two men were holding him upright in his chair and one of them was playing his cards. Johnny crossed the room and looked them over cynically. The redhead behind the drunken man looked up sheepishly. "Is he winnin'?" Johnny asked dryly.

The redhead's flush was deeper. "Well," he said guiltily, "he ain't been holdin' much. Right now he's losin'."

"How much has he lost?"

Red hesitated, then swallowed. "Right at a thousand dollars," he confessed, "maybe a mite over."

Johnny Sutton's right eyebrow tightened. The man did not look like he had a thousand cents, much less dollars. "Did he have that much, little lady?"

"You bet he did!" the girl flashed back at him. "And more, if these blisterin' pickpockets haven't stole it off him!"

Red looked abused, and he let go of the drunken man who slumped over on the table.

"Whose deal is it?" Johnny asked suddenly.

Their eyes were puzzled and wary. "Mine." The speaker was a lean-faced man marked with evil and crookedness.

"All right," Johnny said calmly, "you boys like this game. You started it. Now deal, and don't let any of your mistakes keep him from winning back his money."

"Now, look here — !" The tall man

started to rise but Johnny's left hand dropped to his shoulder and slammed him back in his chair.

"Deal!" Sutton insisted. If he chose to make a fight of it, the result might mean a lot less crime in that part of Texas.

Grudgingly, the man began to deal. It was noteworthy that from that moment the drunken man began to win. Red, devilish in his glee and enjoyment of the reversed situation, bet the old man's hands recklessly. When thirty minutes had passed the tall man glanced at Sutton. "There, now. He's won it all back!" He dropped his hands to the table and started to push back.

"Deal." Johnny's voice was flat and dangerous. "Deal those cards. An' Red, you bet 'em like you see 'em! I like the way you play poker."

"He's got all his money, I tell you!" The tall man's face was wolfish. "I'll be damned if I — !"

Johnny Sutton's eyes fastened on the man, and they seemed to grow flat and lose their shine. With his free hand he reached out and swept all the money from in front of the players into the middle of the table. "You shuffle the cards, fast boy. You like it that way. Shuffle the cards, then you cut for high card with him. Winner takes all!"

"Don't do it, Chiv!" The speaker was a bearded man with a hard set to his jaw. "He can't get away with this!"

"You open your face again," Johnny said calmly, "an' you'll have a mouthful of loose teeth. Shuffle those cards, Chiv. This will teach all of you a lesson you'll remember next time you try to take a harmless old man who's just passin' through! Shuffle an' cut!"

The man looked at the cards with sudden distaste, then, belligerently, he looked up at Sutton. "This time I cut as I want, and it's on the level," he said. "If the old man wins he gets it all, an' if I win, I do."

The girl started forward with a cry of protest, but Sutton waved her back. "All right," he agreed, "but with your permission I'll cut for him." Sutton jerked a thumb toward the old man.

The gambler looked up and his hard eyes brightened with malice. "Why, sure! You cut for him!" He gathered the cards and shuffled them briefly, then slapped the deck on the table and took hold with his thumb and middle finger. "Okay?" he asked, and at Johnny's nod, he cut the cards and showed a queen of hearts, and smiled.

Johnny leaned over and shaped the deck with his fingers, then struck them slightly and split the deck.

At the cut, the gambler's face went white with fury and he grasped the arms of his chair, staring at the ace of clubs Sutton was showing. "Your own deck," Sutton said quietly.

"Lady," Sutton slid suddenly to his feet and stepped back from the table, "pick up the money. Tie it up in something and we'll leave." His black eyes held the gambler's. "Next time," he advised, "don't use a deck with slick aces."

The gambler stared at him, his face taut with hatred and pent-up fury.

As the girl moved toward the door, Johnny Sutton looked the room over, letting each man feel the weight of his attention. "If that girl is bothered again, or if there is any more trouble during my stay in this town, I'll burn the place to the ground, and the ones who are lucky will go to jail."

Deliberately, he turned his back and walked out through the doors. At the wagon the girl turned. "My name is Stormy," she said, "and thanks. I guess Pa an' me ain't much, but we're grateful."

Sutton shrugged. "I was glad to help. If you need me, scream." He pointed toward the window of the room assigned to him. "I'll be up there."

★ ★ ★

The moon floated lazily above the serrated ridges of the scarred landscape below it. A coyote protested its troubles, and then as the moon slid down the sky, the coyote trotted off into the shadows in pursuit of food. Day edged its first skirmishing lines of light along the ridges and Rope Nose George turned over in his sleep and awakened.

All was dark and still but the window showed the first gray that preceded the dawn. Rope Nose George was suddenly wide awake, remembering the seven thousand dollars in the safe and three thousand more, or so it was rumored, in the old man's wagon. Most of this last had been realized from the sale of cattle, the rest from the poker game. Ten thousand dollars was more money than Rope Nose had ever seen. It was also more than had ever been in Paisano at any one time.

And then he heard the horses.

They were walking, and there were more than two of them. With a start, he sat up, realizing on the instant that it was Pink Lucas returning. Vastly disturbed, Rope Nose swung his legs out of bed and felt for his boots. Terrified, he knew he must inform Pink at once about the presence of the

Ranger. He also knew that Pink would try to steal the money and that meant killing Sutton, an act which, he was sure, would put him out of business. Tumbling around in the back of his brain was the idea that he could somehow get his hands on the ten thousand dollars if he could only figure out how to keep from being caught by the Ranger or Pink Lucas.

He got his boots on, struggled into his pants, and hastened to the door. Then he stopped abruptly. *The wagon was gone!*

For a minute he stared, unmindful of the approaching riders, thinking only of the missing wagon. Then he thought of Chiv Pontious. If the gambler had — !

He turned for the stairs to the Ranger's room. He scrambled, panting up the stairs, clutching his unbelted pants with one hand. The Ranger's door stood open and on the rumpled bed was a note.

*"Sorry to leave like this. I got my money."*

Got his money? But? . . . ! Turning, Rope Nose stumbled down the steps and into the saloon. The room was dark and still, and the safe was closed. Hurriedly, he spun the dial and opened the safe. Where the money had been placed was another note.

*"You should be more careful. I read the combination when you opened the safe for me. I've taken my money and you had better keep your boys home."*

The door rattled, and he went to it. Opening it, he found himself pushed aside by Pink Lucas. The big outlaw swaggered to the bar and picked up the bottle left there by Sutton. Pouring a drink, he turned on George. "All right, where is it?"

"Where's what?"

Chiv Pontious had come into the room behind Lucas. He smiled now. "I told you he was scared, Pink. The money's in the safe."

"No, it ain't." George shoved the note at them. "Sutton took it and he's gone, the wagon with him."

"Ten thousand!" Chiv said aloud. "Think of it, Pink! Ten thousand dollars, for the taking!"

Pink slammed the glass down on the bar. "Get fresh horses!" he yelled. "Get 'em fast! We'll have that money! He can't go far with a wagon!"

In the distance, thunder rumbled.

Rope Nose George examined Lucas with heavy-lidded, crafty eyes. "You're right, Pink. They're headed up toward the hills. Let's go get 'em."

"Not you, fat man," Pink said as a clatter of hooves announced the arrival of the remounts. "You're stayin' here, an' keepin' your mouth shut. Come on, men!"

Six miles to the west, Johnny Sutton was leading the wagon into the rough country beyond Tornillo Creek. It was a country cut by many draws that in wet weather ran bank full with roaring water, and it was sprinkling even now. That is, it was sprinkling where Sutton rode. Over the mountains around Lost Mine Peak, heavy thunderheads were losing their weight of water upon the steep slopes of the mountains. Johnny Sutton knew the gamble he was taking and the risk he was running, but to get where he wanted to go he must cross at least two more of the deep draws that cut into the slope leading down into the bottom of Tornillo Flat. There was high ground there where they would be safe, and if his idea worked, it would not only prove safe for him and the Knights, but a trap for any who followed them.

The rain was increasing. Lightning flashed continually. Wheeling his horse, he rode back. "Whoop it up, Pa!" he yelled above the storm. "We've got two more draws to cross!"

Pale-faced, the older man stared at him. "We'll never make it! Look at the rain in those mountains!"

"We've got to!" Sutton replied. "Let's go!"

The horses strained into the harness and gathered speed. The wagon was not heavily loaded, and back along the way they had already thrown out several pieces of furniture. Each one had meant a battle with Stormy, but each time it was a battle Sutton won.

Ahead of them, a deep gash broke the face of the plain, and without hesitation he rode into it. A thin stream trickled along the bottom, but that was merely the result of local rain. What was coming was back up there in those rock-sided mountains, where nothing stopped the weight of rushing water. Whooping and yelling they raced across the draw and the horses lunged up the opposite side. Far off they heard a low roar. Stormy looked quickly at Sutton. "Can't we stop here?" she pleaded.

"Not unless you feel you can hold off a dozen men!" he replied. "Get rollin', old man!"

The team lunged into their collars and the four horses started the wagon moving. It was no more than a half mile to the next draw but the race was on in earnest. Johnny

Sutton rode alongside the horses, whooping it up and slapping them with his rope.

Before them loomed the other draw, all of sixty yards across and the trail showing dimly up the far side. Now the roar filled their ears, but whipping up the horses, Sutton slapped his dun and lunged on ahead. Down the bank he went at a dead run with the wagon thundering behind him. The draw was straight away to the west for all of two hundred yards, and as they hit bottom they saw the water.

It was a rolling gray-black wall at least ten feet high! It was rolling down upon them with what seemed to be the speed of an express train. Sutton whipped the horses and, racing beside them, rushed for the trail. The frightened horses hit the trail up the bank and the wagon bounded like a chip as it struck a stone. Then they were up, and almost in the same instant the water swept by, thundering behind them.

"All right!" Sutton yelled. "Pull up an' give 'em a blow!"

Knight drew up on the lines and the horses quartered around. The draw was running bank full behind them. Then, standing in his stirrups, Sutton pointed.

Behind them, trapped between the two draws, was a small band of horsemen! Rain lashing his face, he laughed grimly. "Got 'em!" he said. "I figured they were close behind!" He rode in close to the wagon and leaned over. "Keep goin', but you can take it easy now. Head for the ranch at Paint Gap. You'll be safe there."

Stormy stood up. "What about you?" she demanded.

"I'm waiting here. I want to watch those hombres. There's one in particular I want to talk to!" He swung the dun and rode away through the rain. Stormy stared after him, then sat down abruptly, her eyes somber.

Johnny Sutton liked the feel of the rain. He was wearing his slicker, but otherwise was thoroughly wet and enjoying it. He rode back toward the draw. The riders had turned and were headed upstream. He grinned, having foreseen that possibility and knowing well what awaited them. As a boy of sixteen he had been punching cattle in this area and had been trapped in the same way. He turned his own horse and followed them. Suddenly, they drew up. The place where they had stopped had been made an island by the two draws running bank full. By the look of the rain they would have no choice but to sit there and wait until the two draws went down, which would be four or five hours by the way the rain was continuing.

They had stopped at the foot of a steep red and grassless slope that led up the sides of a low mesa. The top of that mesa, the last twenty feet, was sheer rock extending from one draw to the other. A horse might scramble up that slope, but nothing could surmount that cliff at the top. Johnny Sutton sat on his horse and chuckled.

From where they sat they could see him plainly and he waved to them. One of the men threw his rifle to his shoulder and fired a shot, but the distance was far too great for it to be effective. Sutton rode forward, not certain whether he would find what he sought or not, but when he came to the bridge of stone, he grinned with satisfaction.

He was now well beyond the mesa that blocked the westward ride of the outlaws, and this stone ledge under which the water ran was in fact a part of that same mesa. Here the water had undermined the solid rock of the ledge and left a natural bridge some fifty feet wide and at least twenty yards along, ample to bridge the draw at that point. Johnny rode across the stone bridge and walked his horse through the rain to the top of the mesa. On this northern side it broke sharply off and was easy of access in several places, as it was from the west, although inaccessible for a rider from either the south or east.

When within some forty yards of the rim below which the horsemen were trapped, Johnny Sutton swung down and drew his rifle from its scabbard, keeping the weapon back under his slicker. He walked up behind some boulders and looked down on the riders standing below. He chuckled, then fired a shot into the ground at their horses' feet. Several animals started to buck. All heads swung around and guns came up.

"Drop 'em, Pink!" he called out. "All of you! I've got you under my gun and I can pick you off like ducks in a barrel! You," Sutton motioned to one of the men, "collect all the guns, an' I *mean* all!"

They sat dead still, staring up at him. Before and behind were roaring rivers, impassable for many hours. East, the ground fell away into a vast flat covered with a stand of water, much of it now treacherous with quicksand. On foot they might climb the stone wall before them; otherwise, there was no escape. Nor was there escape from the deadly rifle that covered them. They were caught in the open and helpless.

"No waiting!" Sutton ordered. "Collect the guns!"

Reluctantly, the outlaw went from man to man, gathering the weapons. Sutton had brought his rope, and now he lowered the end down the wall. "Tie 'em on!" he commanded.

When this was done he hauled the weapons up to him, worked with them a few minutes, and then went back to the rim. "All right, leave your horses and climb up here, one by one!"

"Leave our horses?" Lucas protested. "What becomes of them? How do we travel?"

"On foot."

A burst of profanity answered him, and one man shouted a refusal. Wheeling his horse he dropped low in the saddle and jumped the horse away toward the flat. Yet the horse had taken not even two full jumps when Sutton fired. The man swung loose in the saddle and dropped. Then he struggled to his feet, clutching his bloody shoulder and swearing.

"One at a time!" Sutton repeated. "Start climbin'!"

One by one they climbed up, and one by one he tied their hands behind them, patting them down for knives and other weapons. The last man to come up was Pink Lucas, his red face redder still, his eyes ugly. "I'll kill you for this!" he told Sutton.

Shrugging, Johnny Sutton started them walking northwest through the steady fall of the rain. An hour later he paused and allowed them fifteen minutes' rest. By that time the rain had slowed to a mere drizzle and gave signs of clearing. Then he started them again. Four hours later, wet, bedraggled, and weary, they stumbled into the Paint Gap Ranch yard, and were met by an astonished gathering of cowhands headed by their boss, Charlie Warner, and by Pa and Stormy Knight.

"Well, I'll be forever damned!" Warner stared. "Pink Lucas an' his crowd! How in the thunder did you ever get this bunch?"

Johnny Sutton shrugged wearily. "They got tired of livin' lives of wickedness and decided they would surrender. Isn't that right, Pink?"

Pink Lucas answered with a burst of profanity. Chiv Pontious only stared at Sutton, his eyes evil with murderous desire for a weapon.

Johnny Sutton looked at Stormy, and met her eyes. "You'd better eat something," she said. "You're cold and wet."

"That ain't all," Pink Lucas threatened. "He'll stay cold an' wet."

Johnny Sutton herded the men into the

barn and left a cowhand to watch them. There had been no sign of Red, and secretly he was pleased. He had liked the way Red played Knight's hand the night before. At least, he liked the way he had played it after he, Sutton, moved in.

Sutton walked to the house and dropped the saddlebags against the wall. "I needed Lucas," he said, looking around at Warner. "He's been raiding across the border. I'd been trailing him when I ran into McClary. And that Pontious — he's wanted in New Orleans and Dallas, both places for murder."

"The rain has stopped," Stormy said suddenly. "Maybe we can go on tomorrow."

The rain had stopped. Johnny listened for it, and heard no sound, but he heard another sound — the faint clop, clop of a walking horse. "Somebody coming in?" he asked, turning his head. "Maybe one of your boys?"

"Maybe. There's two still out." Warner got up. "I'll see."

The big rancher turned toward the door. Suddenly he started backing toward them, and Rope Nose George was standing in the door with a shotgun in his hand. He wore two six-shooters, but it was the double-barreled shotgun that stopped Johnny Sutton. "Don't be a fool, George," he said, "you've been out of this."

"I know that," Rope Nose replied solemnly. "I was well out of it, an' then I got to thinkin'. Ten thousand dollars — why, that's a lot of money! It would keep a man a long time, if he used it right, especially down in one o' them South American countries. I just couldn't forget it, so I asked myself, 'where will Sutton go?' And I guessed right."

"George," Sutton said patiently, "you get out of here now and I'll forget this ever happened."

"That's fair. That's mighty fair, ain't it, Mr. Warner? Not many would give a man a break like that. Nevertheless, I ain't a-goin' to do it. Ten thousand — why, I never see that much money! I'll never have me another chance at it. I ain't nervy like that Pink Lucas is. I'm a yaller dog. I know that, Sutton. I always been afeard o' Pink an' his crowd, but why should I set in that durned bar when I could be settin' on a wide piazza down Guatemala way? I know a gent onct who come from Guatemala. He said . . ."

His voice trailed off and stopped. "You!" He pointed at Stormy. "I know that money you got is in that sack. Set it over here.

Then get those saddlebags. Then I'll tie you all up an' drag it."

He chuckled. "I figured you'd come here, so I never went across that Tornillo Flat. I rode straight west without comin' north at all, then dropped south an' crossed the crick afore she got a big head up."

"Better think it over, Rope Nose," Sutton suggested mildly. "We'll get you."

"I done thought it over. I'm takin' two o' Warner's blacks. Nothin' around here will outrun them horses. I'll switch from one to the other an' ride hard to the border. It ain't far, an' once across I'll make the railroad an' head for Guatemala or somewheres. You'll never see hide nor hair o' me again."

With his left hand he gathered up the sacks. The shotgun rested on the back of a chair with the muzzles pointed at Sutton, not ten feet away.

"Now," he waved to Stormy, "you tie these gents up. Tie 'em good an' tight because I'll look 'em over after. Then I'm takin' out. Sure do hate to take your money, young lady, but I'll need it, an' you're young."

Johnny Sutton was the last one tied. The girl drew the ropes about him, then tied a knot and, opening Johnny's hand, placed the end of the rope in it. Instantly, he realized what she had done. She had gambled and tied a slip noose!

Rope Nose called her over and proceeded to tie her hands. Then he picked up the sacks and, with the shotgun, backed to the door. As the door closed after him, Sutton jerked on the rope. His wrists were tied, and he could only pull a little at a time. Sweat broke out on his face and body but he fought with his fingers, struggling to pull the knot loose. He heard a horse walking, then another. He heard one of the outlaws call out from the barn, and Rope Nose replying.

Suddenly the noose slipped, and then he was jerking his arms and shaking loose the loops of rope about his wrists. Swiftly he untied his feet and grabbed for his gunbelts. Whipping them about him, Johnny rushed to the door. Rope Nose had both blacks saddled. He hung the saddlebags and sack on one, then swung to mount the other.

Johnny heard Lucas swearing from the barn, and heard the refusal of Rope Nose to give them aid. Then Johnny stepped out and let the door slam behind him. Rope Nose whirled as if stabbed, the shotgun in his hands. He was all of fifty yards away and his mouth was wide, his eyes staring with incredulous horror.

Suddenly he shouted, almost screamed, "No! No, you ain't goin' to stop me!" He stepped forward and fired the shotgun waist high, and then Sutton fired. The widely scattered pellets of the shotgun clicked and pattered about him as he fired. He shot once, twice.

Rope Nose staggered, dropping the shotgun as the second barrel of shot plowed up earth. Sutton could see the man's fat stomach bulging over his leather belt. He saw the sudden whiteness in the man's face. Saw him step forward, hauling clumsily at a belt gun. He got it out, his eyes wide and staring.

"Drop it!" Sutton shouted. "Drop it, George!"

"No!" the fat man gasped hoarsely now. "No, I won't . . . !"

The gun came waist high and he began to shoot. The first shot went wild, the second kicked up earth at Sutton's feet, and then he saw the muzzle was dead on him, and Johnny Sutton fired a third shot. Rope Nose took a short step forward and kept falling until he hit the hard ground on his face. Then he rolled over and lay staring up at the sky, a spot of mud on his nose.

Sutton ran to him. The man was still alive. His eyes met Sutton's. "Should of knowed I'd . . . I'd never make it," he whispered, "but me, an' I'm a yaller dog, killed in a gun . . . gunfight with Ranger Johnny Sutton!" He breathed hoarsely. "Yessir, let 'em say I was yaller! Let 'em say that! But let 'em remember I faced up to Sutton with a six-gun! Let 'em remember, I died . . . game."

Johnny Sutton stared down at him, a fat, untidy man who had rolled over in the mud. The florid features were pale and the spot of mud might have made him ludicrous, only somehow he was not. It was simply that in this last minute, this moment of death, by his own shady standards at least, he had acquired a certain nobility.

Stormy Knight came up beside Sutton and took his arm. He put his hand over hers and turned away. Why didn't men like this ever learn that it wasn't money in the long run? It was contentment. Or had Rope Nose found contentment in that last moment when he knew he had faced a gun and stood up to it?

"You think it will be all right for us to go on tomorrow?" Stormy was trying to make conversation.

"Sure," Sutton replied, "I think it will.

When you get that ranch, you might write me. I'll come calling."

"I'd like that," Stormy said, and when she smiled, Johnny knew she meant what she said.

# TO MAKE A STAND

W hen the snow began to fall, Hurley was thirty-six hours beyond the last cluster of shacks that might be called a town, and the plain around him stretched flat and empty to the horizon.

The sullen clouds sifted sparse snow over the hard brown earth and the short, dust gray grass. The fall of snow thickened and the horizons were blotted out, and Hurley rode in a white and silent world where he was a man alone.

Had he dared, Hurley might have turned back, but death rode behind him, and Hurley was a frightened man, unaccustomed to violence. He had ridden into town and arrived to see a stranger dismounting from a horse stolen from his ranch only a month before.

Following the man into the saloon, Hurley demanded the return of the horse, and the man reached for his gun. In a panic, Hurley grabbed frantically for his own.

His first shot ripped splinters from the

floor and his second struck the thief through the body and within minutes the man was dead.

Clumsily, Hurley reholstered his gun. Shocked by what he had done, he looked blindly around the room like a man suddenly awakened in unfamiliar surroundings. Vaguely, he felt something was expected of him.

"He asked for it," he said then, striving for that hard, confident tone that would convince them he was a man not to be trifled with. Inside he was quivering with shock, and yet through the startled horror with which he looked upon the man he had killed came the realization that he had actually defended himself successfully in a gun battle. The thought filled him with elation and excitement.

Hurley was not a man accustomed to violence. He carried a gun only because it was the custom, and because in the daily round of activity emergencies might arise with wild steers or half-wild horses when a gun was needed, but he had never dreamed of actually killing a man.

From time to time he heard at the store or the post office some talk of gun battles, but that was in another world than his, and he could remember few of the names he had heard and none of the details.

Hurley had come west from Ohio, where he combined his farming with occasional carpentry work. When he first arrived, he drove a freight team for a season. The one time their wagon train was attacked by Indians the attack broke off before he was able to fire a shot. Leaving the freighting, Hurley had bought a few head of cattle and settled on a small stream with a good spring close by, and true to his Ohio upbringing he put in a crop of corn and a few acres of barley, and planted what was the first vegetable garden in that part of the country. He cut hay in the nearby meadow and stacked it for the winter feeding.

He had wanted no trouble, and expected none. He was a sober, hardworking man who had never lifted a hand in violence in his life.

"He asked for it," he repeated.

"Nobody's going to argue that." Pearson was the saloonkeeper, a man Hurley had several times seen but never spoken to. "But what are you going to do about his brothers?"

Pearson looked upon Hurley with cool, measuring eyes that had looked upon many men and assayed their worth. He found nothing special in Hurley, and of the men in the room, he alone had seen Hurley's success had been born of pure panic and unbelievable luck.

The words failed at first to register on Hurley's stunned consciousness, and when they did register he looked around. "Brothers? What brothers?"

"That's Jake Talbot you killed, and Jake has four brothers, all men mighty big-talking about how tough they are. They're just down the street to Reingold's, and they'll be hunting you."

The momentary elation over his astonishing victory oozed out of him and left Hurley standing empty of all pretense. He looked to Pearson in that moment like a frightened and trapped animal.

"He stole my horse," Hurley protested. "I can prove it."

"Nobody asked for proof. You've got two choices, mister. You can dig in for a fight or you can run."

"I'd better go see the sheriff."

Pearson looked upon him without pity. A man behind a bar cannot afford to take sides. He was an observer, a spectator, and Pearson was not disposed to be otherwise. He viewed all life with complete detachment except as it affected him, personally.

"The sheriff never leaves Springville,"

he said. "Hereabouts, folks settle their own difficulties."

Hurley walked to the bar and put his hands upon it. Jake Talbot . . . the Talbot brothers. They had an outfit somewhat closer in to town than his, and it seemed that half the stories of shootings and knifings he had heard of centered around them. He could recall no details, only the names and their association with violence.

Four of them . . . how could he be expected to fight four men? He was not a brave man and had never pretended to be one. Fear washed over him and turned his stomach sick. Turning swiftly, he went outside and stood staring down the hundred yards of dusty street into the open prairie. Against the four Talbots he would have no chance. He had worked hard since coming here, but had no friends to go to for help or advice.

If they did not find him in town, they would come at once to his ranch and murder him there. Mounting, Hurley rode west, away from town and away from his ranch.

That had been thirty-six hours ago, and now the snow was falling. Thirty of those hours had been in the saddle, and although the bay gelding was an excellent horse the long miles had sapped his strength and the need for rest was desperate.

Hurley got down from the saddle and looped the reins about his arm as he walked. However little he knew about guns and fighting, he knew a great deal about the weather, and he knew his situation was dangerous. At this time of year such a storm as this might be over within hours, and a bright sun might wipe away the snow as if by a gesture. However, such a storm might last for two or three days and the resulting snow remain for weeks.

Until now his mind had been a blank, with no thought but to escape, to get away from the danger of tearing, ripping bullets that would spill his life's blood on the ground — and for what?

Hurley had looked upon the dead face of Talbot and had seen himself lying there, knowing better than most how narrow had been the margin. That he had scored with his second shot had been luck of purest variety, for it had been aimed no more than the first.

The snow fell steadily. The trail he followed was no longer visible, but he could feel the frozen ruts with his feet. It was not a narrow trail, but one a hundred yards or more wide where wagons had cut deep ruts into the prairie sod, yet once away from the road the wagons had traveled, the prairie became flat and smooth. The difference he could tell with his feet . . . until the snow became too deep.

Night offered no warning of its coming, for in this white, swirling world of snow there were no advancing shadows, no retreating light, not even, it seemed, a visible darkening. Only suddenly the night was around them and upon them.

A faint stir of wind sent a chill through Hurley. If the wind started now there would be a blizzard, and dressed as he was even his slim chance of survival would be lost. He had never been farther west than the town, and rarely in town in the short time he had been located on the ranch. From overheard conversations in the stores and the livery stable, Hurley knew there was nothing in the direction he was going for several days of riding.

Finally, he stumbled and stumbled again. Wearily, he turned to the horse and, brushing off the saddle, he mounted again. There was no longer any use in trying to follow the trail through the snow for it had become too deep, so he simply gave the gelding its head.

It might have been an hour or even two

hours later when the gelding stopped abruptly and awakened him from a doze. He peered through the still falling snow, and at first he saw nothing, but then a gate, and some distance beyond it, a cluster of buildings. Actually, they were not buildings, but merely roofs indicating the sod houses below them.

As he got down from the saddle, his legs were so stiff he almost fell, but he managed to fumble the gate open and get his horse inside, and to fumble the gate shut again. He had farmed and ranched long enough to instinctively close all gates behind him.

The house was built into the side of a low hill where drainage was good, and the door he faced was strongly built. There were two windows, both frosted over, but behind them was a faint glow of light. Hurley lifted his fist and dropped it against the door.

The floor creaked inside and then the door opened, and a tall old man held a rifle in his hand. There was an oil lamp on the table, its wick turned low.

"Can you put me up? I'm lost."

The old man's eyes were cold and measuring. "Can't turn a man away in a storm. Go put your horse up."

The door closed in his face, and Hurley

turned away, blinking. There was a dug-out and sod-faced barn not far away and he went to it, kicked back the snow, and forced the door open. It cracked loudly, complaining against the rust and frost in its hinges, and he led the gelding inside and fumbled to light the lantern.

It was a snug barn. The farmer in him appreciated its warmth, the solid construction of the stalls, the strongly made feed bin, and the mangers. He tied the gelding, stripped off saddle and bridle, and then with a handful of hay he wiped the snow and damp from the horse. After he had filled the manger with hay and put a little corn in the feed box, Hurley went to the house.

The single room was square and well built. The plank floor was an unusual feature in a soddy, and it was fitted well. Clothing hung on a row of pegs in the wall, and against the end wall there were four bunks in two tiers, but only one held bedding. There was a glowing kitchen range, and on top of it a teakettle.

The old man was very tall, his wide, thin shoulders slightly stooped, his face deeply lined under the high cheekbones. The furrows in his cheeks seemed to make him look even more grim and determined. He had started to warm some food.

"No weather to travel." Hurley cupped the coffee the old man offered him in his two hands. "Unexpected storm."

"That's fool talk. This time of year a body can expect any kind of weather."

Hurley pulled a chair up to the table and sat down. The chair sat even on the floor, as did the table; both were well made. There was no arguing with the man's comment, for Hurley knew it to be true. "My name is Hurley," he said.

The old man filled his own cup and glanced over the rim at Hurley. "I'm Benton," he said. "What are you runnin' from?"

Hurley stiffened, half angry. He started to protest, but Benton ignored him.

"No man would be caught this far from the settlements without an outfit unless he was runnin' from something, or somebody."

Hurley did not reply. He accepted the offered stew sullenly. He did not like the implication that he was running away.

"I shot a man back there." He tried to make it sound bigger than it was. He wanted to impress this old man, to get under his hide.

"If he's dead, there's no use to run. If he

ain't dead, you better improve your shootin'."

"He was a Talbot . . . with four brothers."

"I know those Talbots," Benton replied. "They're a pack of coyotes."

They ate in silence for several minutes. Hurley stared glumly at his coffee. Benton made it sound petty, like nothing at all. Hurley's killing had made no impression, and the Talbots obviously did not impress him.

"Did you leave anything back there?"

"Yes," Hurley admitted, "I left a good ranch, and a good crop of corn standing, and oats growing. A few head of cattle."

"Where you runnin' to?"

"I never gave it much thought," Hurley admitted. "There were four of them, all rated tough men."

"Were you runnin' when you came out here, too?"

Hurley put down his knife and fork. "Now, see here — !"

Benton never looked up. "A man starts runnin', he doesn't stop. If you run once, you'll run again. Probably you never had as much in your life as you left back there, but you cut out and ran. All right . . . something else happens, you'll run again."

Hurley's features flushed with anger.

Who did this old fool think he was? If it hadn't been for the storm he would have taken his horse and ridden on. "There were four of them," he repeated.

"You said that before, and it don't cut no ice. You didn't even meet up with them. Take it from me, you get four men together and one of them has to take the lead, and nobody wants to be that one. I'd rather face four men any time than one real tough man."

"Easy to talk."

Benton went to the stove for the coffee-pot. "You get yourself a shotgun. You go back there and you walk right in on them. You don't give them any chance to talk, you just tell them if they want trouble they've got it and to cut loose their wolf. They'll back down so fast it will make your head swim."

"And if they don't?"

"Then shoot 'em."

Hurley snorted contemptuously. This old man living out here like a hermit . . . what did he know?

"A man who won't fight for what's his ain't much account," Benton said. "You take it from me."

Hurley started to rise from the table. He was mad clear through.

Benton looked up, his hard eyes level and cold. "You set down, Mr. Hurley. Just set down. I ain't about to be scared of no man who can be run clean out of the country by a passel of tinhorns." The old man grinned sardonically. "Anyway, you ain't about to leave a fireside for that storm out there."

Hurley sat down helpless and angry. Benton gathered the dishes and carried them to the sink, then, pouring water into a dishpan from the teakettle, he began washing the dishes.

The warmth of the room, combined with his weariness, made Hurley nod. His head bobbed several times but he struggled to keep his eyes open. It was comfortable to relax after his long battle against the storm, and outside the sod house he could hear the wind blowing, enough to remind him that had he not found shelter he would have been dead by morning.

Benton indicated a drawer in an old-fashioned bureau. "In that drawer there's blankets. You take the other bottom bunk."

Benton was still puttering around when Hurley dropped off to sleep. Hurley's last thought was: "At daybreak . . . when daybreak comes I'll get out of here."

A blast of icy air awakened him and for

an instant Hurley lay still, fighting to find himself, to realize where he was. The room was dark, swirling with blown snow, and nothing was familiar. Then it all came back to him, and he scrambled out of bed and slammed the door shut.

"What happened?" he asked into the silence, but the silence remained unbroken. Hurley stood still, listening, and he heard no sound but the wind.

Fumbling for his shirt, he found matches and lit one, then the lamp.

Benton's bunk was empty, but it had been slept in.

Hastily, Hurley got into his pants and boots and picked up his coat and shrugged into it. He strapped on his gun belt and, opening a lantern that stood by the door, he lit it. For an instant, he hesitated.

The Talbots might be out there. They might be . . . but his common sense told him they could not be. They would be holed up somewhere, waiting out the storm.

Opening the door, Hurley stepped out into the darkness. The wind was blowing a gale, and he was almost stifled by a blast of wind that blew his breath right back down his throat. Ducking his head, he stepped into the storm and almost tripped over a body, half buried in swirling snow.

Stooping, Hurley picked up the man and carried him to the door, which he opened with one hand, and stepped inside. Then he returned for the lantern.

The body was that of Benton, and a glance told him the old man's leg was broken.

Stretching him out on the bunk, Hurley covered him with blankets and then went to the fire which had been banked against the long hours of night. Stirring the coals, he added fuel and built a roaring blaze to warm the room. He worked swiftly, knowing warmth would be most important to Benton now. Then he crossed the room to the injured man, slit his trouser leg, and pulled the leg into place. He was binding splints when Benton came out of it and tried to sit up.

"Lie still . . . you've busted your leg."

Benton settled back, his face gray with pain. Hurley turned from him and, searching through a cabinet, found a bottle of whiskey. He poured a slug into a glass and handed it to Benton. "Do you good," he said. "Mighty poor stuff to drink if you're going to stay out in the cold, but once inside it warms you up."

Benton drank the whiskey and handed the glass back to Hurley. He settled back, looking around him. "Last thing I recall," he said, "some noise out at the barn. I started out and slipped on the steps. I felt myself falling . . . that was all."

Hurley explained how he had awakened to find the door open and snow swirling into the room.

Then Benton's remark reached his consciousness. "You say you heard a noise at the barn?"

Benton nodded. "You better go see what's wrong."

The Talbots . . . they could be out there. They knew he would come for his horse, and the barn was warm. They could be out there waiting to shoot him down as he came in out of the morning. Or they might have made the noise on purpose to draw someone to the stable.

"It can wait," Hurley replied sullenly. "The door's shut, I can see that."

He got down the coffee and made a pot. How long he had slept he had no idea, but he was fully awake now. If they were really there.

Benton watched him with sardonic amusement as he made the coffee and brought a cup to the injured man. "Don't know whether them Talbots are out there, or not," he said. "You just got to wait and

133

see, or you've got to go out there and find out. Puts a man in a jim-dandy fix."

"Shut up," Hurley said irritably.

He stood over the stove, feeding sticks into the flames and trying to think it out. Even if the storm let up a man would have no chance afoot, for aside from the distance and the cold his tracks would be laid out plain as print for anyone to follow.

He got down the old man's Spencer and checked the loads. Seven shots. He was a good shot with a rifle, and had hunted rabbits and squirrels back in Ohio. The distance to the barn was no more than sixty or seventy feet, point blank range.

After awhile Hurley put the light out and stretched out on his bunk. He could hear deep breathing from Benton's bed and decided the old man must be asleep.

Hurley sat up so suddenly he bumped his head on the upper bunk. *What about Benton?*

Somehow, in the excitement of finding the old man with a broken leg, and his worry about the Talbots being in the stable, he had given no thought to Benton.

Hurley could not leave him. He would have to stay on, he would have to stay and face the Talbots whether they were in the stable or not.

He had escaped death in the storm to

134

trap himself here, a sitting duck to be killed whenever they came upon the place, and he had no chance.

He got out of the bunk and walked to the window. The wind had died down, and here and there he could see a break in the clouds. The barn was a low, squat hovel almost buried in snow. No tracks led to or from it, but there need be no tracks now, for it had blown snow long after they would have entered.

Angrily, he stared at the barn. And then he thought of the obvious idea. He had no business here at all. Suppose the old man had fallen when here alone? He would get along, wouldn't he? Suppose no one had been here to carry Benton in out of the snow? He would be dead by now. By bringing him in, Hurley had repaid Benton for whatever shelter he had gotten here. From now on they were quits and he could leave.

Only he could not go.

He picked up the Spencer, then put it down. If somebody was inside, the length of the rifle would be more of a handicap. What he needed was his pistol.

Hurley paused inside the door, taking a deep breath. Why was he going out there? Was he going to get his horse and run?

He was no gunman, he was a farmer,

and all he wanted to be was a farmer. Suddenly he knew why he was going out there, and it was very simple. He was going out to feed the stock, just as any farmer would do on any winter morning.

*His* stock?

For the first time he thought of his own stock. The cattle were loose to roam, and they were used to bad weather, and this snow wasn't so deep but what they could scratch through it for grass, and there were several haystacks to which he always let down the bars when he left the ranch. The chance of their coming to the stacks was slight, for usually they stayed well out on the range, but if they did there was feed.

Except for his horses, which were all in stalls, in the barn. He had told Anderson he was going into town, and Anderson would water them if he did not see Hurley return before dark. Anderson was a careful man, and he would realize at once that something had gone wrong, hearing the story as soon as anyone. He would care for the horses.

Standing there in the door, Hurley remembered the house he had built with his own hands, the cattle he owned, the horses, fine stock they were, that he had left behind.

Benton was right. He would never have as much again.

Opening the door, he stepped outside into the cold.

The sky was clearing off, and there was a red glow in the east that told him dawn was only minutes away. Facing the barn, Hurley strode toward it. Inside his coat he held his .44, the gun concealed, the hand warmed by contact with his body.

At the barn door he stopped.

There was snow on the door, snow around it. No sign that it had been disturbed since he left it the night before. Unlatching the door he swung it wide, and pulling the .44 from under his coat, he stepped quickly into the barn.

It was, he thought as he took the step, a melodramatic, obvious thing to do. And perfectly foolish, of course, for as he entered the darkness of the barn, he was silhouetted against the snow outside. . . . He moved quickly to one side.

Nothing happened.

From stall to stall he went, and there was no one there. He put his pistol back in its holster and went about feeding and watering the stock. When he had finished, he came out and closed the door behind him. He stood for a minute in the still, cold air watching his breath, and he remembered how long he had been tortured by doubt, how long he had watched the barn, fearing the Talbots might be there.

Was all fear like that? Was it all, or most of it, just imagination? Was Benton right, after all, and the way to meet fear was head-on?

He walked back to the house. On the steps he paused to stomp the snow from his boots. As he did so the door swept open and Benton stood there with a leveled rifle.

Only the rifle was held steady against the doorjamb, and it was pointed past his head at the ranch yard behind him.

Hurley looked up and saw the grim look on the old man's face, saw the old man had dragged himself from bed to cover him while he fed the stock. But he saw much more. Benton was looking past him and Benton said, *"Hold it!* Hold it right there!"

Hurley knew death then. He knew the Talbots were behind him, and he knew there were four of them, and he knew he was fairly caught.

But he was calm.

That, of all things, was the most astonishing. There were, he knew in that moment, worse things than death, and there were few things worse than fear itself.

He turned slowly. "It's my fight, Benton," he said. "You get back in bed."

He stepped down off the step. He was scared. He was really scared, and yet somehow it was not as bad as he had expected. He looked at the four shivering men on their horses, and he smiled. "Are you boys looking for me?" he asked.

They hesitated . . . they were cold and shaky from having spent the night in whatever pitiful shelter had been available out on the prairie. And this man had beaten Jake to the draw, and that bullet had gone dead center. It was one thing to chase down a running man, another to face a man who was ready to fight.

"Jake Talbot was riding a horse stolen from me," Hurley spoke loud in the still air. "When I asked him about it he went for his gun. He asked for it and he got it. Now if you boys have anything to say, have at it."

Joe Talbot looked him over more carefully. They had figured they had him on the run, but he did not look scared now. Not none at all.

They could get him; they were four guns to one. Or two if that old man with the rifle declared himself in, but that fool Hurley, he might just get one of them, or even two while they were killing him. They had taken this ride to kill a man, not to be killed themselves, and each one had deep within him the feeling that the first one to pull a gun would be the one to die.

Silence hung in the still, cold air. A horse stamped a hoof impatiently.

"Jake must have bought that horse off a thief," Joe Talbot said, at last. "We don't know anything about it."

It was a retreat, and Hurley was wise enough to recognize it. He took a step nearer to them. "You have that horse back at my place Monday morning," he said, "and we'll call it quits. Understand?"

They did not like it. They knew what was happening to them and they did not like it at all. After this there could be no more tough talk — folks simply wouldn't pay any attention. They were being backed down and they knew it, but no one of them wanted to be the man to die.

"No need for neighbors to fight," Joe Talbot said. "We didn't have the straight of it."

Joe Talbot made the move, finally, but it was to turn his horse toward the gate. And when he turned, the others turned with him.

"Talbot?"

Joe turned his head carefully to look at Hurley. "Stop by Anderson's and ask him to feed my stock, will you? I've got to take care of my friend here. He's got a broken leg."

At the gate one of the Talbots got down from the saddle and closed the gate carefully, then they rode off, together. It looked like they were not very talkative.

"Hurley?" It was Benton. "Come inside and close the door! You're freezin' the place up! Besides, I want some breakfast."

Hurley stomped his feet again and stepped up in the doorway. He glanced back at the sky. The clouds were blowing off to the north and the sun had already started the icicles dripping. One thing you could say for this country, it didn't take long to clear up.

# THAT MAN FROM
# THE BITTER SANDS

W hen Speke came at last to water, he was two days beyond death.

His cracked lips rustled like tissue paper when they moved, trying to shape a thought. The skin of his face, long burned to a desert brown, had now taken on a patina of crimson.

Yet his mind was awake, and alive within him was a spirit that even the desert could not defeat. Without doubt Ross and Floren believed him dead, and this pleased him, stirring a wry sense of humor.

The chirping of birds told him of water before he saw it. His stumbling, almost hypnotic walk ceased, and swaying upon his feet, he turned his head slowly upon his stiff neck.

The basin remained unchanged, only now he had reached the very bottom of the vast depression, and a jagged knife's edge of rocks, an upthrust from a not too ancient fracture, loomed off to his right.

He had seen a dozen such along the line

of travel, yet there was a difference. The faint, grayish green of the desert vegetation here took on a somewhat deeper green. Yet without the birds he might not have noticed. There was water near.

Through the heat-engendered haze in his skull there flickered grim humor. Floren and Ross thought they had taken from him all that promised survival when they had also taken his gold. They had robbed him of weapons, tools, canteen, food, and water. They had left him nothing.

Better than anyone else he had known what lay before him. After they had gone he had worked to free himself, but when he had succeeded he did not move away. He waited quietly in the shadow of the ledge, gutted of its small hoard of gold. Only when the sun was down did he move, and then he stepped out with a long, space-eating stride, walking away into that vast wasteland, shadowed with evening.

They had left him two things they did not realize would matter. They had seemed but bits of debris in the looted camp: a prospector's gold pan and a storm square from his canvas groundsheet.

Before it grew too dark to travel he had walked eight miles. Stopping then, he scooped a shallow hole in the sand and placed in it the gold pan. Over it he stretched the canvas, and above that he built a small pile of large stones. When his dew trap was complete he lay down to sleep.

Scarcely a spoon of water rewarded the effort, yet he swallowed it and was grateful. Before the sun topped the ridge he had three more miles behind him. Near two boulders he stopped and made a sun shade of a ruined cedar in the space between the boulders. He crawled into this island of coolness and lay down.

Midafternoon of the second day he found a barrel cactus, and cutting off the top he squeezed some water from the whitish green pulp. On the second and third nights he also built his dew traps, and each time got a little water. When he first heard the birds he thought he was losing his reason, yet turning toward the serrated ridge, he stumbled on. At its base, among some desert willows, was a small pool some four feet across . . . but lying in it was a dead coyote.

Swaying drunkenly, he stared hollow-eyed at the dead coyote and the poisoned water. He could go no further, he knew. He must drink, yet, in his weakened state, a case of dysentery would surely kill him. It was not in him to yield, and too well he knew the ways of the wild country and the lessons it taught.

The will that had carried him more than forty miles across the desert moved him then. He dragged the remains of the dead coyote from the water. Then he gathered sticks and built a fire. When he had a small heap of charcoal, he scooped up some water with the gold pan. He covered the water until it was two inches thick with charcoal. Then he stoked his fire and waited. Soon the water was boiling.

The desert night drew darkness around him. The firelight flickered on the rock wall and upon the fragile boughs of the willow, and the smoke drifted and lost itself in the night. Sparks flew upward and vanished.

With a flat stick, he skimmed off the thick scum of charcoal and coagulated impurities. Then he added more charcoal and the water continued to boil. A second time he skimmed it, and only then did he put some aside to cool.

The very presence of water seemed to help. His brain cleared and he thought. He was now halfway across the vast bowl of desert. He was walking toward a place he knew, a ranch with a well of cool, clear water, and a man who would lend him a horse. A horse and a gun.

Forcing himself to ignore the water, he leaned back against the rocks. His lips rustled together and his tongue felt like a dry stick. He closed his aching eyes and waited out the minutes, listening like a prisoner to the faint trickle of water into the pool.

When an hour had passed, he allowed himself his first drink. Dipping up a little of the water he took some in his mouth and held it there, feeling the coolness bringing life back to the starved, shrunken tissues. Slowly he let the water trickle down his throat, feeling the delightful coolness all through him. Even that tiny swallow seemed to reach into every part of his body.

He bathed his lips and face then, taking his time, and finally allowing himself another swallow of the water. Finding in the rock a natural basin that was almost a foot across he used it as a mold, and with a rounded stone he carefully pounded his prospecting pan down into it, forcing the pan into a shape more like that of a bucket. Returning to the fire he boiled more water with charcoal, then poured it into the basin in the rock, repeating the process with his newly made pail. Adding a few more bits of charcoal, he lay back on the ground and was almost at once asleep, knowing that with the dawn the water would be clear and sweet.

Long ago he had established a pattern of awakening, and despite his exhaustion he was stirring long before dawn. It was cold when he opened his eyes, and his body was chilled with the cold of the desert night. Hurriedly, he built a fire and let its warmth permeate his entire being. Then he drank, and after awhile, drank again. Then he turned to the desert.

A fleshy-fruited yucca grew near the water hole and he picked some of the long pods. He ate one of them raw, then roasted the others with some bulbs of the sego lily. When he had eaten these he took a thin, flat sheet of sandstone and began to dip water from the hole. Despite the little water there was, it took him more than an hour to empty the hole.

From time to time he paused to rest. Once, still having his tobacco, he rolled a smoke. He would need no more water than that in his bucket, but if others came along they would not know of the coyote and the poisoned spring. He did not know if his actions would help, but a water hole was a precious thing, to be safeguarded by all who passed.

When the hole was emptied he scraped the bottom with his flat stone, throwing out huge chunks of the mud. He then enlarged the opening through which the water flowed, still only a mere trickle, and finally sat down to eat more of the pods and bulbs, and to drink more water.

Water slowly trickled back into the hole. By night it would be full, and rested, he would start on with the first shadows.

Three days later, he was mounted on a horse. In the scabbard on his borrowed saddle was a Winchester, and thrust into his waistband was a battered but capable Colt.

They had insisted he remain and rest, but Speke would have none of it. Floren and Ross had taken his gold and he had been abandoned to die, yet it was with no thought of actual revenge that he returned to the desert. Nor did he blame his sufferings upon the two thieves whom he had taken into his camp when they had been half dead from thirst. The sufferings he had endured he accepted, as he accepted so much else as a part of life in the desert, yet the gold they had taken was his, and he intended to get it back.

Speke was not a big man but he was tough. The years and the desert had melted away any softness he might have had, and left behind a hard core of that rawhide resilience that the desert demands. Never a gunman, he had used weapons as a soldier in the Apache wars, as a buffalo hunter, and in his own private skirmishes with desert Mohaves or Pimas.

He needed no blueprint to read the plan in the minds of Floren and Ross. They would go first to Tucson.

It was a sufficient distance away. It had whiskey, women, and for a desert town of the era, remarkably good food.

On a sunlit morning not long after day-break, Tom Speke rode his shambling buck-skin into the main street of Tucson. He rode past staked-out pigs, dozens of yapping dogs, a few casual, disinterested burros, and a few naked Mexican youngsters. He was a lean man of less than six feet, not long past thirty but seasoned by the desert, a man with dingy trousers, a buckskin jacket, a battered narrow-brimmed hat, and a lean-jawed look about him.

He swung down at the Shoo Fly, and went into the restaurant. It was a long room of adobe, walls washed with yellow, a stamped earth floor, and tables of pine covered with cheap tablecloths. To Tom Speke, who had sat at a table four times in two years, the Shoo Fly represented the height of culture and gastronomic delight.

He did not order — at the Shoo Fly one accepted what the day offered, in this case jerked beef, frijoles, tomatoes, and stewed prunes (there had recently been a series of Apache raids on trains bringing fresh fruit from Hermosillo) and coffee. All but the coffee and the prunes were liberally laced with chile colorados, and there was still some honey that had been brought from the Tia Juana ranch below the border.

Tom Speke devoted himself to eating, but while he ate, he listened. The Shoo Fly was crowded, as always at mealtimes, and there was much talk. Turning to the kid who was clearing tables, he asked if there was any recent news of prospectors striking it rich in the area. The kid didn't know, but a man up the table looked up and put down his fork.

"Feller down to Congress Hall payin' for drinks with dust. Says he made him a pile over on the Gila."

"Big feller? With blond hair?" A man spoke up from the end of the bar. "Seen him. Looks mighty like a feller from Santa Fe I run into once. They were huntin' him for horse stealin'."

Tom Speke forked up the last piece of beef and chewed it thoughtfully. Then he wiped his plate with a slab of bread and disposed of it in the same way. He gulped coffee, then laid out his dollar and pushed back from the table. The description was that of Floren.

The sun stopped him on the step, and he waited until his eyes adjusted themselves to the glare. Then he walked up the street to the Congress.

Pausing on the step he eased the position of the Colt, then stepped inside and moved away from the door. Early as it was, the place was scattered with people. One game gave the appearance of having been on all night. Several men stood at the bar. One of these was a giant of a man in a stovepipe hat and a black coat. Speke knew him for Marcus Duffield, one-time town marshal and now postal inspector, but still the town's leading exponent of gun-throwing.

Speke glanced around. There was no sign of Ross, but Floren's big blond head was visible. He was sitting in the poker game, and from the look of it, he was winning.

Speke moved down the bar to Duffield's side. He ordered a drink, then jerked his head at Duffield. "An' one for Marcus, here."

Duffield glanced at him. "Goin' to be some shootin' here right sudden," Speke said quietly. "I figured to tell you so's you wouldn't figure it was aimed at you." He indicated Floren by a jerk of his head. "Feller there an' his partner come into my camp half dead. I gave 'em grub an' water. Second day they throwed down on me, tied me up, an' stole my outfit, includin' three pokes of gold."

"Seen the gold," Duffield said. "Didn't figure him for no miner."

He glanced over his shoulder. "Better wait'll he finishes this hand. He's holdin' four of a kind."

Speke lifted his glass and Duffield acknowledged it. They drank, and Tom Speke turned around and then moved down the bar. He waited there, watching the game, his eyes cold and emotionless. Floren raked in the pot on his four queens and started to stack the money.

And then he looked up and saw Speke.

He started to move, then stopped. His eyes stared, his face went sickly yellow.

A card player noticed his face, took a quick look at Speke, then carefully drew back from the table. The others followed suit.

"You won that with my money, Floren," Speke said carefully. "Just leave it lay."

Floren took a quick look around. His big hands rested on the arms of his chair, only inches from his gun. One of the players started to interrupt, but Duffield's bold black eyes pinned the man to the spot. "His show," Duffield said. "That gent's a thief."

Floren touched his lips with his tongue. "Now, look," he said, "I — "

"Ain't aimin' to kill you," Speke said conversationally, "nor Ross. You stole my outfit an' left me for dead, but all I want is my money an' my outfit. Get up easy an' empty your pockets."

Floren looked at the money, and then at Speke. Suddenly his face seemed to set, and an ugly look flared in his eyes. He started to rise. "I'll be double d— !" His hand dropped to his gun.

Nobody had seen Ross come in the door. He took one quick look, drew, and fired. Even as Speke thumbed back the hammer, he was struck from behind. He staggered, then fell forward.

Floren stood, his unfired gun in his hand, and looked down at Speke. Ross held the room covered. Floren lifted the muzzle of his gun toward the fallen man.

"Don't do that," Duffield said, "or you'll have to kill every man in this room."

Floren looked up at him, and hesitated.

"Don't be a fool," Ross said, "pick up your money and let's go."

It was two weeks before Speke could leave his bed, despite excellent care by Semig, a Viennese doctor attached to the Army. It was a month before he could ride.

Duffield watched him mount the buckskin. "Next time don't talk," he advised. "Shoot!"

Tom Speke picked up the trail of Floren and Ross on the Hassayampa and followed them into Camp Date Creek. Captain Dwyer of the Fifth Cavalry listened to Speke's description, then nodded. "They were here. I ordered them out. Ross was known to have sold liquor to the Apaches near Camp Grant. I couldn't have them around."

Swapping the weary buckskin for a zebra dun mustang, Speke returned to the trail.

At Dripping Springs Speke drew up and swung down. Cherokee Townsend came from his cabin with a whoop of pleasure. The two had once traveled together across New Mexico. In reply to his questions, Townsend nodded. " 'Bout two weeks back," he said. "Didn't take to 'em much. Big fellow is ridin' a bay with three white stockings. The other one an appaloosa with a splash of white on his right shoulder. They headed for Prescott."

Townsend was, he said, staying on. "Watch out for 'Paches," he said. "They are out an' about. I've buried twenty-seven of them right on this place."

Speke rode on, sparing his horse but holding to the pace. He saw much Indian sign.

In Prescott the two had remained more than a week. They had left town headed west. Everywhere he was warned of Indians. The Apaches were out, and so were the Hualapais and Mohaves. There were rumors of an impending outbreak at Date Creek, and General Crook was going down to investigate.

Neither Floren nor Ross was a man of long experience in the West. During their time in his camp, before they had robbed him, he had seen that. They were men who had come west from Bald Knob, Missouri. Tough men and dangerous, but not desert-wise.

On the second day out of Prescott, Speke found two Indian ponies. Badly used, they had obviously been released by Indians who had gone on with fresher, stronger horses. Speke caught up the two ponies and led them along with him, an idea forming in his brain.

On the third day he spotted them ahead

of him, and he deliberately created dust off to their left and behind. That night he left his own horse and rode one of the others, and took the other unshod horse around their camp. He left four separate sets of tracks across their trail for the following day.

Moving on cat feet, he slipped down to the edge of the camp. A small fire was burning. Floren was asleep, and Ross sat nearby. Waiting for more than an hour with Indian patience, he finally got his chance. He slipped the muzzle of his rifle through the strap of a canteen and withdrew it carefully. He could have stolen the other also, but he did not. He made his way some distance, then deliberately let a small gravel slide start. Glancing back, he saw Ross come to his feet and leap from the firelight.

It was the beginning of his plan. He watched them draw up when they reached the tracks of the unshod ponies the following morning. To anyone, this certainly meant Indians. Indians often rode horses shod at trading posts or stolen from the white settlers, but white men almost never rode an unshod horse for any length of time. The tracks were headed west and south. Floren and Ross pulled off the trail, working north. Remembering the country ahead of them, Speke was satisfied.

In the four nights that followed, he succeeded in alarming their camp with stealthy
noises at least twice a night. He left pony
tracks ahead of them and near the camp.
Steadily, they bore off to the north, trying
to avoid the unseen Indians.

They were worried by the Indians they
believed were congregating nearby, they
had but one canteen between them, and
they were getting only disturbed sleep when
they slept at all. It was a calculated war of
nerves. Twice Speke lay on a bluff or behind a rock near the camp and heard them
arguing fiercely.

Ahead of them on the following morning,
he built a signal fire. He used a blanket to
simulate Indian signals, then went south a
few miles and did the same thing. They
were now well to the north of Ehrenberg
and headed for Hardyville. At dusk he lit
two more signal fires and used the smoke,
then put them out and worked closer to
the camp of the two outlaws.

Floren was thinner, haggard, hollow-
eyed. Ross was tighter, snappish and shifty.
They built a tiny fire to make coffee, and
Speke waited. When Ross reached for the
pot, he fired rapidly — three times.

The first shot struck the fire and threw
sparks, the second drilled the coffeepot —

Speke could see the sudden puff of steam and smoke when the coffee hit the fire — and the third shot struck a log on which Floren was seated.

Following the shots there was silence. Evidently the firing had caught both men away from their rifles. Moving a little, Speke watched the fire, relaxed and at ease. He had suffered from these men, and now he expected to recover his gold, and to do it, if possible, without killing.

Yet they had planned for him to die, and only the presence of Duffield and the rest had saved him in the saloon. It was not a consideration of mercy that moved him, rather a complete indifference to the fate of the two men. He wanted his gold; this he had worked for, slaved for. Whatever they had won gambling he would consider his — won with his money and payment for this long trek.

Day dawned with low clouds and a hint of rain. He saw them move out slowly, and knew they had spent an uncomfortable and altogether miserable night away from their bedrolls. Twice during the day he sent them into hiding with quick shots from ambush, not aimed to kill.

Twice he heard them bickering over the canteen, and an idea came to him. He knew they kept the gold close to them, so to get at it was scarcely possible, but there was something else he could get. And that night he stole one of their horses.

At dawn, after a quiet sleep on the desert, Tom Speke was awake. Gathering his horses, he left them concealed in the shelter of an upthrust of rock, and then moved closer to watch.

Already an argument was ensuing. One canteen, one horse, thirty pounds of gold, and two men.

Coolly, Speke rolled a smoke. He could have written the story of what was to happen now. Harassed beyond limit, their nerves on edge from constant attack, from sleepless nights, and from uncertainty as to their enemies, the two were now facing each other. In the mind of each was the thought that success and escape could belong to one man, and one only.

Floren was saddling the horse. Then he picked up the gold and tied it behind the saddle. He seemed to be having trouble. Ross dropped his hand to his gun — he failed to calculate on the shadow, and Floren turned and fired.

Ross staggered, took a step back, then yelled something wild and incoherent. He went down to his hands and knees and

Floren swung into the saddle and rode away.

Ross remained on his hands and knees. Speke drew deep on his cigarette and watched Floren go. He was heading northwest. Speke smiled and got up, then went back for his own horses. When he had them he walked down to Ross. The man had fallen, and he was breathing hoarsely.

Working with swift sureness, Speke carried the smaller man into the shade of a cedar and, ripping open his shirt, examined the wound. Ross had been struck on the top of the hipbone, knocking him down and temporarily shocking him into a state of partial paralysis. The bullet had torn a hole in his side, a flesh wound, from which blood was flowing.

Heating water, he bathed the wound. Then, making a decoction from the leaves of creosote bush, he used it as an antiseptic on the wound. Then he bandaged it crudely but effectively. Ross revived while he worked, and stared at him. "You . . . is it?"

"Uh-huh."

"Figured we'd lost you."

"Ain't likely."

"Why you helpin' me?"

Speke sat back on his heels. He nodded at the horse he had stolen. "I'm leavin' you that horse and a canteen. You head out of here. If I ever see you again, I'll kill you."

He got to his feet and started for the horses. Ross stared after him, then tried to lift himself to an elbow, managed it. "You leavin' me a gun?"

"No."

"Then I'm a sittin' duck for Injuns."

Speke smiled a rare smile. "Maybe you'll be lucky."

He walked his horse away on Floren's trail. He was in no hurry. Before them lay the breaks of the Colorado. Soon Floren would be stopped by the canyon itself. Speke had been long in the desert, and the desert teaches patience. There was no escape for Floren.

For days Speke had directed his smoke columns and his actions to cause the two outlaws to pull farther and farther north, until now Floren was in a cul-de-sac from which there was no way out except back the way he had come. But Floren would not know this. He would waste time looking.

It was a hot still day when the search ended. A day of a high sun and the reflecting heat from the face of vast plateaus of rock and the cedar-clad hillsides. Lizards panted even in the shade, their mouths held open, their sides pumping at the hot, thin air.

Floren was hollow-eyed and frightened. Whichever way he went he faced awesome canyons, and the only water was far, far below. Only a few drops slopped lonesomely in his canteen, and the horse he rode was gaunt and beaten. He swung down, and his heels hit hard, and he stared over the brink into the vast canyon below.

Trapped . . . Seven times he had found new routes, and each had ended in a cliff. Seven times he tried and seven times he failed. And now he knew there was no way to turn but back. He turned toward the horse, and as if expecting him, the animal went to its knees, then rolled over on its side. Fiercely, Floren swore. He kicked the horse. It would not rise, it could not rise. Better yet without the horse he could take the gold and find a way down the cliffs. Then a raft . . . feverishly, he rushed at the horse and stripped off the pack of gold. He started to take his rifle, then shrugged. It would only be in the way.

Shouldering the gold, he walked to the cliff's edge. There was no way over at that point. He turned, then stopped abruptly. One hundred yards away was Speke. The prospector held a Winchester cradled in his arm.

Speke said nothing. He just stood there, silent, still, alone.

Floren touched his lips with his tongue. He held the gold sack in his right hand. Anyway, at that range . . . a pistol . . . he looked toward his rifle. Too far away.

Speke shot from the hip, and the sack jerked in Floren's hand. Another shot. Speke moved a step forward and Floren dropped the sack and drew. He fired quickly, hastily. He missed. . . .

Speke fired again and Floren felt the bullet tug at his shirt. He took a hasty step back, then fired again himself. The bullet struck far to the left. Speke swung his rifle and fired. Rock fragments stung Floren's cheek. He jerked his head back up.

Speke said nothing. He worked the lever on his rifle and waited. Floren started forward, and a bullet kicked up sand ahead of him. He took a hasty step back.

The edge . . . could not be far behind. He glanced back and Speke fired swiftly, three shots. They scattered rock around his feet and a ricochet burned Floren's face. He was no more than six feet from the edge.

"You ain't goin' to make me jump!" he shouted angrily. He threw up his gun and fired.

Speke waited a minute, then walked swiftly

forward and picked up the gold. He backed away, then dropped the sack and fired. His Winchester '73 carried eleven bullets and he was counting them.

The shot whipped by Floren's face, so close it drew blood.

Floren was frightened now. His face was drawn and white. He stared with wide eyes and haggard mouth. Speke picked up the gold again and backed to his horse. Lashing it behind the saddle, he swung into the leather.

As he did so, he dropped the lead rope of one of the Indian ponies. "Help yourself," he said, and rode slowly away.

Floren started after him, shouting. Tom Speke did not turn his head or glance back. He merely rode on, remembering Tucson and the Shoo Fly. He would enjoy a meal like that now. Maybe, in a week or so . . .

He had lots of time . . . now.

# LET THE
# CARDS DECIDE

W here the big drops fell, we had placed a wooden bucket retrieved from a corner of the ancient log shack. The long, earth-floored one-room cabin smelled of wet clothing, wood smoke, and the dampness brought on by unceasing rain. Yet there was fuel enough, and the fire blazed bright on the hearth, slowly dispelling the dampness and bringing an air of warmth and comfort to the cheerless room.

Seven of us were there. Haven, who had driven the stage; Rock Wilson, a mine boss from Hangtown; Henry, the Cherokee Strip outlaw; a slender man with light brown hair, a sallow face, and cold eyes whom I did not at first know; the couple across the room; and myself.

Six men and one woman — a girl.

She might have been eighteen or a year older, and she was one of those girls born to rare beauty. She was slim, yet perfectly shaped, and when she moved it was to unheard music, and when she smiled, it was for you alone, and with each smile she seemed to give you something intimate, something personal. How she had come to be here with this man we all knew. We knew, for he was a man who talked much and talked loud. From the first, I'd felt sorry for her, and admired her for her quiet dignity and poise.

She was to become his wife. She was one of a number of girls and women who had come west to find husbands, although why this girl should have been among them I could not guess. She was a girl born for wealth and comfort, and her every word and movement spoke of breeding and culture. Yet here she was, and somehow she had gotten into the hands of Sam Tallman.

He was a big fellow, wide of shoulder and girth, with big hands and an aggressive manner. Not unhandsome in a bold way, he could appear gentle and thoughtful when it suited him, but it was no part of the man and strictly a pose. He was all the girl was not: rough, unclean, and too frank in his way of talking to strangers of his personal affairs.

That Carol Houston was becoming disillusioned was obvious. That is, if there had been any illusions to start. From time to time she gave him sharp, inquiring glances, the sort one might direct at an obnoxious stranger. And she was increasingly uneasy.

The stage was headed north and was to have dropped several of us here to meet another stage heading west. We were going to be a day late, however, for our coach had overturned three miles back on the muddy trail.

Bruised and shaken, we had righted the stage in the driving rain and had managed to get on as far as the shack. As we could not continue through the night, and this place was at least warm and dry, we made the best of it.

There seemed no end to the rain, and in the few, momentary lulls we could hear the measured fall of drops into the bucket, which would soon be full.

Now in any such place there comes a time when conversation slowly dies. The usual things have been said, the storm discussed and compared to other storms, the accident bewailed, and the duration of our stay surmised. We had exchanged destinations and told of our past lives, and all with no more than the usual amount of lying.

Dutch Henry produced some coffee, and I, ransacking the dismal depths of the farther cabin corners, a pot and cups. So the good, rich smell of coffee permeated the room with its friendly sense of well-being and comfort.

My name, it might be added, is Henry Duval. Born on Martinique, that distant and so lovely island noted for explosive mountains and women. My family had been old, respected, and until it came to me, of some wealth. By profession I had been a gambler.

This was, for a period of nearly a century, the usual profession of a young man of family but no means. Yet from gambling I had turned to the profession of arms, or rather, I had divided my time between them. The riverboats started me on the first, and the revolutions and wars of freedom in Latin America on the second. Now, at thirty-five, I was no longer occupied with either of these, but had succeeded in building a small fortune of my own in handling mining properties.

But let us be honest. During my gambling days I had, on occasion, shall we say, encouraged the odds? An intelligent man with a knowledge of and memory for cards, and some knowledge of people, can usually win, and honestly — when the cards run with him — but of course, one must have the cards. So when they failed to come of themselves, sometimes I did, as I have said, encourage them a bit.

Haven, the stage driver, I knew slightly. He was a solid, dependable man, both honest and fearless. Rock Wilson was of the same order, and both were of the best class of those strong, brave, and often uneducated men who built the West. Both had followed the boom towns — as I once had.

Dutch Henry? You may have heard of him. They hanged him finally, I believe. He was, as I have said, an outlaw. He stole horses, and cattle, and at times robbed banks or stages, but all without malice and without unnecessary shooting. And he was a man of rugged good nature who might steal a hundred today and give it away tomorrow.

The sallow-faced man introduced himself. His accent was that of the deep South. "My given name is John. I once followed the practice of medicine." He coughed into a soiled handkerchief, a deep rattling tubercular cough. "But my ahh . . . condition made that an irony I could no longer endure." He brushed a speck of lint from the frayed cuff of his faded frock coat. "I am now a gentleman of fortune, whatever that may mean."

Henry made the coffee. It had the strong, healthy flavor of cowpuncher coffee, the best for a rainy night. He filled our cups, saving the best for the lady. She smiled quickly, and that rugged gentleman of the dark trails flushed like a schoolboy.

Tallman was talking loudly. "Sure hit the jackpot! All them women, an' me gettin' the best o' the lot! Twenty o' them there was, an' all spoke for! Out in the cold, they said I was, but all right, I told 'em, if there's an extry, I get her! An' this one was extry!"

The future Mrs. Tallman flushed and looked down at her hands.

"How did it happen, Miss Houston?" I asked her. "Why didn't they expect you?"

She looked up, grateful for the chance to explain and to make her position clearer. She was entitled to that respect. "I wasn't one of them — not at first. I was coming west with my father, in the same wagon train, but he died of cholera and something happened to the little money he had. We owed money and I had nothing . . . well, what could I do?"

"Perfectly right," I agreed. "I've known some fine women to come west and make good marriages that way."

Good marriage was an expression I should not have used. Her face changed when I said that, and she looked down at her hands.

"Should o' heard the others howl when

they seen what I drawed!" Tallman crowed. "Course, she ain't used to our rough western ways, an' she ain't much on the work, I hear, but she'll learn! You leave that to me!"

Haven shifted angrily on his bench and Rock Wilson's face darkened and his eyes flashed angrily. "You're not married to her yet, you say? I'd be careful if I were you. The lady might change her mind."

Tallman's face grew ugly. His small eyes narrowed and hardness came into his jowls. "Change her mind? Not likely! You reckon I'd stand for that? I paid off her debts. One o' them young fellers back yonder had some such idea, but I knocked that out of him mighty quick! An' if he'd gone for a gun, I'd o' killed him!" Tallman slapped his six-shooter. "I'm no gunman," he declared, "but I get along!"

This last was said with a truculent stare around the room.

More to get the conversation away from the girl than for any other reason, I suggested poker.

John, the ex-doctor with the sallow cheeks, looked up sharply, and a faint, wry smile hovered about his lips. The others moved in around the table, and the girl moved back. Somehow, over their heads, our eyes met. In hers there was a faint pleading, an almost spoken request to do something . . . anything . . . but to get her out of this. Had we talked an hour she could not have made her wish more clear.

In that instant my resolution was made. As John picked up the cards I placed my palm flat down on the table in the old, international signal that I was a cardsharp. With a slight inclination of my head, I indicated Tallman as the object of my intentions, and saw his agreement.

Tallman played with the same aggressive manner of his talk, and kept a good eye on the cards that were played. We shifted from draw to stud and back again from time to time, and at first Tallman won.

When he had something good you had to pay to stay in the game, and he rode his luck hard. At the same time, he was suspicious and wary. He watched every move closely at first, but as the game progressed he became more and more interested and his vigilance waned. Yet he studied his cards carefully and took a long time in playing.

For me, there were no others in the game but Tallman and John. Once, when I had discarded, I walked to the fire and added a few sticks, then prepared more coffee and put the pot on the fire. Turning my head I saw Carol Houston watching me. From my chair I got my heavy coat and brought it to her. "If you're cold," I whispered.

She smiled gratefully, then looked into the flames.

"I do not wish to intrude on something that is none of my business." I spoke as if to the fire. "It seems that you might be more comfortable if you were free of that man."

She smiled sadly. "Can you doubt it? But he paid bills for me. I owe him money, and I signed an agreement to marry him."

"No one would hold you to such an agreement."

"He would. And I must pay my debts, one way or another. At the moment I can see no other way out."

"We'll see. Wait, and don't be afraid." Adding another stick to the fire, I returned to the table. Tallman glanced up suspiciously, for he could have heard a murmur, although probably none of the words spoken between us.

It was my deal, and as I gathered the discards my eyes made note of their rank, and swiftly I built a bottom stock, then shuffled the cards while maintaining this stock. I placed the cards in front of Henry for the cut, then I shifted the cut smoothly back and dealt. John gathered his cards, glanced at them, and returned them to the table before him. Tallman studied his own, then fidgeted with his money. I tossed in my ante and we started to build Tallman. We knew he liked to ride hard on a good hand and we gave him his chance. Finally, I dropped out and left it to the doctor. Tallman had a straight, and Doc spread his cards — a full house, queens and tens.

From then on we slowly but carefully took Tallman apart. Haven and Wilson soon became aware of what was happening. Neither John nor I stayed when either of them showed with anything good, but both of us rode Tallman. Haven dropped out of the game first, then Wilson. Henry stayed with us and we occasionally fed him a small pot. From time to time Tallman won, but his winnings were just enough to keep him on edge.

Once I looked up to find Carol's eyes on mine. I smiled a little and she watched me gravely, seriously. Did she guess what was happening here?

"Your bet, Mistah Duval." It was John's soft Georgia voice. I gathered my cards, glanced at them, and raised. Tallman saw me and kicked it up. Henry studied his cards, shrugged, and threw them in.

"Too rich for my blood," he said, smiling.

John kicked it up again, then Tallman raised. He was sweating now. I could see his tongue touch his lips, and the panic in the glance he threw at John when he heard the raise was not simulated. He waited after his raise, watching to see what I would do, and I deliberately let him sweat it out. I was holding three aces and a pair of sixes, and I was sure it wasn't good enough. John had dealt this hand.

My signal to John brought instant response. His hand dropped to the table, and the signal told me he was holding an ace.

Tallman stirred impatiently. Puttering a bit, as if uncertain, I raised twenty dollars. The southerner threw in his hand and Tallman saw my raise, then felt in his pockets for more money and found none. There was an instant of blank consternation, and then he called. He was holding four queens and a trey when he spread his hand.

Hesitating only momentarily, I put my cards down, bunched together.

"Spread 'em!" John demanded impatiently, and reaching across the table he spread my cards — secretly passing his ace to give me four aces and a six.

Tallman's eyes bulged. He swallowed and

his face grew red. He glared at the cards as if staring would change their spots. Then he swore viciously.

Coolly, I gathered in the pot, palming and discarding my extra six as my hand passed the discards. Carefully, I began stacking my coins while John gathered the cards together.

"I'm clean!" Tallman flattened his big hands on the table. He looked around the room. "Who wants to stake me? I'll pay, I'm good for it!"

Nobody replied. Haven was apparently dozing. Rock Wilson was smoking and staring into the fire. Henry yawned and looked at the one window through which we could see. It was faintly gray. It would soon be morning.

From the ceiling a drop gathered and fell with a fat *plop* into the bucket. Nobody spoke, and in the silence we realized for the first time that the rain had almost ceased.

"What's got into you?" Tallman demanded. "You were plenty willin' to take my money! Gimme a chance to get even!"

"No man wants to play agin his own money," Wilson commented mildly.

My winnings were stacked, part of it put away, yet of what remained the entire six hundred dollars had been won from Tallman.

"Seems early to end a game," I remarked carelessly. "Have you got any collateral?"

He hesitated. "I've got a — !" He had started to put up his pistol, but changed his mind suddenly. Something inside me tightened when I realized what that might mean.

Tallman stared around, scowling. "I guess I ain't got — " It was time now, if it was ever to be time. Yet as the moment came, I felt curiously on edge myself. "Doesn't she owe you money?" I indicated Carol Houston. "And that agreement to marry should be worth something."

Even as I said it, I felt like a cad, and yet this was what I had been building toward. Tallman stared at me and his face darkened with angry blood. He started to speak, so I let a string of gold eagles trail through my fingers and their metallic clink arrested him, stopped his voice in his throat. His eyes fell to the gold. His tongue touched his lips.

"Only for collateral," I suggested.

"No!" He sank back in his seat. "I'll be damned if I do!"

"Suit yourself." My shrug was indifference itself. Slowly, I got out my buckskin money bag and began gathering the coins. "You asked for a chance. I gave it to you."

I'd played all night for this moment but I was now afraid I'd lost my chance.

Yet the sound of the dropping coins fascinated him. He started to speak, but before he could open his mouth Carol Houston got suddenly to her feet and walked around the table.

"If he won't play for it with you, maybe he will play with me." She looked at Tallman and her smile was lovely to look upon. "Will you, Sam?"

He glared at her. "Sit down! This here's man's business!" His voice was rough. "Anyway, you got no money! No tellin' what you'd be doin' if I hadn't paid off for you!"

Dutch Henry's face tightened and he started to get to his feet. John was suddenly on the edge of his chair, his breath whistling hollowly in his throat, his eyes blazing at the implied insult. "Sir! You are a miserable scoundrel — !"

"Wait!" Carol Houston's voice stopped us.

She turned to John. "Will you lend me six hundred dollars?"

Both Dutch Henry and I reached for our pockets but she ignored us and accepted the money from the smaller man.

"Now, Sam. One cut of the cards. One

hundred dollars against the agreement and my IOU's . . . Have you got the guts to do it?"

He started to growl a threat, but John spoke up. "You could play Duval again if you win." His soft voice drawled, "He gave you quite a thrashing."

Yet as John spoke, his attention, as was mine, was directed at the face of Carol Houston. What happened to our little lady? This behavior did not, somehow, seem to fit.

Tallman hesitated, then shrugged. "Yeah? All right, but I'm warning you." He shook his finger at John. "I'm paying no more of my wife's debts. If she loses, you lose too. Now give me the damn cards."

She handed him the deck and he cut — a queen.

Tallman chuckled. "Reckon I've made myself a hundred," he said. "You ain't got much chance to beat that."

Carol Houston accepted the cards. They spilled through her fingers to the table and we helped her gather them up. She shuffled clumsily, placed the deck on the table, then cut — an ace!

Tallman swore and started to rise.

"Sam, wait!" She put her hand on his arm. He frowned, but he dropped back into his seat and glared at me.

Carol Houston turned to me, her eyes quietly calculating. The room was very still. A drop of rain gathered on the ceiling and fell into the bucket — again that fat *plop*. The window was almost white now . . . it was day again.

"How much did you win from Sam, Mr. Duval?"

Her face was without expression. "Six hundred dollars," I replied. "Not more than that."

She picked up the cards, trying a clumsy shuffle. "Would you gamble with me for that money?"

John leaned back in his chair, holding a handkerchief to his mouth. Yet even as he coughed his eyes never left the girl. Dutch Henry was leaning forward, frankly puzzled. Neither Wilson nor Haven said anything. This seemed a different girl, not at all the sort of person we had —

"If you wish." My voice strained hard not to betray my surprise. I was beginning to understand that we had all been taken in.

She pushed the entire six hundred dollars she had borrowed from John into the middle of the table. "Cut the cards once for the lot, Mr. Duval?"

I cut and turned the card faceup — the nine of clubs.

She drew the deck together, straightened it, tapped it lightly with her thumb as she picked it up, and turned — *a king!*

Stunned, and more by the professional manner of the cut than its result, I watched Carol Houston draw the money to her. With careful hands she counted out six hundred dollars and returned it to John. "Thank you," she said, and smiled at him.

His expression a study, John pocketed the money.

Haven, who had left the cabin, now thrust his head back into the door. "All hitched up! We're goin' on! Mount up, folks!"

"Mr. Haven," Carol asked quickly, "isn't there a stage going west soon?"

" 'Bout an hour, if she's on time."

The six hundred she had won from me she pushed over to Sam Tallman. Astonished, he looked at the money, and then at her. "I — Is this for me?"

"For you. It is over between us. But I want those IOU's and the marriage contract."

"Now wait a minute!" Tallman roared, lunging up from his chair.

He reached across for her but I stopped him. "That money is more than you deserve, Tallman. I'd take it and get out."

His hand dropped and rested on his pistol

181

butt and his eyes narrowed. "She's goin' with me! I'll be *damned* if I let any of you stop me!"

"No, suh." It was John's soft voice. "You'll just be damned. Unless you go and get on that stage."

Tallman turned truculently toward the slighter man, all his rage suddenly ready to vent itself on this apparently easier target.

Before he could speak, Dutch Henry spoke from the doorway. "You'll leave him alone, Tallman, if you want to live. That's Doc Holliday!"

Tallman brought up short, looking foolish. Doc had not moved, his right hand grasping the lapel of his coat, his gray eyes cold and level. Shocked, Tallman turned and stumbled toward the door.

"Henry Duval, you quit gambling once, did you not?"

She held my eyes. Hers were clear, lovely, grave. "Why . . . yes. It has been years . . . until tonight."

"And you gambled for me. Wasn't that it?"

My ears grew red. "All right, so I'm a fool."

Until that moment I had never known how a woman's face could light up, nor what could be seen in it. "Not a fool," she said gently. "I meant what I said by the fire — up to a point."

We heard the stage rattle away, and then I looked at Carol.

A smile flickered on her lips, and then she picked up the cards from the table. Deliberately, she spread them in a beautiful fan, closed the deck, did a one-hand cut, riffled the deck, then handed them to me. "Cut them," she said.

I cut an ace, then cut the same ace again and again. She picked up the deck, riffled them again, and placing them upon the table, cut a red king.

Picking up the deck I glanced at the ace and king she had cut. "Slick king and a shaved ace," I said. "Tap the deck lightly as you cut and you cut the king every time. But where did you have them?"

"In my purse." She took my hands. "Henry, do you remember Natchez Tom Tennison?"

"Of course. We worked the riverboats together a half dozen times. A good man."

"He was my father, and he taught me what I did tonight. Both things."

"Both things?"

"How to use cards, and always to pay my debts. I didn't want to owe anything to Sam Tallman, not even the money you

183

took from him, and I didn't want to be the girl you won in a poker game."

Dutch Henry, the Cherokee Strip outlaw, slapped his thigh. "Women!" he said. "If they don't beat all!"

It was almost two hours before the westbound stage arrived . . . but somehow it did not seem that long.

# RICHES BEYOND DREAM

It was June when they arrived at the adobe on Pinon Hill. There had been little change since Kirby Ann had last been there . . . the trees Tom Kirby planted the year before he died were taller, and bunch grass grew where the lawn should be.

Kirby Ann got out of the jeep and looked at Bob. The ride had tired him . . . a serious wound and a year in a Red Chinese prison camp had wrecked his health. He needed the sun, they told him, with rest and quiet. Well, he could get that here. Maybe it was all they could get here.

"It's a roof, honey," Bob said quietly. "We can fix up the place." He took her hand and they walked to the edge of the hill. "I always loved it here," she said.

Before them lay the long valley, dotted now with cloud shadows, and beyond the valley a rugged hill, and beyond more hills, more valleys, more peaks and ridges.

"Tom built for the view," Kirby Ann said, "and would you believe it? When he

185

was declared mentally incompetent, this was one of the reasons. Because he built an expensive house in a lonely place, and then wouldn't allow a road to be built leading to it."

"He was a good old man," Bob said. "I liked him."

Long after Bob was asleep, Kirby lay awake, remembering. This place had been left to her by her great-uncle Tom. It had been written into his will before his grandchildren had him declared incompetent and took over the handling of his affairs.

They had taken his house in town, the orchard he planted with his own hands, the ranch, and the mine. It was the silver they really wanted, and Blake, his eldest grandson, believed it came from the long-unworked Kirby Silver Mine on the edge of town.

There was never any argument about the adobe. Nobody wanted a house in such a lonely place. Yet when she came for her first visit she found they had been there, too, spading up the yard and blasting rock in the hill, feverishly searching for the silver lode. For the source of the fabulous *planchas de plata* he had sold to the bank in Topa.

Blake Bidwell had been coldly furious

after the funeral. "The old fool! He should have been declared incompetent years ago!"

"He was always soft in the head," Archie Moulton said sourly, "but I never dreamed he'd die without telling us."

"And not even to tell Kirby!" Esther was aghast. Esther was always aghast. "And she did so much for him!"

Kirby Ann had sat very still, her coffee growing cold. Not a thought for the poor old man who had died in that narrow windowless room that smelled of disinfectant, died still dreaming of the hills he loved so well.

He had given them all so much. Blake his first car. Archie and Esther a restaurant business. Jake a start in the bank.

And that was to say nothing of the other, intangible things he had tried to give them. His love of wild things, of trees, flowers, of the lonely desert and the enchanted hills. Of them all, she alone shared his love for these. He had, because of this, wanted her to have the adobe.

He never tired talking of the desert. Only at the end had his thoughts turned more and more to mining. Again and again he told her how to stake a claim, build the cairn, post the notices, and register it.

"A staked claim is property, Kirby Ann," he said, winking at her. "Lucky I didn't have one or they'd have taken that, too.

"Now don't you forget what I've told you. Like me, you love the desert. Someday you may find something . . . someday when you need it worse than now."

Had there been a hint in that? There would never be a time when they would need it worse than this very day. The money Bob would get from the government would help only for a while. It would be months and months before he could work. She searched her memory but could find nothing in the old conversations but the nostalgic wanderings of an old man nearing death.

He had loved the desert, and he knew the lines of ancient beaches where seas and lakes had been. He knew where lay the best beds of agate, jasper, or garnet. He had followed the old, mysterious trails of prehistoric Indians marked by forgotten piles of desert-varnished stones. He had known the plants of the desert, the cacti, the flowers, the herbs and grasses.

She remembered the town's excitement when he first brought in the ore, the sheets and balls of almost pure silver. When men failed to track him, and when his own grandchildren failed to probe his secret,

188

they began to believe he had uncovered a rich vein in the long abandoned Kirby Silver Mine . . . and he let them think so. Not long after, the twins, Blake and Jake, working with Esther and Esther's husband, Archie Moulton, began the move to have him declared incompetent.

They took over the mine and they spent thousands on engineers who probed and estimated and explored to no purpose. And the old man would have no more to do with them.

When she had received the deed to the house, there had been a note inside that she was to keep. Remembering it, Kirby Ann got it out of her overnight bag to show to Bob in the morning.

*You been good to me, Kirby Ann, patient with a tired old man. Marry Bob and spend your June honeymoon here — never sell it or give it away. Enjoy the flowers, and remember what I taught you about them. They ask only care, and they give so much in beauty, and in riches beyond dream.*

Sitting before the kitchen window, they ate their first breakfast in the adobe. " 'Mighty purty sight,' Great-uncle Tom used to say," she told Bob. " 'Come June the purtiest I ever did see.' "

"If we only had the money to fix it up," Bob agreed. "I'll work around, but I'll have to take it slow at first."

Bob lifted his coffee cup, nodding toward the far hill. "Honey, what's the yellow over there across the valley?"

Kirby Ann looked. "It's buckwheat. It blooms in late June. . . .

"Bob," Kirby Ann said, her eyes narrowing, "we were never here in *June!* We postponed our wedding, and our honeymoon was in September."

He chuckled. "I know that. I didn't have any money in June, and not much more in September."

She got to her feet. "Bob, get the jeep. We're going over there."

Twenty minutes later they stood in the patch of buckwheat, golden and beautiful in the morning sun. It was all about them, and at their feet, thicker than elsewhere, it cloaked and disguised an old mine working. Bob held in his hand a chunk of ore, seamed with silver.

"When I was only a child he told me," she said. "It's an old prospector's saying: 'Look where the buckwheat grows — it has affinity for silver.' "

# WEST OF DRY CREEK

On a late afternoon of a bitterly cold day he returned to the hotel and to his room. There was a narrow bed, a straw mattress, an old bureau, a white bowl and pitcher, and on the floor a small section of rag rug. The only other article of furniture was a drinking glass.

Beaure, short for Beauregard, took off his boots with their run-down heels and stretched out on the bed with a sigh. He was dog-tired and lonely, with nothing to do but wait for the storm to blow itself out. Then he would ride a freight out of town to somewhere and hunt himself a job.

Two days ago he had been laid off by the Seventy-Seven. After a summer of hard work he had but sixty-three dollars coming to him, and nobody was taking on hands in cold weather. It was head south or starve.

Beaure Hatch was twenty-two, an orphan since fourteen, and most of the time during those eight years he had been punching cows. Brute hard work and nothing to show

191

for it but his saddle, bridle, an old Colt, and a .44–40 Winchester. Riding company stock all the time, he did not even own a horse.

The Spencer House was the town's second-best hotel. It occupied a place midway between the Metropole, a place of frontier luxury, and the hay mow of the livery barn, where a man could sleep if he stabled his horse there.

When a man had time to kill in Carson Crossing he did it at the Metropole, but to hang out there a man was expected to buy drinks or gamble, and a few such days would leave Beaure broke and facing a tough winter. He crumpled the pillow under his head and pulled the extra blanket over him. It was cold even in the room.

It was late afternoon when he went to sleep with the wind moaning under the eaves, and when he awakened it was dark. Out-of-door sounds told him it was early evening, and his stomach told him it was suppertime, yet he hesitated to leave the warmth of the bed for the chill of the room.

For several minutes he had been conscious of a low mumble of voices from beyond the thin wall, and then the sound broke into understandable words and he found himself listening.

"It ain't so far to Dry Creek," a man was saying, "otherwise I wouldn't suggest it in weather like this. We'll be in a rig and bundled warm."

"Couldn't we wait until the weather changes?" It was a girl's voice. "I don't understand why we should hurry."

Irritation was obvious in the man's reply. "This hotel ain't no place for a decent girl, and you'll be more comfortable out at the Dry Creek place. Big house out there, mighty well furnished."

Beaure Hatch sat up in bed and began to build a smoke. It was twenty miles to Dry Creek through a howling blizzard . . . and when that man said there was a comfortable house on Dry Creek he was telling a bald-faced lie.

Beaure had punched cows along Dry Creek and in its vicinity all summer long, and in thirty miles there were two buildings. One was the Seventy-Seven line shack where he had bunked with two other hands, and the other was the old Pollock place.

The Pollock ranch had been deserted for six or seven years, the windows boarded up. A man could see inside, all right, and it was still furnished, left the way it had been when old man Pollock went east to die. Everything was covered with dust, and it would be icy cold inside that big old place.

The well was working — he had stopped to water his horse not three days ago — but there was no fuel around, and no neighbors within fifteen miles.

It was no place to take a girl in midwinter after telling her what he just had . . . unless, and the thought jolted him, she was not expected to return.

"But why should we go now?" she was protesting, "and why don't you want to talk to anyone? When I sell the place people will certainly know it."

"I explained all that!" The man's voice was rough with anger. "There's folks want that range, and it's best to get it settled before they can start a court action to prevent it. If you get tied up in a lawsuit it may be years before the estate is settled. And you say you need the money."

"I should think so. It is all I have, and no relatives."

"Then get ready. I'll be back in half an hour."

The door closed and after a long silence he could hear the girl moving around, probably getting dressed for the drive.

Beaure finished his cigarette and rubbed it out. It was not his business, but anybody driving to the old Pollock place on a night like this was a fool. It was nigh to zero now, with the wind blowing and snow in the air. A man with a good team and a cutter could make it all right . . . but for what reason?

Beaure got to his feet and combed his hair. He was a lean, broad-shouldered young man with a rider's narrow body. He pulled on his shabby boots and shrugged into his sheepskin. Picking up his hat, he also made up his mind.

He hesitated at her door, then knocked. There was a sudden silence. "Is that you, Cousin Hugh?"

"No, ma'am, this here is Beauregard Hatch, ma'am, an' I'd like a word with you."

The door opened and revealed a slender young girl with large gray eyes in a heart-shaped face. Her dark auburn hair was lovely in the reflected lamplight.

"Ma'am, I'm in the next room to you, and I couldn't help hearing talk about the old Pollock place. Ma'am, don't you go out there, especially in weather like this. There ain't been nobody on the ranch in years, and she's dusty as all get-out. Nor is there any fuel got up. Why, ma'am, you couldn't heat that ol' house up in a week."

She smiled as she might smile at a child.

"You must be mistaken. Cousin Hugh says it is just as it was left, and of course, there is the housekeeper and the hands. Thank you very much, but we will have everything we need."

"Ma'am," he persisted, "that surely ain't true. Why, I stopped by there only a few days ago, and peeked in through the boarded-up windows. There's dust over everything, and pack rats have been in there. It ain't none of my business, ma'am, but was I you, I'd sure enough ask around a mite, or wait until the weather breaks. Don't you go out there."

Her smile vanished and she seemed to be waiting impatiently for him to finish what he was saying. "I am sure you mean well, Mr. Hatch, but you must be mistaken. If that is all, I have things to do."

She closed the door in his face and he stood there, feeling like a fool.

Gloomily, he walked down the hall, then down the steps into the lobby. The fire on the hearth did nothing to take the chill from the room. What the Spencer needed was one of those potbellied stoves like at the Metropole, one with fancy nickel all over it. Sure made a place look up — and warmer, too.

It was bitter cold in the street and the

snow crunched under his boots. Frost nipped at his cheeks and he ducked his face behind the sheepskin collar. When he glimpsed Abram Tebbets's sign, he knew what he was going to do.

Abram was tilted back in his swivel chair reading Thucydides. He glanced at Beauregard over his steel-rimmed spectacles, and lowered his feet to the floor. "Don't tell me, young man, that you've run afoul of the law?"

"No, sir." Beaure turned his hat in his hand. "I reckoned I might get some information from you. I been savin' a mite and figured I might buy myself a place, sometime."

"Laudable." Abram Tebbets picked a pipe from a dusty tray and began to stoke it carefully with a threatening mixture. "Ambition is a good thing in a young man."

"Figured you might know something about the old Pollock place."

Abram Tebbets continued to load his pipe without replying. Twice he glanced at Beaure over his glasses, and when he leaned back in his chair there was a subtle difference in his manner. Beaure, who could read sign like an Apache, noticed it. He had known Tebbets for more than a year, and it had been the lawyer who started him reading.

"Settin' your sights mighty high, Beaure. That Pollock place could be sold right off, just anytime, for twenty thousand dollars. The Seventy-Seven would like to own it, and so would a lot of others."

"Who owns it now?"

"Heirs to old Jim Pollock. His granddaughter was named in the will, but she dropped out of sight a few years back, and it's believed she died back east somewhere. If she doesn't show up in a few weeks it goes to Len Mason, and after that to Hugo Naley."

Beaure knew them both by sight, and Naley a little better than that. Mason lived in a small shack over on the Clearwater. He had been a prospecting partner of Jim Pollock's when the latter first came west. Hugo Naley was foreman of the Slash Five. The granddaughter's name, Tebbets informed him, was Nora Rand.

If he explained to Tebbets what he had overheard, Tebbets would advise him, and rightly, that it was none of his business and to stay out of it. Still, the old man might be able to help.

That girl had no business going out there alone, and he was not going to stand by and see her do it. He remembered Hugo Naley from the roundup. He was a burly, deep-voiced man with an arrogant, hard-heeled way about him, and the punchers had him down as a bad man to cross.

There was a jingle of bells in the street and Beaure turned quickly to look from the window, a fact not lost on Abram Tebbets. In the lights that fell from windows to the snow, Beaure saw it was a cutter containing two people. Beaure went down the stairs two steps at a time.

Abram Tebbets stepped past his chair into the living room of his apartment, and glanced from the window in time to see the cutter and its two passengers disappearing into the snow along the river road. At the distance and in the vague light there was no possibility of making them out. The horses and rig looked like one belonging to the livery barn.

The wind moaned under the eaves and snow swirled in the now empty street. It was a bad night to be out . . . Beaure Hatch was going into the livery stable.

Sighing, Tebbets put aside his pipe and shouldered into his buffalo coat. That Beaure was thinking of buying a place was logical — it was a thought that came to many cowhands, and Beaure was more canny than the average. That he had saved any money at his wages was ridiculous.

Crossing to the Metropole, Tebbets ordered a drink. "Has Len Mason been in?"

"Len? Ain't seen him in a week or more. And not likely in this storm."

Beaure Hatch was a quiet young cowpuncher and not inclined to go off on tangents. Tebbets tossed off half his whiskey and scowled at the glass.

"Suppose everybody will be staying out of town, and don't know as I blame them."

"Naley was in from the Five. He didn't stay long."

Hugo Naley . . . scowling, Tebbets crossed to watch the checker game. Dickerson was the station agent, and he had played checkers in the Metropole every night for years.

"Quiet," he replied to Tebbets's question. "No passengers today, and only three last night. A couple of hands returning from Denver and some girl . . . a pretty little thing."

The big red horse Beaure rented from the livery stable had no liking for the storm, yet he forged ahead into the snow, evidently hopeful of a good bait of corn and a warm barn at the end of the trip.

The wind was stronger once clear of the

town. Here and there it had swept the road free of snow, but there were drifts. The cutter had a good start and was making time. Beaure took out his muffler and tied it around his hat and under his chin, and with his collar around his ears, he could keep fairly warm.

After awhile he dismounted and led the horse. His feet tingled with the cold that was in them. Only where the cutter went through a large drift were there visible tracks. Suppose they didn't go to the Pollock place at all? Try as he might, Beaure could not think of an alternative along this road.

Beaure wiped the red horse's eyes free of the snow that had gathered on his lids. It was bitter cold, and night had turned to solid blackness through which the wind howled and the blown snow snapped at the skin like tiny needles.

If Hugo Naley was planning to do away with the girl — and Beaure could think of no other reason for his lies — then he had chosen a perfect time. The girl would have been seen at the station and at the hotel, but it was unlikely anybody would think of her again.

She had taken her belongings, and nobody would have seen them leave town in this storm. If the girl never came back, who would there be to know?

But how could Naley hope to profit? Len Mason was due to inherit before Naley. Unless something happened to Mason, too. Living alone as he did, it might be weeks before anyone knew. Mason was nearly eighty, and he lived far out of town on a lonely part of the range. A number of times his friends had tried to get him to move to town. The girl was supposedly dead, and Mason's death would surprise no one.

There was no question of seeing any more. The snow was swirling all around, and all sense of direction was lost. He must have been traveling a couple of hours, and during the first hour he had made good time. He could be no more than ten miles from Carson Crossing now, which would put him in the midst of a broad plain. Roughly a mile ahead would be the first of the timber. If he could get into that timber, the trail would be well defined by the trees themselves.

He put the wind on his left side and pointed the horse straight ahead, keeping the wind against the left side of his face. Suddenly they were floundering among the drifts at the edge of the woods, and Beaure recognized a huge old lightning-struck cottonwood, and knew he was less than a mile from the Pollock house. Turning into the wind, he rode along the edge of the timber. He had not kept to the trail, but despite the storm had made good time. Through a break in the storm he glimpsed a dark bulk ahead, and turned his horse into the trees.

Here the blowing snow was less, the fury of the wind was cut down, and there were places where he found relatively little snow.

Beaure drew up, snuggling his cheek against the sheepskin collar. Now that he was here he had no idea what he meant to do or could do. Had they arrived? He saw no light.

Thrusting his hand inside the coat he felt for his six-gun, touching the butt lightly. He also had his Winchester in the scabbard with an old bandanna tied around it to keep the snow out. He had no desire to go up against Hugo Naley, yet he surely couldn't allow anything to happen to that girl.

He sat in his saddle looking toward the Pollock house, and suddenly he began to feel foolish. Suppose he was wrong? Suppose Hugo had fixed the house up? Even had a fire going?

He peered through the snow. There was

no smell of smoke, but in this wind it would be hard to tell.

There was a large stone stable, but that would be the very place Naley would head for. However, there was an old adobe out back where cowhands occasionally kept their horses and slept themselves when in the vicinity. It was back from the house, but it was tight, and there might even be a little hay.

Keeping under cover of the trees, Beaure Hatch rode north until he could cut across to the adobe. He opened the door and led his horse inside.

Suddenly, it was very still. He struck a match and looked around. The small building was dark and still. There was hay heaped in a corner, and there were four stalls in the small building. He led his horse into a stall, loosened the cinch, and put hay into the manger.

He took a handful of hay and rubbed his horse dry, and then peered out toward the house. No light was visible.

Suppose they had not even come here? Suppose Naley had taken her to his own place? He was owner of a small spread over at the head of Brush Canyon. No sooner had the idea occurred to Beaure than it was dismissed, for in this weather such a trip was not to be considered.

He had been aware of a peculiar smell for several minutes, and now he struck another match and looked slowly around. He walked to the next stall and peered in. Nothing. Nor was there anything in any of the other stalls. Nevertheless, he did smell something, and suddenly he knew what it was — it was fresh earth.

He went quickly to the corner of the old barn where a door opened into the old lean-to behind it. This was the only place he had not looked.

Opening the door, he stepped in, and struck a match. Before him gaped a hole. It was six feet long, and all of six feet deep, and it was freshly dug. The top layers of frozen earth had been hacked away with a mattock, which stood nearby, alongside the shovel. And Beaure needed no second glance to recognize them. They were the tools he had often seen on Len Mason's place. In fact, he had borrowed that shovel several times to help dig steers out of bogs, scooping mud away from their legs before pulling them out with a rope. He knew the scarred handle, the red spot on the end that Mason put on his tools to mark them against theft.

The match burned down to his fingers

and he dropped it into the grave, for grave it was . . . or was intended to be.

He walked back through the darkness to the window and peered out at the snow-blanketed house. While he waited here, murder could be done.

But what about Len Mason? Was he in on it, too?

He shucked his gun and checked it, wetting his cold lips with his tongue. No getting around it, he was scared. He had never faced any man with a gun. He had never used a gun for anything but potshots at rabbits, and once he had killed a rabid coyote.

Thrusting the pistol back into its holster, he buttoned his coat and went out into the storm, closing the door behind him.

The wind tore at his coat, lashed his face with hard driven particles. The snow was more than knee deep in the ranch yard as he plodded across it to the wall of the house. He had never been inside and had no idea whether it was advisable . . . or even how to get in.

He started around the house, then stopped. Dimly he could see the big barn, and a darker square showed through the white. The big door had been opened! Closed now, but the snow that had been blown against the boards had fallen off as it was moved.

A stir of sound came from within the old house. Turning swiftly, Beaure ran around to the back. The old slanting cellar door was partly broken, and he lifted it against the weight of snow and went down the steep steps into the cellar.

Above him the floor creaked. Feeling his way in the unfamiliar darkness, he found the steps and crept up them. Carefully, he tried the door that led into the house. It was unlocked, but stuck tight by dampness.

"I was warned not to come here."

"You're a liar — Who could warn you?"

"A cowboy . . . he overheard us through the partition. He has the room next to mine, and he told me this place had been closed for years."

"Do you take me for a fool? In the first place, cowhands don't stay in hotels. When in town they sleep in the livery stable."

Beaure could hear sticks breaking. Hugo Naley was making a fire. If he was going to kill her, why was he waiting? And why build a fire at all?

He shivered, answering his question with his own bitter chill. His fingers were stiff and his face raw from the cold outside. He tried to warm his face in his hands, then realized he would need warm, pliable fingers to handle a gun, and thrust both hands inside his coat.

"Nobody knows you are alive, Nora, and they haven't kept a guest register at that hotel for years. Now if you had stopped at the Metropole, I'd have been in trouble."

The breaking of sticks continued. He was stomping on heavier sticks to break them, and Beaure thought he might time his pushing of the door with one of these attempts, but there was no rhythm to them and he was afraid to try.

"If you got outside you'd just die in the snow," Naley was saying, "so you'd better be satisfied. You ain't been treated rough, and I don't aim to treat you so. Once I get this place all to myself I can have women, all the women I want . . . Anyway, you're too skinny for my taste."

Beaure was angered. She was not skinny! Fact was, she was a mighty shapely little filly — willowy, maybe, but not skinny.

He heard a scrape of a boot and the snap of a clasp knife opening. Nora screamed, and Beaure lunged against the door.

It gave suddenly under his weight, and he stumbled into the room and fell to his knees. He grabbed at the fastenings of his coat, and hearing the click of a gun hammer he looked up into the round muzzle of Hugo Naley's pistol.

"Well . . . you're Hatch, ain't you? What are you doing here?" Without taking his gun off Beaure, Hugo Naley folded his knife closed and stowed it in his pocket.

Beaure got to his feet very carefully. Nora was unwinding a freshly cut rope that had bound her wrists, her eyes were wide and frightened. He must look almighty foolish, falling into a room that way, and he wasn't cutting much figure as a rescuer. "Waiting for the Dutchman," he said. "I was hunting up some wood, figured to build me a fire and warm up until he got here. Reilly sent the Dutchman and me to work cattle out of Smoky Draw before they get buried."

Beaure was amazed at himself. The lie made more sense than anything he had done so far, and it had come to his lips very naturally. It was just plausible enough to be true.

Naley's pistol was steady. "Reilly told me he was letting most of the Seventy-Seven hands go," he said.

Beaure had no idea what to do. Saying he had a chance, what was there he could do unless he could get his gun out?

He would have no chance in a fight with Hugo. Around the Seventy-Seven chuck wagon they said Hugo Naley was a mean man in a fight, and Beaure had not fought since that scrap with the mule skinner in Gillette, Wyoming, three years ago. Naley would outweigh him by forty pounds.

"I'm finishing out the week." He had expected to do just that, but Reilly let them all go without saying aye, yes, or no. "The Dutchman said he would meet me here."

Naming the Dutchman — that was a good thing, too. Dutch Spooner was a tough man, just about the toughest on the Seventy-Seven, and no nonsense about him. Beaure had no idea that the Dutchman would side him against anyone, but they had worked together.

"All right," Naley said, "we'll wait for him. I think you're lying."

Nora watched him cautiously from across the room. Obviously, she was thinking about his warning in town and was wondering just what he was up to. That was a question to which Beaure wished he had a better answer.

"Say," he asked innocently, "what are you all doing here, and what was that yelling about?" He casually unbuttoned his jacket as he moved toward the fire, wanting his hands warm. Only Naley outguessed him and sidestepped suddenly, bringing the barrel of his six-shooter down on Beaure's head. He saw it coming and tried to duck, catching a glancing blow that dropped him to his knees. Before he knew what was happening, Naley put a foot between his shoulders and held him down while he slid his six-shooter out of its holster.

"That was the meanest thing I ever saw!" Nora Rand's face was white with anger. "You — you dirty coward!"

"Shut up," Hugo Naley said impatiently. "Shut up, Nora, I've got thinking to do."

Beaure had slumped down by the fire, and feeling the warmth soaking the chill from him, he remained there. He needed to get the stiffness of cold out of his muscles, and he needed time to think. So far he had acted the blundering fool. Through the throbbing pain in his skull, that fact stood out with pitiless clarity.

"He's going to kill us," Nora whispered. "He wants to inherit this ranch from my grandfather, and you're in it, too."

She was right, and the worst of it was there just wasn't anything anybody could do about it. Nobody knew the girl was here, nobody knew Beaure was. He had been paid off and had told everybody he was leaving, so nobody would be looking for either the girl or himself, and they could drop from sight and nobody the wiser.

Out of the slit of his eyes he looked up at Hugo Naley and was awed by the man's size. His face might have been carved from oak.

Naley was trying to think it out. Beaure knew that Naley placed little faith in the lie about the Dutchman, but it was a likely story because all the range knew the Seventy-Seven had lost cattle by their bunching up in narrow draws which filled up with many feet of snow. There was a better chance for them in the wider valleys and canyons where the snow drifted less deep.

The Dutchman was a notoriously difficult, taciturn man. Hard-headed, opinionated, and obstinately honest, he was a man without humor and without fear. Moreover, it had been rumored that the Dutchman did not like Hugo Naley.

Beaure wished there was something he could do. Naley was so all-fired big and mean — and he had both guns.

The wind moaned under the eaves, and Beaure thought of that icy grave in the lean-to. Naley could bury them together, fill in that grave, and scatter straw over it, and come spring nobody would know the difference. Nobody ever went into that old lean-to, anyway.

The fire was warming him. Beaure thought of that. They were fairly trapped, but so was Naley. No man would be fool enough to try to cut across country in weather like this, and if he stopped by any of the ranches they would be curious as to why he was out. No passersby were likely in this weather, but somehow Naley had to be rid of them both.

"Suppose you do get rid of me?" Nora asked. "What about Len Mason?"

Naley shot her a glance out of his ice-blue eyes, but he did not comment. Beaure had a feeling that Naley had his own reasons for not worrying about Mason.

That livery stable man . . . He wouldn't worry about his horse for a day or two, and if the horse showed up without a rider, if Naley simply tied the stirrups up and let it loose, the hostler might curse Beaure out for leaving the horse find his way back alone, but he probably wouldn't suspect any foul play.

Beaure sat up. "I want to see you try that on the Dutchman," he said. "I just want to see you try."

Naley walked to the window and peered out into the blinding snowstorm. Beaure looked at the broad back and studied the idea of jumping him, but realized the floor would creak and Naley would turn and let him have it.

Yet Naley was worried. Was it the storm? Or was he buying that story about the Dutchman?

"You'd better call this off, Naley. You kill us and you'll hang. I saw you and the girl in town today, and others did too."

Naley ignored him, walking restlessly from window to window. Obviously he thought little of any attempt Beaure might make against him. It was the storm that worried him, for the wind was increasing. The cold was also increasing.

Beaure thought about the fuel situation and understood why Naley was worried. If the storm lasted three days, they would be burning the house itself. There were some deadfalls at the edge of the woods, but finding and cutting them up in this weather would be impossible, even if there was an ax available.

Beaure studied the situation and liked it none at all. Of course, Naley could break up the old stable out there. Not that there was much wood, except in the lean-to.

He leaned over and tossed a couple of pieces of broken board on the fire.

"Looks like the Dutchman should be here," Beaure commented thoughtfully. "This is the only shelter anywhere around."

Naley turned angrily. "Shut your mouth!" He laid a hand on his gun. For an instant Beaure felt a cold that was not from the winter storm. Naley was on a hair trigger in that instant, and prepared to kill him.

Nora got up.

The movement distracted Naley and he glanced at her, then swung his eyes quickly back to Beaure, who had remained where he was.

"It's going to be a cold night," Beaure said. "We'd all better be thinking about that."

It was at least ten degrees below zero. He thought of the horse out there in the stable. It would be warmer than they were, for it was a tight, well-built old building of adobe, and heavily thatched. Now it was covered with snow and snow had drifted against the walls. The horse would be warm enough.

The big old house was too high in the ceiling, and the rooms were big and hard to heat.

The noise was faint . . . but they all heard it. A faint call in the momentary lull of the wind.

Naley swore and turned swiftly to the window, peering out into the storm. When he turned from the window, he said, "Somebody's out there. If it's that damn Dutchman, I'll — !"

Beaure felt a sudden panic. Who could it be? Whoever it was would walk in out of the cold right into Naley's gun, and Beaure knew suddenly that Naley was through debating; he was primed and ready. A passerby stopping in for shelter might have been the salvation that they were hoping for — after all, how many people did Naley think he was going to kill? — but now Beaure had set him up to think that the toughest hombre in the county was about to come through the door. Whoever it was, really, was about to be shot down without ceremony.

Unwittingly, Beaure had put the newcomer in a trap. Expecting only shelter, he would walk right into a bullet.

Naley was facing the door and waiting.

Beaure felt sick. He should have known that his argument that the Dutchman would work Smoky Draw was a good one. He was just the man who would be given the job; he was that dependable. He glanced at Nora and she was looking at him. He turned his eyes back to Naley. He was going to have to try. He might get killed, but it was the only chance for all of them.

Naley moved a step toward the door, squaring himself a little for it. Suddenly there was a stamping on the porch outside, as somebody knocked the snow from his boots.

Naley eared back the gun hammer, and the click was loud in the room. At the same instant, the knob started to turn and Beaure threw himself at Naley.

The big man turned like a cat, firing as he turned. The hammer was back and the slightest pressure fired the gun — an instant before it was lined up on Beaure Hatch. And then Beaure hit him.

He hit him in a long dive, his hands grabbing for a hold. Naley clubbed with the gun, and fell back, off balance. Before he could bring the gun down in a line with Beaure, the young cowpuncher jumped, grasping the wrist with both hands and smashing it hard against the wall.

The gun fell, and both men got up. Naley circled toward the gun and Beaure went into him, taking a smashing blow over the eye. Surprisingly, the blow did not hurt as much as he expected. Beaure swung his own fist and caught Naley at the angle of the jaw. The big man bobbed his head, and Beaure spread his legs wide and cut loose with two roundhouse swings.

Naley staggered, and then Beaure closed in, taking another punch but landing both fists.

"All right, Beaure. Let him alone."

It was Abram Tebbets, and he was holding a six-shooter on Hugo Naley.

Beaure backed off, breathing hard and sucking a bloody knuckle.

Tebbets stepped forward and scooped Naley's gun from the floor.

"He's got my gun under his coat," Beaure said. Tebbets stepped in, whipped open the coat with his left hand, and took the gun. He was deft, sure, capable.

"You sure handle that gun like you know how," Beaure said. Abram Tebbets glanced at him. "I studied law while I was marshal of a cow town," he said, "and I was six years in the Army, fighting Indians."

Beaure walked over to Nora. "Are you all right?"

"I'm sorry I didn't listen to you." She put her hand on his sleeve. "Will you forgive me for all the trouble I've caused?"

"Yes, ma'am. I'm just glad this all worked out. I was afraid my talking about the Dutchman nearly got Mr. Tebbets killed," Beaure said. "I was just a-yarning, hoping to worry him."

"You did all right," Nora said.

"You know, it's funny you mentioned him," Tebbets commented. "He broke a leg early this morning and will be laid up for the winter. The Seventy-Seven foreman was in town looking for you. If you want it, you have a job."

Beaure knelt and added fuel to the fire. It looked like they were going to have to tear down that lean-to, after all.

"I'll stay," he said, glancing around at Nora. "Seems like I'm just getting acquainted."

Beaure felt gingerly of his face, where it was puffed from a blow. "Thing that surprises me," he commented, "Naley didn't punch near so hard as that mule skinner up in Gillette."

# MARSHAL OF CANYON GAP

H e rode down from the hills in the morning, a tall, rawboned young man with the quiet confidence of one given to hard work and responsibility. He had a shock of rusty brown hair, gray eyes, and a way of moving in which there was no lost motion.

Sitting in the sunlight on the main street of Canyon Gap, I was sorry to see him come. He was a man who looked like he'd been long on the road. He also looked like trouble aplenty, and I was a man who didn't like trouble at all.

He rode into town on a rawboned buckskin and dismounted at Bacon's hitch rail. All the time he was tying that horse, he was looking up and down the street while seeming to be almighty busy with that knot.

By the time he had his horse tied he knew the location of every man on the street, and every window. I'd not seen Jim Melette before, but he was no tenderfoot, no pilgrim. A man isn't marshal of a cow town for ten years without sizing up the men who come to town, and learning to estimate their capacity for trouble.

He stepped up on the boardwalk, a big man in fringed shotgun chaps and a blue wool shirt, wearing a black flat-brimmed hat. For a moment, his eyes caught me with full attention, and then he turned his back on me and went into the store.

That store didn't worry me so much. What I was thinking about was the saloon. Brad Nolan was over there with Pete Jackson and Led Murry.

Brad was a headstrong, troublemaking man who had a way of bulling about that showed he figured he made mighty big tracks. Trouble was, he'd never done anything to entitle him to that attitude, and he was aching for a chance. Brad was feeling his importance, and for four or five years I'd been watching him put on muscle and arrogance until I knew trouble couldn't be avoided.

Lately he had been swaggering around and I knew he was wondering how far he'd get trying me on, but he'd seen me shoot holes through too many aces and no man wants to buck that kind of shooting.

Pete Jackson was worse because he was a talker. He never knew when to keep his mouth shut, and never considered the results of his loose talk, and such a man can cause more trouble than three Memphis lawyers.

Led Murry was an unknown quantity. He was new in town, and I hadn't made up my mind what to think about Led . . . there was something that happened a short while back that had me wondering if he wasn't the worst of the lot, but I wasn't sure. I just knew he never said much and he had crazy eyes, and that worried me.

Brad Nolan seemed the one inclined to start trouble, but he had seen me toss a playing card in the air, draw, and put a hole in it dead center before it hit the ground. It kept him and a lot of others from starting anything.

It was time I had some tobacco. Not that I didn't have some, but Melette was buying supplies and I figured it might be a good thing to know more about him. Also, he was a fine figure of a man and that Ginnie Bacon was working for her pa this morning.

Jim Melette was looking at the trousers when I came in, and Ginnie, she was looking at him.

Lizzie Porter was there and she was talking to Ginnie like she'd been put up to it. "Who's taking you to the pie supper, Ginnie?"

"I don't know," Ginnie said, looking at Melette. "I'm waiting to be asked."

"What about Brad? Isn't he taking you?"

"Brad? Oh . . . Brad. I don't know yet."

"All I can say is" — Lizzie never said all she could say, but she tried hard enough — "I hope that Ross woman doesn't come." Melette didn't react much but I've watched a good deal of human nature in my time and I could tell he was suddenly on point.

"Oh, she won't come! Who would bring her? Not after the way she was treated last time." Ginnie was watching Melette, who was studying some new boots now. "She's pretty enough if you like that snooty type, too good to talk to anyone . . . and she must be thirty, if she's a day."

Jim Melette went to the counter and took a list from his pocket, and Ginnie gave him one of her dazzling smiles. "What's about this pie supper?" he asked.

"It's tomorrow night." Ginnie was batting her eyes like an owl in a hailstorm and Ginnie was a mighty pretty girl. "We'll all be there. They auction pies, you know, and if you buy a girl's pie you get to sit with her. There's dancing, too. You do dance, don't you?"

"Sometimes . . . I can hold a girl while she dances. Who's this Ross woman you mentioned?"

"Her?" Ginnie wrinkled her nose. "She's nobody. She moved into the house on Cottonwood Hill a few months ago, and the only visitors she has around seem to come of a night, at least there's lots of horse tracks in and out of her gate. Nobody wants her around, but she came to that last social, bold as brass."

That Ginnie . . . she could make a sieve out of the truth without half trying. Truth was, nobody did want Hanna Ross, nobody but the men. The women looked down their noses at her because she was a stranger who lived alone, but so far as I'd seen none of them had tried to be neighborly.

Thirty years old, Ginnie said, but Hanna Ross couldn't be a day over twenty-four, and was one of the finest-looking girls I'd seen in a coon's age, and believe me, I've seen aplenty.

Ginnie saw me coming to the counter for my tobacco. It was high time because I'd about worn out that saddle, what with turning it and studying it and picking at the stitching. "Oh! Marshal, have you met Mr. Melette?"

He turned around giving me a straight,

hard look. "I haven't met the marshal," Melette said, "but I've heard of him."

"Name's McLane," I said. "Folks call me Mac."

"Seems to me I remember you," Melette said. "You've walked the boards of this town quite some time, haven't you, Marshal?"

Inside I stiffened up . . . that there phrase "walked the boards" might have been an accident, but from the smile around his eyes it seemed to me there was something behind it.

"Ten years," I admitted, "and we've had less trouble than most towns. The way I figure is to anticipate trouble and take steps."

"Good idea." Jim Melette gathered his supplies. "What do you do when trouble comes that you can't avoid?"

When he said that I had a chill . . . for ten years that had been my nightmare, that trouble might come that I couldn't sidetrack or outsmart, and I wasn't as young as I used to be.

"Don't ever worry about that," Lizzie said. "Ben McLane had killed fourteen outlaws before he came to Canyon Gap. Many a time I've seen him toss a card in the air and shoot the spots out."

"That's shooting," Melette agreed. "I've only seen one man who could do that. Of course, I was just a youngster then, must have been thirteen, fourteen years ago."

He picked up the rest of his supplies and walked out and I stood there looking at my hole card, and it had suddenly become a mighty small deuce. After all these years, while things shaped up mighty fine, I'd come to believe I was set for life in Canyon Gap. The town liked me and I liked the town, and one way or another, I'd kept the peace. Now it looked like the whole show was going to bust up right in my face.

Walking to the door, I watched Melette stow his stuff in his saddlebags and a sack he had tied behind his saddle. Then he dusted off his hands and started across the street.

A man can only keep the peace by working at it, so I stepped out on the walk. "Melette!" He turned slowly when I spoke his name. "I wouldn't go over there if I were you. There's trouble over there."

Figured first off he'd tell me to mind my own affairs, but instead he walked back to me, and then I was really scared because I thought he'd have something personal to say, and one thing I did not want to do was talk about myself. Not to him.

"All right, McLane, I won't," he said. "Will you tell me where Hanna Ross lives?"

He had called her Hanna, although her first name had not been mentioned inside, so my hunch was right. Trouble *was* coming to Canyon Gap in the person of Jim Melette. He knew more than he was letting on. I pointed the way up the street to her house.

"For a stranger," I said, "you seem to know a lot about folks. Why do you want to see Hanna Ross?"

He was stepping into the saddle. "Why, Mac, I think I used to know her, so I sort've figured I'd stick around for that pie supper and if Hanna Ross will go with me, I'll take her. You keep the peace, Mac!" And he trotted his horse off toward Cottonwood Hill.

Standing there in the street I knew I was scared. For ten years nobody had come to Canyon Gap who knew me, and I'd begun to believe no one ever would. The days of gun battles were about over, tapering off, anyway, and I'd begun to feel that I had it made, as we used to say in the goldfields.

It seemed to me that I was going to get it from two directions unless I was very careful. Ginnie Bacon had been flirtin' around Brad Nolan for the past several months trying to see what kind of trouble she could help him get into. He was spoiling for a fight, and from the way she'd acted toward Jim Melette there in the store, it seemed like she might try to get the two of them to go at it.

The other thing that had me worried was that I knew who'd been leaving all those tracks around Hanna Ross's house . . . it was that crazy-eyed Led Murry. I didn't know what that meant, but I was afraid. Nolan and Murry were some trouble separately, but together they were downright dangerous.

Something like this had happened a time or two before, but I'd been able to break up the dangerous combinations before they realized their strength. Divide and rule, that was my motto, and I made it a point to know about people, and whenever I saw fellers getting together who might cause trouble, I got a girl betwixt 'em, or jealousy about something else, and usually I'd managed to split 'em up.

There's more ways to keep the peace than with a gun, and I'd proved it in Canyon Gap, where there hadn't been a gunfight in ten years . . . and in the month before I took over there had been three. Nor in all that time had I drawn a gun on a man.

Cottonwood Hill was right up there in

plain sight at the edge of town, and from town everybody could see who came or went from the place, so Lizzie Porter saw Jim Melette ride through the gate up there, and she went right back in to tell Ginnie.

No need for me to read the playscript to know Ginnie would get mad . . . she had practically offered herself to Melette for the pie supper, and he had walked away and gone to see Hanna Ross.

Things were bunching up on me.

Ten years it had been, and I'm a man likes a quiet life. When I rode into this town on the stage and saw the snow-capped mountains round about, the shaded streets and pine forests on the hills around, and that stream running right through town, I decided this was the place to spend my declining years. The fact that they mistook me for a gunfighter and offered me the marshal's job had provided me with a living.

Now, between Hanna Ross, Ginnie Bacon, the Nolan outfit, and Jim Melette, I could see the whole thing blowing up in my face. It was too late for me to hunt up a new town, and I liked this one. And I never had been able to put by much in the way of money.

Worst of all, suppose Jim Melette told around town what he knew about me?

*  *  *

They had ten coal-oil lamps with bright reflectors behind them to light the school-house for the pie supper and dance, and they had two fiddlers and a guitar player out there on the floor.

Pete Jackson, Brad Nolan, and Ginnie were there, thick as thieves, the men passing a flask back and forth, Ginnie talking fast and flashing her eyes. Led Murry was there, too, a-settin' against the wall, missing nothing but a-watching everything.

Outside by the hitch rail I waited to fend off trouble, for I could see the storm making up, and I wasn't thinking only of me. I was thinking of the town. There I was when a livery rig came into the yard and Jim Melette got down and helped Hanna Ross to the ground.

"Jim!" My thumb was tucked in my belt, gunfighter fashion. "I want to talk to you!"

Excusing himself, Jim came over to me. "Don't go in there," I said, "as a favor to me. Brad Nolan's in there and he's spoiling for trouble. So's Murry."

"Sorry, Mac," Melette said. "I've nothing against you, but Hanna and I must go in there. We both figure to live around here the rest of our lives, and we might as well bring matters to a head right now."

"That's one way," I said, "but the wrong way. You two just dig in and hold on and folks will come around. You go in there and you'll make trouble."

"We're going. You don't understand the situation," he said.

"Now, look here!" It was time to be tough. "I — !"

"Mac," Jim lowered his voice, "don't you pull that act on me. When I was no more than thirteen I saw you on the stage in *Ticket-of-Leave-Man,* and a year later I saw you in *Lady of Lyons.*"

"So I've been an actor. That isn't all I've been. Now look!"

From my pocket I took an ace of hearts. "Boy, I want to show you something."

It was time to go into my act, and it was a good act, which had kept more than one tough man from making me trouble.

He stopped me. "Let me show *you* something," Melette said. He took the card from my hand and tossed it into the air. He didn't draw and fire as I had so often, but when the card fell he reached over and grasped my arm. I started to struggle, then let up, knowing it was no use. He knew my secret and he was going to have his say about it. Jim Melette slid two fingers into the cuff of my coat, plucking the hidden card out of its hidden clip.

"After I saw you demonstrate your shooting act in front of the theater one day I figured you for the greatest shot ever, but then a stable boy who used to work on the stage showed me how it was done. You just go out in the hills and shoot holes in fifty cards at three-foot range or whatever's necessary and then just carry them around in a holdout, and when you pick up the tossed up card, palm it and hand over one that's already been shot."

"Nobody around here has ever guessed," I said bitterly. This was what I'd been afraid of for years, and now just when I needed some luck, things were catching up with me.

"What are you going to do, Melette?"

"I'm going to go in there and have it out with Led Murry. If any of the others want a piece of it, that's their lookout."

Have it out with Led Murry . . . I'd been thinking it was Brad Nolan who was going to be the bigger problem. "You said that I didn't understand — exactly what is it that I don't understand?" I asked.

"Jim and I are married." Hanna Ross had walked over to us. "We've been married for three years."

"We were living near Denver, but I had to go to Mexico on business. I had an accident in a little mountain village. I was laid up a long time."

"I didn't know what had happened. I thought he was dead." She whispered it, looking off into the night.

They told me their story. In hushed tones, Melette's voice often rough with anger, they recounted how Led Murry had seen Hanna on the street in Denver and begun following her around. He'd asked her if he could come courting, but when she had told him that she was married he refused to leave her alone. He lurked around their house and spied on her at night. When she complained to the constables he would disappear for awhile, but sooner or later he was back. All this time Jim Melette was helplessly trying to recuperate south of the border. He tried to send Hanna letters, but was not surprised that none of them were ever received.

Then one night Led Murry broke into Jim and Hanna's house and tried to force himself on her. She fled, and thinking that her husband was dead, she changed back to her maiden name. Finally she found her way to my town, and became the mysterious woman that we all knew as Hanna Ross.

The story had all the elements of a great play, and when Led Murry appeared in our town it was obvious that that play had become a tragedy. Like a character from a Shakespeare play, he had become a man obsessed.

"After a long time I made it back from Sonora," Jim said, "and the postmaster in Denver helped me find where Hanna had gone. Now that I'm here, I've got to put a stop to this.

"Led's a bad man, McLane. He's an outlaw, but the law never caught up with him but once and he served his time for that. He's a mighty fast man with a gun. Tonight I'm going to see how fast. I'm going to tell him to leave us alone or start shooting."

"No." I spoke sharply. "I'm marshal here, actor or not. Maybe I'm an old fraud, but if you start trouble you'll go to jail. You leave Led Murry to me. He has assaulted a good woman. The next jury he stands in front of will send him away for life."

Melette looked at me like he figured I'd lost my good sense, and I knew there was no sense, good or otherwise, in what I had in mind. When a man has taken a marshal's salary for ten years, he can hide the first time real trouble shows. My whole life was based on being something I wasn't, but fool that I was, I hoped I wasn't a coward, too.

"You're crazy, McLane. You can't arrest him without shooting."

"Marshal?" Hanna Ross spoke up. "He knows . . . Led Murry knows that you . . . well, that you did that fake shooting in the Buffalo Bill show. I threatened to go to you when he showed up, and he said you were a fraud!"

"He'll kill you," Jim Melette said. "You leave him to me."

Before he could say more I turned my back on him and walked to the hitch rail where I could be alone.

This was my town. Sure, I'd become marshal because I could play the part, but in the ten years that passed I'd bought my own home, had shade for my porch, and flowers around the garden fence. When I walked along the street folks spoke to me with respect, and passed the time of day.

When first I came to this town I was an old actor, a man past his prime and with nowhere to go but down. For most of my life I'd been dressing in cold, draughty dressing rooms, playing worn-out roles in fourth-rate casts, and all that lay ahead of me was poorer and poorer roles and less and less work. But then I'd come to Canyon Gap.

There had been a time when I'd played with a few of the best, and in the olio between acts I'd do card tricks, juggle eight balls or eight dinner plates, or sing a fair song. The one thing I could still do best was juggle . . . there's a place it pays a man to keep up, keeps his hands fast and his eyes sure. Even a town marshal may someday have to give up and go back to doing what he knows.

When I first came to town, the boy that took my bags to my room saw a Colt pistol in my bag . . . it had fourteen notches on it. That started the story that I was a gunfighter, but it was nothing more than a prop I'd carried when I was with the Bill show.

Whatever I was in the past, I was town marshal now, and I'd been playing the role too long to relinquish it. There was an old adage in the theater that the show must go on. Undoubtedly, that adage was thought up by some leading man who didn't want the understudy to get a chance at his part, but this show had to go on, and I wasn't going to fail the people who had trusted me.

There's something about playing the same role over and over again. After awhile a man can come to believe it himself, and over most of those ten years I'd been a good marshal because I'd come to believe I was the part I was playing. Only tonight I could fool myself no longer. I was going up against a man whom I couldn't hope to bluff.

So up the steps I went and into the schoolhouse, and I crossed the room to where Led Murry was sitting with his back to the wall. And as I was crossing the room I saw one of my problems eliminated.

Jim Melette saw me coming and knew what I was going to do, and he started across the room to stop me. He had taken only two steps when Brad Nolan stepped out in front of him. "Look here, Melette, I — "

Jim Melette hit him. He hit Brad in the belly and then he hit him on the chin, and Brad Nolan went down and he didn't make any show of getting up. What Brad had been looking for all these years he'd gotten in one lump, and it knocked all the muscle out of him.

"Led." I spoke clearly. "Get on your feet. You're under arrest."

He looked at me and he started to smile, but it was a mean smile. Nothing pleasant about it.

"Am I, now? Why, Marshal? Why me?"

"You've assaulted Hanna Ross, a citizen of this town. I'll have nothing of the sort in

Canyon Gap. Get on your feet and drop your gun belts!"

He just sat there, smiling. "Marshal," he said, "you're a two-bit fraud. I'm going to show this town just what a fraud you are."

It was dead still in that room. Sweat trickled down my cheeks and I felt sick and empty inside. Why in the world hadn't I stayed outside and let well enough alone?

"After I get through with you, I'll have a talk with good old Jim and Miss Hanna. But first I'm going to kill you, Marshal."

They were watching, all of them, and they were the people of Canyon Gap, the people of my town. To them I was tall, straight, and indomitable, and though I might be an old man, I was their marshal whom they believed to have killed fourteen men. To myself I was a man who loved peace, who had never drawn a gun in anger, and who had rarely fired one, and who was suddenly called upon to face the results of the role he had created.

My audience, and an audience it was, awaited my reply. Only an instant had passed, and I knew how these things were done, for often I had played roles like this upon the stage. Only to this one there could be but one end. Nonetheless, I owed it to myself, and to the people who had kept me marshal of their town, to play the role out.

"Led Murry," I said coolly, "stand up!"

He stared at me as if he were about to laugh, but there was a sort of astonished respect on his face, too. He stood, and then he went for his gun.

Fear grabbed at my stomach and I heard the smashing sound of a shot. Led Murry took an astonished step forward and fell to the floor, then rolled over on his back. The bullet had gone through his throat and broken his spine.

Then somebody was slapping me on the back and I looked down and there was a gun in my hand. A gun with fourteen notches filed in the butt, a gun that had fired more blank rounds than live.

There was still the scene. Coolly, I dropped the pistol into my holster and turned my back on Led Murry. Inside I was quivering like jelly. True, we had been only ten feet apart, and it was also true that all my life I'd worked at juggling, sleight of hand . . . I'd had fifty years of practice.

"Marshal!" It was Lizzie Porter. "You were wonderful!"

"He was a danger to the community," I choked. "I deeply regret the necessity."

Inside I was shaking, more scared than

I'd ever been in my life, but I was carrying it off . . . I hoped.

It was Jim Melette who forgot himself. "McLane," he protested, "you were on the stage! You're no — !"

"Ah, the stage!" Interrupting him as quickly as I could, I handed him an old quote from the show, when I had appeared onstage as a companion of Buffalo Bill. " 'I was shotgun messenger for the *Butterfield* stage, scouted for George Armstrong Custer, and rode for the Pony Express!' " I squeezed his arm hard and said, "Forget it, Jim. Please. Forget it."

And then I walked out into the night and started for home, my heels hitting the ground too hard, my head bobbing like I was drunk. Right then it hit me, and I was scared, scared like I'd never been in my life. I had no memory of drawing, no memory of firing . . . what if I hadn't been lucky?

No question about it, I was getting too old for this. It was time to retire.

Of course, I could always run for mayor.

# HOME IS THE HUNTER

N ot even those who knew him best had ever suspected Bill Tanneman of a single human emotion.

He had never drawn a gun but to shoot, and never shot but to kill.

He had slain his first man when a mere fourteen. He had ridden a horse without permission and the owner had gone after him with a whip.

Because of his youth and the fact that the horse's owner was a notorious bully, he was released without punishment, but from that day forward Bill Tanneman was accepted only with reservations.

He quit school and went to herding cattle, and he worked hard. Not then nor at any other time was he ever accused of being lazy. Yet he was keenly sensitive to the attitudes of those around him. He became a quiet, reserved boy who accepted willingly the hardest, loneliest jobs.

His second killing was that of a rustler caught in the act. Three of his outfit, including the foreman, came upon the rustler with a calf down and tied, a heated cinch ring between two sticks.

The rustler dropped the sticks and grabbed his gun, and young Bill, just turned fifteen, shot him where he stood.

"Never seen nothin' to match it," the foreman said later. "That rustler would have got one of us sure."

A month later he killed his third man before a dozen witnesses. The man was a stranger who was beating a horse. Bill, whose kindness to animals was as widely acknowledged as his gun skill, took the club from the stranger and knocked him down. The man got to his feet, gun in hand and took the first shot. He missed. Bill Tanneman did not miss.

Despite the fact that all three killings had been accepted as self-defense, people began to avoid him. Bill devoted himself to his work, and perhaps in his kindness to animals and their obvious affection for him he found some of that emotional release he could never seem to find with humans.

When riding jobs became scarce, Tanneman took a job as a marshal of a tough cow town and held it for two years. Many times he found himself striding down a dusty street to face thieves and troublemakers of every stripe. Always he found a strange and powerful energy building in him as he went to confront his adversaries. One look at that challenging light in his eyes was enough to back most of them down. Surprisingly enough, he killed not a single man in that time, but as the town was thoroughly pacified by the end of his two years, he found himself out of a job.

At thirty years of age he was six feet three inches tall and weighed two hundred and thirty compact and bone-tough pounds. He had killed eleven men, but rumor reported it at twice the number. He had little money and no future, and all he could expect was a bullet in the back and a lonely grave on Boot Hill.

Kirk Blevin was young, handsome, and had several drinks under his belt. At nineteen he was his father's pride, an easygoing young roughneck who would someday inherit the vast BB holdings in land and cattle. Given to the rough horseplay of the frontier, he saw on this day a man riding toward him who wore a hard, flat-brimmed hat.

The hard hat caught his gleeful attention and a devil of humor leaped into his eyes. His gun leaped and blasted . . . a bullet hole appeared in the rim . . . and Bill Tanneman shot him out of the saddle.

Tanneman's gun held the other riders, shocked by the unexpected action. From the dust at Tanneman's feet Kirk managed a whisper. "Sorry, stranger . . . never meant . . . harm."

The words affected Tanneman oddly. With a queer pain in his eyes he offered the only explanation of his life. "Figured him for some tinhorn, gunnin' for a reputation."

Milligan, who rode segundo for Old Man Blevin, nodded. "He was a damn fool, but you better make tracks. Seventy men ride for Blevin, an' he loved this kid like nothin' else."

That Tanneman's reason for shooting had been the best would be no help against the sorrow and the wrath of the father. Curiously, Bill Tanneman's regret was occasioned by two things: that Kirk had shown no resentment, and that he had been a much-loved son.

For behind the granite-hard face of the gunfighter was a vast gulf of yearning. He wanted a son.

To see the handsome youngster die in the road had shocked him profoundly, and he was disturbed about the situation in general — he had no wish to fight against the man whose son he had accidentally killed. He thought of trying to speak to the old man, but did not intend to die, and the idea of having to shoot his way out of such a meeting chilled him to the core. The boy had given him no choice, but further tragedy must be avoided at all costs.

He swung swiftly into the hills, and with all the cunning of a rider of the lone trails, he covered the tracks and headed deeper and deeper into the wild vastness of the Guadalupes. He carried food, water, and ample ammunition, for he never started on the trail without going prepared for a long pursuit. When a man has lived by the gun he knows his enemies will be many and ruthless. Yet this time Bill Tanneman fled with an ache in his heart. No matter how justified his shooting, he had killed an innocent if reckless young man — the one bright spot in the life of the old rancher.

For weeks he lost himself in the wilderness, traveling the loneliest trails, living off the land, and only occasionally venturing down to an isolated homestead or mining claim for a brief meal and a moment or two of company.

Finally summer became autumn, and late one afternoon Bill Tanneman made his camp by a yellow-carpeted aspen grove in the shallow valley that split the end of a long ridge. From a rock-rimmed butte that stood like a watchtower at the end of the line of mountains, he scanned the surrounding country. Below him the slope fell away to a wide grass-covered basin several miles across. On the far side, against a low ring of hills, there was a smear of wood smoke and a glint of reflected light that indicated a town. Here and there were a few clusters of farm or ranch buildings. Noting that human habitation was comfortingly close yet reassuringly far away, he retired to his fire and the silence of the valley.

It was past midnight when he heard the walking horse. Swiftly he moved from under his blankets and, pistol in hand, he waited, listening.

The night was cold. Wind stirred down the canyon and rustled softly among the aspen. The stars were bright, and under them the walking horse made the only sound. A weary horse, alone and unguided.

It came nearer, then, seeming to sense his presence, the horse stopped and blew gently through his nostrils. Tanneman got cautiously to his feet. He could see the vague outlines of a man on the horse, a man slumped far forward, and something behind him . . . a child.

"What's wrong, kid?" He walked from the deeper shadows.

"It's my father." The voice trembled. "He's been shot."

Gently, Bill Tanneman lifted the wounded man from the saddle and placed him on the blankets.

He heated water from his canteen, and while the child looked on, he bathed the wound. It was low down and on the left side. From the look of the wound it had been a ricochet, for it was badly torn. Tanneman made a poultice of prickly pear and tied it on, yet even as he worked he knew his efforts were useless. This man had come too far, had lost too much blood.

When at last the wounded man's eyes opened, they looked at the dancing shadows on the rock wall, then at Tanneman.

"The kid?"

"All right." Tanneman hesitated, then said deliberately, "Anybody you want to notify?"

"I was afraid . . . no, there's nobody. Take care of the kid, will you?"

"What happened?"

The man breathed heavily for several minutes, then seemed to gather strength. "Name's Jack Towne. Squatted on the Centerfire. Big outfit burned me out, shot

247

me up. It was all I had . . ."

Tanneman built a fire and prepared some stew, and when it was finished he dished some up for the child. He looked again at the dying man's run-down boot heels, the worn and patched jeans, the child's thin body. "I'll get your place back," his voice was rough, "for the kid."

"Thanks, anyway." The man managed a smile. "Don't try it."

"What was the outfit?"

"Tom Banning's crowd. It was Rud Pickett shot me."

Rud Pickett . . . a money-taking killer. But a dangerous man to meet. And Banning was a tough old hide-hunter turned cattleman, taking everything in sight.

"Your kid will get that ranch. I'm Bill Tanneman."

"Tanneman!" There was alarm in the man's eyes as he glanced from the big gunfighter to the child.

The big man flushed painfully. "Don't worry, he'll be all right." He hesitated, ashamed to make the confession even to a dying man. "I always wanted a kid."

Jack Towne stared at him, and his eyes softened. He started to speak, but the words never came.

Bill Tanneman turned slowly toward

the child. "Son, you'd better rest. I — "

"I'm not a son!" The voice was indignant. "I'm a girl!"

Tanneman watched the child with growing dread. What was he going to do? A little girl would take special treatment, but he didn't even know where to start. A boy, now . . . but this was a *girl*. How did one talk to a girl kid? He spoke seldom, and when he did his voice was rough. This was a situation that was going to take some thought.

Thompson's Creek was a town of two hundred and fifty people, two saloons, one rooming house, one restaurant, and a few odds and ends of shops, and at the street's end, a livery stable.

Betty Towne and Bill Tanneman rode to town the next evening. Tanneman remained cautious, as was his nature, but his mind was stubbornly set on the problem of the little girl. Their horses stabled, he brushed his coat and hat while the child gravely combed her hair, then joined him to bathe her hands at the watering trough.

"Let's go eat," he said, when she had dried her hands.

Her little hand slipped confidently into his and Bill Tanneman felt a queer flutter where his heart was, followed by a strange glow. A little more proudly he started up the boardwalk, a huge man in black and a tiny girl with fine blonde hair and blue eyes.

This had been her father's town, and it was near here that he had been shot, driven from the ranch where he had worked to create a home. And in this town were men who would kill Tanneman if they knew why he had come.

The life of Bill Tanneman had left him with few illusions. He knew the power of wealth, knew the number of riders that now rode for Tom Banning, and knew the type of man he was, and the danger that lay in Rud Pickett. Yet Tanneman was a man grown up to danger and trouble, knowing nothing else, and for the first time he was acting with conscious, deliberate purpose.

On the street near the café were tied several horses, all marked with the Banning brand. Tanneman hesitated for a moment, then led the girl toward the door. As they entered the café, he caught the startled glance of a woman who was placing dishes on the table. The glance went from the child to the weather-beaten man with white hair who sat at the end of the table. The man did not look up.

Also in the room there were three cowhands, one other man more difficult to place, and a tall, graceful girl with a neat gray traveling dress and a composed, lovely face.

At the sight of the man at the head of the table, Betty drew back and her fingers tightened convulsively. She looked up at Tanneman with fear in her light blue eyes. Deliberately, Tanneman walked around the table and drew back the two chairs on Banning's right.

The rancher glanced up irritably. "Sorry, that seat's reserved." His glance flickered to the girl and then back to Tanneman, his eyes narrowing. . . .

Ignoring him, Tanneman seated Betty, then drew back the chair nearest the rancher. For an instant their eyes met, and Tom Banning felt a distinct shock. Something within him went still and cold.

Reassured by the presence of Tanneman, Betty began to eat. Soon she was chattering away happily. She looked up into the lovely gray eyes opposite her. "This is my Uncle Bill," she said. "He's taking me home. At least, where we used to live. Our house was burned down." She glanced nervously toward the head of the table, fearful that she had said too much.

Tanneman was stirred by a grim humor.

"Don't worry, honey. The men who burned it are going to build you a new house, a much bigger, nicer one. It will belong to you."

One of the cowhands put down his fork and looked up the table. Banning's eyes were on Tanneman, a hard awareness growing in them. The cowhand started to rise.

"You work for Banning?"

"Yeah."

"Then sit down. If you figure on lookin' up Rud Pickett, don't bother. I'll hunt him myself."

Coolly, Tanneman helped himself to some food. "I despise a man," he stated calmly, "who hires his killing done. I despise a man who murders the fathers of children. A man like that is a white-livered scoundrel."

Tom Banning's face went white. He half started to rise, then slid back. "I'm not packin' a gun," he said.

"Your kind doesn't." Tanneman gave him no rest. "You hide behind hired guns. Now you listen to me: I'm here to take up for Jack Towne's daughter. You rebuild that house you burned, you drive his stock back. You get that done right off, or you meet me in the street with your gun. Not your hired men — you, Tom Banning."

He forked a piece of beef and chewed silently for a minute, and then he looked up. It was obvious that he had everyone in the café's attention. "This here little girl's father was murdered by riders, at Tom Banning's orders. That will be hard to prove, so I don't aim to try. I know it, an' everybody else around here does, too.

"He robbed this little girl of her daddy and her home. I can't give back her father, but I can give back her home."

Tom Banning's face was flushed. The girl was looking at him with horror, and he quailed at the thought of what she must be thinking. In his youth a fire-eater, Banning had come more and more to rely on hired guns, yet this man had called him personally, and in such a way that he could not avoid a meeting. That the stranger had done so deliberately was obvious. And now Tanneman pointed it even more definitely.

"Ma'am," Tanneman glanced up at the older woman, "give that fellow some more coffee." He indicated the cowhand who had started to rise. "He's worked for Banning awhile, I take it, and now he's got him a chance to see who his boss is, whether he's ridin' for a coward or a game man."

The directness of the attack took Banning by surprise, and once the surprise was over, he began to worry. This was no brash youngster, but a mature and dangerous man. If he tried to leave the man might order him to sit down, and then he must submit or risk actual physical combat.

Tanneman turned to the child and began cutting her meat. He talked to her quietly, gently, and the girl across the table was touched by the difference in his voice.

Kate Ryerson, who owned the restaurant, offered to give the child a bed. Slipping from her chair, Betty slipped her arms around him and kissed his rough cheek. "Good night, Uncle Bill."

The tall girl at the table met his eyes and smiled. "You seem to have a way with children."

Bill Tanneman felt himself blushing. "Don't guess I do, ma'am. It's that youngster. She has a way with me."

When the child was gone, the girl with the gray eyes filled her cup. "I think this should be investigated by the United States Marshal, and if these charges are correct Mr. Banning should be charged with murder and theft."

Tom Banning started to speak, then held his peace. For the first time he was really frightened. Guns, even turned against him, were something he understood and against which he could take measures. Explaining his ruthless killings to a jury and being torn apart by a prosecuting attorney was another thing.

When he finished his meal he got up quietly, but Bill Tanneman ignored him. With his cowhands, Banning walked from the room.

Penelope Gray studied the big, hard-featured man across the table with attention. She remembered with warmth the queer wonderment in his eyes when he looked at the child. Instinctively, she knew this man was lonely for a long time.

"You've never been married?"

"I reckon no woman would want my sort of man."

"I think you're a very good man." She touched her fingers to his sleeve. "A man who would risk his life for the rights of a child who was no kin to him — that's a pretty fine sort of man."

Bill Tanneman remained seated after the girl retired, one thing holding his attention. Skilled at reading men, he had seen that Penny's threat of the law had frightened Banning much more than his own warnings. Asking for pen and paper, he sat down and wrote a letter to Dan Cooper.

It had been long since he had seen

Cooper. A sheriff then, Cooper had been pursuing him after a shooting until the sheriff's horse put a foot in a prairie dog hole and broke a leg. It was wild country and the Comanches were riding. Tanneman had turned back, disarmed Cooper, and let him ride double until within a mile of town. Cooper was a judge now, and a power in Territorial politics.

At daybreak, he routed out the storekeeper and bought an express shotgun and fifty rounds for it. He loaded the shotgun and stuffed his pockets with shells. Then he saddled his horse and headed for the Towne place.

It was still early . . . quail called in the mesquite as he rode by at a space-eating canter. He found the Towne place as Kate Ryerson had described it, a flowing spring, a small pool, the weed-grown vegetable garden, and the charred ruins of a cabin.

His fighter's eyes surveyed the terrain. An old buffalo wallow could be a rifle pit . . . that pile of rocks . . . but he must not think in terms of defense, but of attack.

He was tying his horse in the brush behind the spring when he heard approaching hoofs. He turned swiftly, his rifle lifting. It was Penny Gray.

His voice was rough when he stepped into

the open. "You shouldn't have come. There may be trouble, and this is no place for a woman."

"I think it is, Bill. Banning and his men are coming. Anyway" — a half smile played on her lips — "you need a woman . . . more than you know."

The words caught him where he lived and he turned away angrily. How did women know where to strike? How to hurt? Even when they did not want to hurt.

And then he heard horses, many of them.

Tom Banning and a dozen riders came into the little valley and rode toward them. With something like panic, Bill saw Penny get her rifle from its scabbard. "Stay out of this!" he ordered.

Banning drew up. The presence of the girl disconcerted him. He had never killed a woman, nor did he believe his riders, other than Rud Pickett, would stand for it. Had it just been the two of them, now . . .

"Send that girl back to town!" he demanded angrily. "I'm fightin' men, not women!"

"Then don't fight, Mr. Banning." Penny's voice was serious. "Although it seems that your morals are not so pure as you'd like to let on. You took away everything that little girl had!" She glanced at Tanneman.

"I came of my own free will. You do what you have to."

Banning chewed his mustache, and then Tanneman said, "You try any killing here today, Banning, and you'll never live to see it. My first bullet tears your heart out." He raised his rifle and took the slack out of the trigger.

"He may not believe me, Tascosa." Tanneman's eyes flickered briefly to a raw-boned cowhand behind Banning. "Tell him who I am."

Tascosa shifted in his saddle, liking the effect his remark would have. "Boss, this here's Bill Tanneman."

Tom Banning felt the shock of it. Tanneman . . . the killer. No wonder he had not been worried by Rud Pickett.

Tom Banning sat very still feeling the cold hand of death. Whatever else he loved, he loved living, and this man would kill him. Not all his men, all his power, all his money and cattle could keep that bullet from his heart.

He was whipped and he knew it. He reined around. "Come on, boys."

"Banning!"

He drew up but did not look around. "You've one week to start building a six-room house with two fireplaces, corrals, and a barn. You'd best get busy."

Dust lifted from the trail as they walked their horses away. Defeat hung heavy upon their shoulders.

"You've won."

Tanneman shook his head. "Banning would have gambled if you were not here."

One week . . . He was stalling for his letter to reach Dan Cooper, stalling because he did not want to kill again.

Tanneman was worried by the tall, cool-eyed young woman who rode beside him back to town. What was her interest in this? Who was she, anyway? What was she doing here?

The town knew and the town waited. Rud Pickett was coming in . . . Banning's hands would get Tanneman. The showdown would be something to see.

Tanneman was used to waiting. Trouble had been his way of life.

On the second day, four Banning riders appeared and entered the saloon. Bill Tanneman followed them in and ordered a drink. The riders felt his presence and knew why he was there. They respected him for it. He was letting them know that if they wanted him, he would not be hard to find.

The fifth day dawned. It was hot, dry, brittle. The heat left a metallic taste in the mouth, and there was no wind. Sweat broke out at the slightest move, yet men remained indoors despite the heat. When they appeared briefly on the street it was to hurry.

At noon, Tom Banning rode into town with fifteen men at his back. They left their horses at the corral and loitered along the streets, smoking idly.

Tanneman heard of their arrival and ordered another cup of coffee. Kate Ryerson brought it to him, and Penny watched him, her lips tight and colorless.

He pushed back his chair. Betty got up quickly. "Where are you going, Uncle Bill? Can I come?"

"Not this time." He touched her hair with his hand. "You stay with Penny."

It was the first time he had used her name, and when he looked up she was smiling at him. He turned quickly away and went out, swearing at himself.

He had to do this job, but he no longer looked forward to it. Once out in the still heat none of his old daring returned, the challenge, the urge to look death in the eye and laugh. How long had it been since he had felt that? That old love of a fight for a fight's sake. What happened to it? To love a fight as he had, one had to accept death, and that was something he found he could no longer do. Bill Tanneman knew what he had to do and he was ready, but he no longer enjoyed it. All he could do was put on a good show.

Every eye saw him, every eye knew. This was Bill Tanneman, almost a living legend. Nobody wanted to be in his shoes now, yet all envied him a little. Each one wished that *he* could step out into a street of enemies with that air, and look as formidable as he looked now.

Tom Banning waited in the saloon. Rud Pickett was beside him. They could have guessed to the instant when Tanneman appeared on the street. And then his shadow darkened the door.

Outside there was movement, the stir of many boots as Banning men converged on the saloon.

Bill Tanneman faced them, faced Banning and Pickett, as they turned from the bar. He was utterly calm, utterly still. Only his eyes moved, alert, watchful. These two men and a dozen more. Would the dozen fight if Banning and his gunman were dead? If they did, Tanneman would surely follow them into the grave. A grim smile tightened across his teeth.

"Here it is, Tom," Tanneman said quietly, "and I see you're hiding behind a hired gun to the last."

Rud Pickett moved out a little from the bar. He was going to draw. He was going to draw now . . . only he didn't. He looked into the cold gray eyes of Bill Tanneman and the seconds ticked by.

"Any time, Rud."

That was it. Now . . . only he was frozen. He wanted to draw, he intended to draw . . . but he did not draw.

There was a stir at the door and a tall white-mustached man stepped into the room. His voice was sharp. "Stop this right now!"

Sweat broke out on Rud's face. Hesitantly, his eyes wide and on Tanneman's face, he stepped back. He started to turn and saw the contempt on the bartender's face. Banning did not look at him.

The man with the white mustache walked to the bar between Tanneman and Banning. "I'm Judge Dan Cooper," he said. "We'll settle this without guns."

Tom Banning cleared his throat. He was white and shaken. Slowly, Cooper began to explain. The old days were gone. Banning would face a court in the capital. Cooper suggested that if Banning were to do as Tanneman had asked he would recommend some leniency to the court, but like it or not Banning would stand trial for murder. "The sheriff'll have to come down to make the arrest," Cooper said. "You can try to run away if you want, but I figure with all you got you'll try to fight it out in court."

Banning walked from the room. Rud Pickett was on the steps. Banning did not pause. "You're fired," he said, and walked on.

Rud Pickett stared at him, then turned and stumbled off the steps. The sun was not on his shoulders as he walked slowly away up the street. He was not thinking, he was not feeling, he was just walking away.

The bat-wing doors opened and Penny came in. "Bill? You're all right?"

The tension was slowly going out of the big man. "I'm all right. I'm going up to my room, get myself a long night's sleep. I'd . . . I'd like to see you tomorrow, maybe go riding, if you would."

"I'd enjoy that. You just let me know when, Bill." He smiled a tired smile and turned toward the stairs.

Thoughtfully Cooper looked from one to the other. "He's been a lot of things, Penny, but he's a good man. I've always known that."

"So do I," she replied seriously. "I knew

it when I first saw him with Betty . . . and I knew he was my man."

The next morning the sound of curses and hammering echoed back from the quiet hills. Fifteen tough cowhands were hard at work on Betty Towne's new six-room house.

# RAIN ON THE
# HALFMOON

J im Thorne came down off the Mules at
daybreak with a driving rain at his back. But
when he rode out of the pines on the bench
above Cienaga Creek he could see the bright
leap of flames through the gray veil of the
rain.

Too big to be a campfire and too much
in the open. The stage bearing Angela
should have left twenty minutes ago, but
Dry Creek Station was afire.

Leaving the trail, Thorne put his horse
down the slope through the scattered pines,
risking his neck on the rain-slick needles.
He hit the flat running, and crowded the
dun off the trail to the more direct route
across the prairie.

Flames still licked at the charred timbers
with hungry tongues when he came down
the grade to Dry Creek, but the station was
gone. Among the debris, where the front of
the building had been, lay the blackened
rims of the stage wheels and the remains of
the hubs, still smoldering.

His mouth dry with fear, Jim Thorne drew up and looked around, then swung in a swift circle of the fire. There was but one body in the ruins, that of a belted man. The glimpse was all he needed to know, it was the body of Fred Barlow, station tender at Dry Creek.

Where, then, was Angela? And where was Ed Hunter, who drove the run?

A splatter of footprints in the mud pointed toward the stable, and at their end he found Hunter.

The driver had been shot twice, once in the back while running, the second fired by someone who had stood above him and deliberately murdered the wounded man.

There was, nowhere, any sign of Angela.

Keeping to the saddle, he swung back. With a rake handle he poked at the ruins of the stage, rescuing a burned valise from which spilled the charred remnants of feminine garments. They were Angela's.

She had, then, been here.

He sat his saddle, oblivious to the pounding rain. Angela had reached the stage station, had obviously seen her valise aboard the stage. She must have been either in the stage or about to get in when it happened.

Apaches?

A possibility, but remote. There had been

no trouble in almost a year, and the body of Ed Hunter was not mutilated.

The nearest help was in Whitewater, fifteen miles north. And with every minute they would be taking Angela farther and farther away.

Wheeling the dun, he rode again to the stable. The horses were gone. He swung down and studied the floor. At least one man had been in here since the rain, for there was mud, not yet dry, on the earth floor.

Four stage horses habitually occupied the stalls, but there was ample evidence that eight horses had been stabled there the night before. Knowing Barlow shod the stage horses, and his shoes were distinctive, Thorne studied the tracks.

The four draft horses were easily identified. Three of the other horses were strange, but the fourth had at least one Barlow shoe. The stalls of the four strange horses were not muddy, which meant the riders must have stabled their horses before the rain began.

It was not unusual for Barlow to stable the horses of travelers, but the horse with the Barlow shoe implied at least one of the riders had passed this way before.

Jim Thorne walked to the door and built

a smoke. Going off half-cocked would not help Angela. He must think.

Four men had arrived the previous night. Angela must have arrived earlier and probably went to bed at once. Trouble had apparently not begun until after the arrival of the morning stage.

Fred Barlow and Ed Hunter had both known Angela. Both were old friends of his, and solid men. They would have seen no harm come to her. Therein, he decided, lay the crux of the situation.

Angela was not merely pretty. She was steady, loyal, sincere. But Angela had a body that drew the eyes of men. Suppose one of the strangers made advances? Barlow would allow no woman to be molested, and Hunter was stubborn as well as courageous.

Suddenly, Jim Thorne saw it all. And as suddenly as that, there was no remaining doubt. The Ottens and Frazer.

They were a Tennessee mountain outfit, surly, dangerous men who made no friends. Quarrelsome, cruel, and continually on the prowl after women. They had settled on the Halfmoon six months before.

"Tough outfit," Barlow had commented once. "Wherever they come from they was drove out. An' left some dead behind, I'll gamble."

Jim Thorne had seen them. Lean, rangy men with lantern jaws and swarthy skin. The odd man, who was Frazer, was thickset and sandy. The leader was Ben Otten, a man with thin, cold lips and a scar on his cheekbone.

They raised no cattle, lived on beef and beans, rode a lot at night, and made a little whiskey, which they peddled.

A month after they arrived in the country, they had killed a man down at Santa Rita. Three of them had boxed him and shot him down. There had been some trouble over at Round Mountain, too, but since it was known that trouble with one meant trouble with all, they were left strictly alone.

When Angela left him, she had come here to catch the stage, just as she told him in the note she left on the table. The Ottens and Frazer must have ridden in; they often stayed over at the station when the weather was bad, although they were tolerated rather than welcomed guests. One of them had started some kind of trouble, and Barlow had been killed. They had murdered Hunter, burned the station, then taken Angela and left.

Tearing a sheet from his tally book, Jim wet his stub of pencil and wrote what he surmised and where he had gone. The stable door opened inward so he left the note fastened to the door out of the rain. Then he walked to the corner of the blacksmith shop, and drawing aside an old slicker that hung there, Jim took down Barlow's backup gun.

It was a Roper four-shot revolving shotgun with several inches sawed off the barrel. Checking the loads, he hung it under his slicker and walked back to the dun. It had undoubtedly been this gun Ed Hunter was running for when shot down.

Hesitating, Jim Thorne then walked back to the stable, sacked up some grain, and tied it behind the saddle under his bedroll. Then he led the dun outside and swung into the leather.

It was a twenty-mile ride to Halfmoon the way he would go, but almost thirty miles by the route they would be taking. He was quite sure the Ottens had not been in the country long enough to have scouted the route up Rain Creek and over the saddle to West Fork.

Two of his friends lay dead, a stage station burned, his wife kidnapped. There was in his heart no place for mercy.

Angela was an eastern girl, lovely, quiet, efficient. She had made him a good wife, only objected to his wearing a gun. She had heard that he had killed a man, a rustler. But that had been in Texas and long ago. There had been no black mark on their marriage until the arrival of Lonnie Mason.

Jim Thorne had recognized him for what he was at first sight. Deceptively shy, good-looking, and not yet twenty, Lonnie Mason had seemed a quiet, inoffensive boy to Angela. Jim Thorne had seen at once that the man was a killer.

Several times he had stopped by the ranch, talked with Angela, and in his eyes a veiled taunt for Jim. He had heard of Jim Thorne, for while Thorne had killed but one man, he had been a Ranger in Texas, and he had won a reputation there. And a reputation was bait for Lonnie.

It had come unexpectedly. Some stage company stock had drifted, and Thorne had gone with Fred Barlow to find it. They had come upon Lonnie and another man with a calf down and an iron hot . . . a Barlow calf.

Lonnie had grabbed for his gun, incredibly fast, but Jim Thorne had not forgotten what he had learned on the Neuces. Lonnie went down, shot through the heart, and one of the stranger's bullets cut Barlow's belt before Thorne's guns saved the rheumatic elder man's life.

Angela was profoundly shocked. Jim would never forget the horror in her eyes when he rode into the ranch yard with the bodies over their saddles, en route to the sheriff.

She would listen to his explanations, but they never seemed to get through to her. It was incredible that Lonnie had been a thief, ridiculous that he might be a killer. Jim Thorne had simply been too quick to shoot. She had known this would happen if he continued to wear a gun. Fred Barlow had tried to explain, but all she could remember was that her husband had killed two men, one of them that soft-voiced boy with the girlish face.

They argued about it several times and Jim had become angry. He said things he should not have said. He declared she was no fit wife for a western man. To go back east if that was how she felt. It was said in anger, and he had been appalled to return one day to find her gone.

Low clouds, heavy with their weight of rain, hung above Haystack when he skirted the mountain and rode into Rain Canyon. Taking the high trail above the roar of run-off water, he cut back into the hills. The dun was mountain-bred and used to this. Thunder rolled down the canyons, crashing from wall to wall like gigantic boulders rolling down a vast marble corridor. Ponderous echoes tumbled among the stern-walled mountains.

The pines were no longer green, but black with rain. The dun plodded on, and squinting his eyes against the slanting rain, he stared ahead, watching for the saddle he must cross to West Fork.

When Jim Thorne reached the saddle, the rain was sweeping across in torrents. On either side loomed the towering peaks of more than ten thousand feet each. The saddle was itself over eight thousand feet, and at this point was almost bare of timber, rain blackening the boulders and falling in an almost solid wall of water.

Pushing on, Jim watched the lightning leaping from peak to peak, and striking the rocky slopes with thunderous crashes. Rain pounded on his shoulders until they were bruised and sore, and several times the dun tried to turn away from the pelting rain, but Jim forced the horse to move on, and soon the saddle was crossed and they began the descent.

From an open place in the timber, Jim Thorne looked over toward Halfmoon. The country between was an amazing spider web of broken canyons and towering peaks. It was a geological nightmare, the red rocks streaked with rain and the pines standing in somber lines, their slim barrels like racked guns against the dull slate gray of the sky and the surrounding rock. He pushed on, and the dun had an easier trail now, picking its way surefooted down the mountain.

The Ottens would have slower going of it, for they must go around, and knowing the country less well, they would be picking their way with care. Suddenly he saw a deep crack in the earth on his right. Swinging the dun, he walked the horse down through the pines and found the narrow trail that led to the canyon bottom.

Below him there was a tumbling mass of roaring white water, along the edge of which the trail skirted like an eyebrow. The dun snorted, edged away, and then, at his gentle but persistent urging, put a tentative hoof on the trail, starting down. A half hour later the trail left the gorge and slanted up across the mountain, and then around through a small park between the hills, and when he drew up again he was in thick pines above Halfmoon.

Finding several pines close together that offered shelter from the downpour, Jim

Thorne slid to the ground, and removing the bit, hung on the nose bag with a bait of grain. Leaving the dun munching the grain, he worked his way along through the trees and looked down on the high mountain park.

There was the old cabin as he had remembered it, a long, low building with a stable and corrals some fifty yards away. He squatted on his heels against the bole of a tree and built a smoke. The rain had dwindled away to a fine mist, and he waited in the growing dusk, watching the trail.

It was almost dark when he saw them coming. Six riders and several stolen horses loaded down with packs. They had taken time out to loot the stage station before firing it. With his field glasses he studied their faces, looking first at Angela. She looked white and drawn, but defiant. One of the men pulled her down off of the horse and took her inside. The others stripped the horses of their saddles and turned them into a corral.

There was but one door to the cabin, and no windows. There were portholes for defense, but they offered no view of the interior. There was only one means of entering the cabin, and that was right through the front door.

He sat down on the edge of the hill and studied the scene with cold, careful eyes. He knew what he was going to do. It was what he had to do — go in through that door. And quickly . . .

Angela Thorne rubbed her wrists and stared around the long room.

Along both sides of the opposite end were tiers of bunks, two high, and wide. Several were filled with tumbled, unwashed bedding. A bench was tipped over at the far end, and there were muddy boots, bits of old bridles, a partially braided lariat, and various odds and ends lying about. The air was hot and close, and smelled of stale sweat.

Frazer was bending over the fire, warming up some beans in a greasy pot. Dave Otten, a darkly handsome man with a wave of hair above his brow, had pulled off his boots. He grinned at her from the nearest bunk, his hands clasped behind his head.

It had been Dave who had grabbed her when she refused to reply to his opening remarks, and Barlow had struck his hand away.

One of the others had knocked Barlow down and started kicking him. Dave had left her and walked over and joined the kicking. It had been slow, methodical, utterly brutal. Ed Hunter had come to the door at her scream, and had wheeled and rushed for the stable. . . . Ben Otten had walked to the door, lifted a gun, and deliberately shot him down.

Then he had walked outside, and a moment later there was another shot.

By that time Barlow was lying on the plank floor, his face a bloody wreck, all life gone.

They forced her up on a horse. Through the open door of the station she could see two of them shoveling embers out of the stove, dumping them on the floor and piling them under the curtains. Jude set the stock loose as the roof of the building, despite the rain, went up in a rush of flame. On the way back to his horse he picked up a burning shingle and tossed it into the stagecoach.

Dave Otten laughed as he watched the flames. He was still laughing as they set out on the trail that led into the mountains.

Now Ben Otten slowly rolled a smoke and watched his brother stretch out on the bunk. "Dave," he said slowly, "you get them horses saddled come daybreak. We're takin' out."

Dave rolled up on his elbow. "Ain't no

need, Ben," he protested. "Who'd figure it was us? Anyway, what could they prove?"

Jude rolled his tobacco in his jaws and spat expertly at the fire. "Folks won't need to prove nothin'," he said. "They'll know it was us, an' they'll come. Ben's right."

"If you are wise," Angela said suddenly, "you'll give me a horse and let me go right now. My husband will be coming after you."

Dave turned his head and looked at her with lazy eyes. "Never figured you for married."

"You'd better let me go," she repeated quietly.

Ben Otten lighted his cigarette. "We ain't worried by no one man. But folks get riled up when you mess with their womenfolks. It's them in Whitewater that worries me."

She sat very still. Ben Otten was the shrewd one. If only she could make him see . . . "My husband will know where I am. By now he has found the station burned. He will know what happened."

Dave chuckled, that lazy, frightening chuckle. "Ain't likely. Left him, didn't you? I heard some talk betwixt you an' Barlow. Didn't know what it meant until you said you was married."

"I left him a note."

Ben Otten was watching her. He seemed to be convinced she was not lying. "Better hope he don't foller you."

In desperation she said, "He can take care of himself. He was a Ranger in Texas."

Otten's back stiffened and he turned on her. "What was his name?"

She lifted her chin. "Jim Thorne."

A fork clattered on the hearthstone. Frazer put down the pot and got up. He didn't look well. "Ben, that's him. That's the feller I was tellin' you about. He kilt Lonnie Mason."

Nobody spoke, but somehow they were impressed. Despite her fears she felt a wild hope. If they would only let her go! Let her ride away before Jim could get here . . . for she suddenly realized with a queer sense of guilt that he would come, he would not hesitate.

She saw his face clearly then, cool, quiet, thoughtful. The tiny laugh wrinkles at the corners of his eyes, the little wry smiles, the tenderness in his big, hard hands.

"He done a good job." That was Silent Otten. The oldest one except for Ben, the one who never talked. "Lonnie was a dirty little killer."

"But fast," Frazer said. "He was fast. An' Baker was with him."

He squatted again by the fire.

Ben Otten drew on his cigarette. "Maybe she's right," he said. "Maybe we better let her go."

Dave came off the bunk, his eyes ugly. "You crazy?" His voice was hoarse. "She's mine, not yours! I ain't a-lettin' her go."

Ben turned his black eyes toward Dave and for a long minute he looked at him. "You forgettin' who got us into this mess?" he asked softly. "It was you, Dave. If'n you'd kept your hands off her, we'd still be safe here, an' no trouble. I'm gettin' so I don't like you much, Dave. It was you make us leave Mobettie, too. You an' women."

"She'd tell off on us," Jude Otten said. "Come daybreak we better get shed of her. They'd never prove nothin' then."

Ben Otten frowned irritably. The idea of anybody proving anything angered him. They would not try to prove. They would decide, and there would be a necktie party. He drew on the last of his smoke. No chance for —

The door opened and the lamp guttered, then the door closed and they all saw the tall man standing inside. He had rain-wet leather chaps on, and crossed belts. Under his slicker something bulked large. With his left hand he lifted his hat just a little, and Angela felt a queer little leap in her throat.

"You boys played hob," Jim Thorne said quietly.

"It was you that played hob," Ben said, "comin' here."

"Got the difference." Jim Thorne's voice was quiet. But as he spoke the muzzle of the sawed-off four-shot Roper tilted up. "You boys like buckshot?"

Frazer was on his knees. He came in range of the gun. So did Ben and Jude. Frazer looked sick and Jude sat very quiet, his hands carefully in view.

"So what happens?" Ben asked quietly.

"I'm takin' my wife home," Thorne said quietly. "The rest is between you boys an' the town."

"You're takin' nobody." Dave rolled over and sat up, and his .44 was in his hand. "Drop that shotgun."

Jim Thorne smiled a little. He shook his head.

Ben Otten's eyes seemed to flatten and the lids grew tight. "Dave, put that gun down," he said.

Dave chuckled. "Don't be a fool, Ben. This here's a showdown."

"Three for one," Thorne said quietly. "I'll take that."

"Put down that gun, Dave." Ben's voice was low and strange.

Dave laughed. "You don't like me much, Ben. Remember?"

"Dave!" Frazer's voice was shrill. "Put it down!"

Angela sat very still, yet suddenly, watching Dave, she knew he was not going to put down the gun. He would risk the death of his brothers and of Frazer — he was going to shoot.

Ben knew it, too. It was in his face, the way the skin had drawn tight across his cheekbones.

Jim Thorne spoke calmly. "I've seen a man soak up a lot of forty-four lead, Dave, but I never saw a man take much from a shotgun. I've got four shots without re-loadin', and pistols to follow. You want to buy that?"

"I'll buy it." Dave was still smiling, his lips forcing it now.

Angela was behind and to the left of Ben, a little out of range. She was opposite Dave. And beside her, scarcely an arm's length away, was Silent.

Angela's fingers lifted. That gun . . . if she . . . and then Silent slid the six-gun into his hand. "Put your gun down, Dave," he said. "You'd get us all kilt."

Dave's eyes flickered, and hate blazed suddenly in their depths. He swung toward Angela. "Like h— !" He started to rise and thrust the gun toward her, and Silent Otten shot his brother through the body.

Dave's gun slid from his fingers to the floor and blood trickled down his arm. He looked around, his face stunned and unrealizing, looking as if awakened from a sound sleep.

Jim Thorne did not fire. He stood widelegged in the door and said quietly, "Better for you boys. Now set tight." He did not shift his eyes, but he spoke quietly. "Angela, get up and come over here. Don't get between me an' them. I ain't aimin' to kill nobody if I can help it."

Angela got shakily to her feet, and nobody else moved. Ben was staring at Jim. "If it wasn't for that shotgun — !" His voice sounded hoarse.

She walked around Ben, fearing he might try to grab her, but he did not. She moved to her husband's side, and Jim said quietly, "Just open the door, Angela, and get out — fast."

The Roper four-shot was out in the open now, and Jim Thorne had both hands on it. "You're through around here," he said. "You'd better scatter and run. There'll be a hangin' posse after you."

"There's time," Ben Otten said thickly. "We'll catch up to you. You hadn't no time to go to Whitewater."

" 'Bout an hour after I left Dry Creek," Jim Thorne replied, "the stage bound for Whitewater came through. I left a note on the stable door. By now there's fifty men headed for here. You ain't goin' to get away, but you can try."

Angela opened the door, the lamp guttered again, and Jim sprang back, jerking the door to and then leaping to catch Angela's hand. Quickly, he sprang around the corner of the house and ran for the woods. Stopping at the corral gate he threw it open, and waving his arms he chased the animals through the gate while trying to keep an eye on the cabin.

Below them a door banged and there was a shout, then running feet. In the stable door a light flared. Whipping his shotgun up, Thorne dropped three quick, scanning shots at the area of the light. The match went out and there was darkness and silence.

Jim Thorne led the way up to the bench where he had left the dun. Riding double and leading the spare horse, they turned up the slope toward the saddle between the peaks. Angela spoke softly in his ear. "Will they follow?"

"No." He took his poncho from the bedroll and put it around her shoulders. "Unless they can catch up those horses."

"Then they'll be caught?"

"Most likely."

They rode in silence for several minutes. Somewhere off over the hills they heard the sudden clatter of the hooves of many horses. There was a long silence then, and after the silence, a shot, then a rattle of shots . . . silence . . . then a single shot.

The water in the canyon was much lower. Hours later, they reached the flat again. Angela leaned against him, exhausted. "You want to ride into Whitewater?" he said. "You can catch a stage there."

"I want to go home, Jim."

"All right," he said.

In the gray cold light of a rain-filled dawn, they rode across a prairie freckled with somber pools. He reached a hand down to hold her hand where it rested at his waist, and they rode like that, across the prairie and past the blackened ruins of the stage station, and up to the mountain and into the pines.

# STAGE TO
# WILLOW SPRING

H e was a medium-tall man with nice hands and feet, and when he got down from the stage he stood away from the others and lit a small Spanish *cigarro*. Under the brim of the gray hat his features were an even sun-brown, his eyes gray and quiet.

Under a nondescript vest he wore a gray wool shirt, and a dark red bandanna that was worn to exquisite softness. His boots had been freshly heeled, and when he walked it was with the easy step of a woodsman rather than that of a rider. His gun was thrust into a slim, old-fashioned holster almost out of sight behind the edge of his vest.

Koons saw him there when he came out to the stage, and he took a second look, frowning a little. There was a sense of the familiar about the man, although he was sure he had never seen him before.

Avery was standing alongside the stage watching them load the box. Koons was pleased to see Avery. They were carrying a small shipment of gold and he liked to have a steady man riding shotgun.

There were five passengers to ride inside and a sixth riding the top. Everybody along the run knew Peg Fulton. She was sixteen when her parents died and she married a no-account gambler who soon ran off and left her. She had gone to a judge for a divorce, an action much frowned upon. She had since been treated as a fallen woman, although there was no evidence to prove it. Koons regretted his part in what had happened to Peg. He had believed he was too old to marry her but the gambler, who was also his age, had not hesitated. Peg's father had been a dry farmer named Gillis, and she came of good stock.

Bell was a fat, solid little man who had been riding the stages for eight years, a drummer for an arms outfit. Gagnon had a couple of rich claims in Nevada and carried himself with the superior feeling of one who is a success — without realizing his good fortune was compounded of ninety percent luck. The man riding the top was a stranger, an unwashed man with weak eyes and a few sparse hairs trying to become a beard. He carried a Spencer .56 and wore a Navy Colt.

The last passenger came from the stage

station, and Koons looked again, surprised at her beauty. She had dark, thick hair and the soft skin of a girl of good family and easy living. Her traveling dress was neat and expensive and she had a way of gathering her skirt when about to get into the stage that told Koons she was a lady.

Bell moved over to Koons. "See the fellow in the gray hat?"

"Who is he?"

"That's Scott Roundy, the Ranger who went into Mexico after Chato."

"Him?" Koons looked again. Curiosity impelled Armodel Chase to pause on the iron step of the stage, listening. "Of course he's not a Ranger any more, but they say he's killed ten men. Wonder if he knows about Todd Boysee?"

"Likely. Wonder what he's doin' up here? Seems mighty far off his range."

"Boysee will ask him."

Gagnon had been listening, and he said, "He doesn't look so tough to me."

Bell glanced at him irritably. "That's what Chato thought. That Mex killed nine, ten men in gunfights, murdered a dozen more. Roundy followed him to Hermosillo and shot him to death in a cantina."

"I heard the Rurales don't like that sort of thing."

"Huh!" Bell said. "They were so glad to get rid of Chato they looked the other way."

Armodel gathered a skirt again, and suddenly beside her there was a low question — "May I?" — and a hand to help her. She accepted it naturally, without coy hesitation, then glanced at the man. It was Scott Roundy.

He got into the stage and sat opposite her beside Peg Fulton. A whip cracked, the stage jolted, then lunged and they were off, and the dust began to rise behind them. The weather was comfortable, even slightly warm in the direct sun, but after a few minutes the shade had a frosty bite to it that indicated winter was waiting just beyond the horizon. This was a country of rolling hills, sparse grass, and piñon-crested ridges. In the shallow valleys there were scattered oaks.

Peg Fulton's head nodded and after awhile fell to Roundy's shoulder. Awakening with a start, she apologized and he said quietly, "That's all right, ma'am. I don't mind."

Armodel looked at him thoughtfully but said nothing. She saw his eyes stray to her several times, and then she dozed a little. It seemed hours later when she awakened to find the stage had come to a stop. Dust climbed into the coach and settled upon their clothes. Koons came to the door. "Might get down a few minutes. One of the mules is a mite sick. Thought I'd let him rest up a little."

Avery walked to a point where he could see over the edge of the arroyo, and with a glance toward him, Roundy moved over to Armodel. "Would you like to have a seat, ma'am? There's a flat rock under the oak."

After she seated herself she saw Peg Fulton looking around helplessly, and she said quickly, "Won't you sit here with me? There's room enough."

Peg thanked her and sat down. Gagnon's eyes flashed irritably and he muttered something to Bell, who ignored it. The passenger with the Spencer had squatted on his heels with his back to the rear wheel of the coach and was smoking.

"Are you traveling far, Mr. Roundy?" The blue-green eyes met his. "I am Armodel Chase, and I am going to Willowspring."

"Not far . . . I am stopping there also. If I can be of service, please call on me."

Gagnon spoke abruptly. "Ma'am, being new to the West I am afraid you do not know the character of the young woman beside you. I believe I should — "

"And I believe you shouldn't!" The

blue-green eyes were dark and cool. "Miss Fulton and I are comfortable here, and I do not believe that a woman's marital misfortune is any reason to withhold one's friendship or civility." Peg bit her lower lip and averted her eyes, but her hand sought out Armodel's and for a moment gave it a tight squeeze.

She caught the faint smile on Scott Roundy's face as Gagnon turned away, his back stiff with offended righteousness.

Later, back on the stage, Armodel studied Roundy when he was not looking. His was a quiet, thoughtful face, his smile almost shy. It was preposterous that this man could have killed ten men.

Gagnon broke the silence, speaking abruptly to Roundy. "What you figure to do when Boysee braces you?"

"Excuse me, I don't know what you are talking about."

Armodel felt the chill in the Ranger's voice, saw the flicker of irritation there.

"Aw, you heard of Todd Boysee! He's marshal of Willowspring. Killed seventeen or eighteen men. They say he's hell on wheels with a six-gun. He killed Lew Cole."

"Cole's been asking for it for years."

"Maybe he thinks you have, too."

Scott Roundy's voice was cold. "I don't

care to continue the conversation, my friend. Todd Boysee's business is his own. I'm sure he won't look for any trouble where there's none to be had."

Gagnon could not resist a final word. "He'll meet the stage." He smiled without warmth. "We'll see then."

Bell opened his eyes. "Nothin' to that talk, Roundy. Boysee's a good man. The men he's killed had it comin'. He's kinda touchy about strangers wearin' guns, though."

The conversation lapsed. Atop the stage they heard the passenger with the Spencer moving around. The air grew noticeably colder and the wind seemed to be mounting. A gust almost lifted the stage. "A norther," Bell said, "bad place to meet it. All flat country for miles."

Scott Roundy lifted the curtain and peered out. Darkness had fallen, but there was sifting snow in the air, and a scattering of it on the ground.

He sat back in his seat and closed his eyes. It was always the same. Once they knew you were a gunfighter they would not let it alone. Men had been killed in utterly senseless battles created by idle talk, the sadistic urge to see men kill, or the simple curiosity of mild men eager to see champions compete. It was an age-old, timeless curiosity that would live as long as men had the courage for battle. He had heard the endless arguments over what would happen if Hickok shot it out with Ben Thompson, or Wyatt Earp with John Ringo, or Boone May with Seth Bullock. Men compared their respective talents, added up their victories, exaggerated the number they had killed.

It was starting again now. "Charlie Storms," Gagnon was saying, "is one of the fastest men alive. Never saw him beat. I don't think Earp would have a chance with him."

Bell, who heard everything, opened his eyes again. "Charlie Storms is dead," he said quietly, "Luke Short killed him in Tombstone."

"Short?" Gagnon was contemptuous. "I don't believe it."

"I heard it, too," Peg Fulton said quietly.

Armodel looked again at Scott Roundy. He was leaning back and had his eyes closed, apparently hearing nothing. Yet he was awake. She had seen his eyes open slightly only a minute or two before. How he must feel to hear this talk. Would that man be waiting for him? If so, what would happen? Half frightened, she looked at Roundy. To think that he might soon be dead!

"None of them are as good as they're cracked up to be," Gagnon said, staring at Roundy. "Meet the right man an' they take water mighty fast."

Roundy's eyes opened. "Did you ever face a gun?" he asked mildly.

"No, but — "

"Wait until you do." Roundy closed his eyes and turned his shoulder away from Gagnon.

Through the crack of the curtain he could see the snow was falling fast, but most of it was in the air. For some time now, the stage had slowed to a walk.

Bell was not asleep. Scott Roundy and Todd Boysee. It would be something to see — and something to tell. He knew how avidly men gathered about to hear stories of a famous gun battle. Concannon had seen the fight between Billy Brooks and the four brothers who came to Dodge hunting him. He had been at the restaurant window when Brooks stepped to the door and killed all four of them in the street. It was history now, but Concannon could hold a crowd any time, just telling of it. Long as he had been in the West, he had known all the great names among gunfighters, but he had never seen a shoot-out between two top men.

This Roundy was cool. He had killed Con Bigelow at Fort Griffin, and Bigelow was ranked with the best. Roundy beat him to the draw and put two slugs into his heart. Bigelow had been a wanted man who laughed at the Rangers and evaded them, until that afternoon when cornered by Scott Roundy.

Roundy hunched into the corner. Irritably, he was thinking of the talk. They never let up. Always after a man.

Todd Boysee . . . no longer a youngster. That meant a cagey and straight-shooting man. But what kind of a man? Was he like Jeff Milton or Jim Gillette, who shot only when absolutely necessary? Or was he a reputation hunter like Old John Selman who had killed more than one man under doubtful, to say the least, circumstances. Some of those hard-bitten old town marshals felt the simplest way to maintain their position was to kill any man who threatened it, even by his presence.

He wanted no trouble, but it would pay to be careful. Once a man had a reputation with a gun there was no rest short of the grave.

The stage rumbled on through the night. During a momentary stop he got blankets out and spread them over the knees of Peg and Armodel. Then he relaxed again in his corner. There was the estate to settle, or he would just ride on through Willowspring. He suddenly knew he did not want to stop. Yet, even if he did not want to, he must. If the idea got around that he had taken water for any man, he would have to kill a half dozen who would want to build reputations at his expense.

He settled down to get some sleep. Outside the snow fell and the wind rocked the stage, moving slowly to keep to the ill-defined trail.

Old Todd Boysee was a grim and hard-bitten man. He had found Willowspring a roistering boomtown with two and three killings a night. He had killed four men during his first month on the job, and two later that year. After that there had been little trouble.

Occasionally he laid a pistol barrel over the head of some malcontent who believed he could tree the town, and once he had faced down a mob who intended to lynch a prisoner. Lately, it was becoming difficult. Twice in the past year men had come to town hunting him, one a pink-faced youngster who believed himself a dangerous man, the other a burly loudmouth who believed, and said, that Todd Boysee was too old for his job.

Both of them were buried now, out on Boot Hill. The boy had too much nerve for his skill, and the loudmouth, who might have backed down at the last minute, might also have come back to take a shot from ambush. Todd Boysee had not lived to become fifty-four by taking chances. By the ages of gunmen he was an old man, but his hand was sure, his aim straight.

It was snowing lightly and the wind was blowing when he walked down to the Gold Star. A snow-covered rider was at the bar, pouring a glass of whiskey. He glanced up at Boysee. "Here he is now," he said. "Ask him."

A heavy-set rancher with ill-fitting false teeth turned to Boysee. "Todd," he said, "we was just a-talkin'. Who do you reckon is best man with a gun? Wyatt Earp or Scott Roundy?"

Boysee pulled the end of his white mustache and his cold eyes measured the rancher. He did not like talkative men. "I have no idea," he said coldly.

A thin-legged man with amazingly narrow hips and a long, loose jaw said, "Roundy's comin' up the trail. Jess seen him gettin' on the stage."

The rancher was watching Boysee, his watery blue eyes eager. "Wonder what he's comin' *here* for? He used to be a Ranger, but this ain't Texas."

Boysee ignored them, waiting for the bartender to set up his evening drink. They were loafing, loose-mouthed men who would be better off at home. The rancher had been one of those in the lynch mob he had stopped, and Todd Boysee had not forgotten it. Yet when he found a rustler on his place he ran for help instead of bracing the man then and there.

Yet, what *was* Scott Roundy coming here for? This was far from his usual haunts. It made no kind of sense, and Todd Boysee had made it his business to know about men like Roundy. The man's reputation was good. He had never killed but in performance of his duty, although he was always in the dangerous spots. A couple of times he had not even fired until shot at. A man who did that had a streak of weakness in him. Given a break, men would kill you sooner or later. You had to shoot first, and shoot to kill.

"You still goin' to meet the stage?" Jess asked.

The word "still" angered Boysee. His cold blue eyes flashed. "I'll meet it," he said.

He took up the bottle and poured a drink. It was the one drink he permitted himself.

When he closed the door behind him he heard the buzz of excited voices. The fools! What did they know!

Bitterly, he stared into the night and the snow. There should be an easier way to make a living, but how? It was all he knew. He was too old now to punch cows, and who would give him a job? He had no money, only the little house and the garden behind it. Had Mary lived, he might have broken away from this life. She had wanted him to leave it.

What could he do, live on charity? Quitting was not an escape, anyway. The name would follow him, and they would still come hunting him, believing if they killed Todd Boysee it would make them feared. Little did they know.

He had been a buffalo hunter at seventeen, a scout with the Army at nineteen, an express messenger riding shotgun on the stages at twenty. At twenty-five he became a town marshal, and he had followed it since, working a dozen towns before he had settled in Willowspring.

Gifted with natural speed of hand and eye, he had improved by constant practice. For a time he savored the reputation it had given him, and then it had turned to ashes in his mouth after he killed a man he need not have killed. Finally, even that memory grew dim and he killed to live, to survive.

Every cow outfit that came up the trail had at least one man who fancied himself a gunhand. You stopped them or they stopped you. It was too bad, he reflected again, that Mary had not lived. He was fifty-four now, but looked and acted ten years older.

Why was Roundy coming here? What was there for him in Willowspring? It was foolish to think he was coming here to hunt him . . . but was it? Those fools back in the saloon believed it.

He walked down the street, a tall, very straight man. In this town he was the Law. It was all he had left. He never touched a gun except against strangers. Here, all he ever needed to do was to speak, quietly, sternly. He took out his big silver watch. Mary had given it to him for his birthday. He had been pleased. He had always wanted a watch. The wind moaned cold when he stopped at the corner. The sky was a flat black, without stars. It would be bitter cold on the plains tonight.

The stage was stopped when Armodel

opened her eyes. Scott Roundy was gone, although she had not heard him go. Bell was sitting up, wide awake. "What is it?" she asked.

"We're lost. The stage has been circling."

"But how could they get off the trail?"

"No fences, no telegraph posts, just a couple of wheel tracks, mostly grassed over. We're the second stage since the Indians burned the White Creek Station, last summer."

Outside in the snow, Koons stood beside Avery and Roundy. "If you're sure we passed Three Oaks," Roundy said, "we're south of the Wall."

"Didn't know you knew this country. The Wall's north of the trail, but circlin' wide as we done we'd have hit it."

"So we're south." Roundy was sure. "Bear south some more to North Fork Canyon."

"Don't know the place," Koons said.

"I'll find it." Roundy suggested to Avery, "We go ahead and let Koons line up on us. That would keep us in a straight line."

It had been a long time. The wind moaned along the plains, stirring snow from the grass . . . this place he would not forget, he had never forgotten, no matter how many the years. His name was different, but he was the same.

"And when we get there?"

"A stone cabin and fuel. At least, there was fifteen years ago, and a stone cabin doesn't rot. Anyway, the place is sheltered."

Koons turned. "All right," he said.

The stage lurched into motion and headed south, away from the wind. When they had been proceeding slowly for almost an hour the ground suddenly began to slope away, and after awhile Roundy did not go on ahead but stood and waited, and when Avery came up they guided the coach into the arroyo.

The stage bumped along over frozen earth and occasional rocks, and then a black cliff reared before them, and against the face they could see the rock house. It was barely visible under the overhang.

"Bring the mules inside!" Roundy yelled. "There's a cave back of the house and room enough!"

The first mule balked at the dark opening, but when it finally entered the rest followed. Koons stabled them at a tie-pole in the cave and returned to find a fire going in the house. Roundy was kneeling beside it, and Armodel Chase stood beside him.

Koons stared at Roundy curiously. "Never knowed of this place," he said.

Roundy nodded at the bottom bunk in the tier of two. "I was born in that bed," he said, "in gold rush days."

Armodel stared at him, and looked again at the bunk. Her eyes went around the bare room. There were two tiers of beds, a table, two benches, a chair. There was an iron pot beside the fireplace. Her mind returned to her own comfortable home. Hers no more.

"My mother is buried in the trees across the creek," he said. "She only lived a few days."

Koons brought more fuel and added it, stick by stick, to the fire. "All Injun country then," he said. "Must have been."

"It was during a lull in an attack when I was born," Roundy said. "Wagon broke down up on the trail. The rest of them were gold-hungry and anxious. Only one wagon would stay with us."

Avery brought coffee from the stage and they started getting water hot over the fire. Gagnon was not talking, but Bell was curious. It was like so many tales he had heard, yet he never tired of listening. He probably had heard more Western history in his years of traveling than any man alive, and sometimes he passed the stories on.

"What happened?" Armodel searched the

quiet face, thinking of how his mother must have felt, dying here, never knowing if her child would live, never knowing if he would grow up to become a man. Suddenly, she knew that gunfighter or not, his mother would have been proud.

"My father and the people who stayed," he said, "they started Willowspring."

Koons shifted his feet. "Then," he took his pipe from his mouth, suddenly disturbed, "you must be Clete Ryan's nephew."

"Yes," he said.

Peg Fulton looked across the fire at Koons, and she started to speak, then stopped, looking helpless. Koons got up and walked toward the back of the cave. Peg would know, of course. Peg was a Gillis, and they had lived neighbors to the Ryans. Gillis worked for Clete, time to time, for Dave, too, before Mary got married and Dave went east.

He did not remember Roundy, but he remembered the story. The boy's father had been an Army officer, and he had taken the boy to Fort Brown, Texas. After that they never heard of them again.

The man with the Spencer rifle brought in an armful of fuel from outside and sat down near the fire, keeping back a little, and giving the others room. Despite the cold, the stone cabin was tight and the place was warming up.

Peg moved around and took over the coffee making from Avery. Koons watched her, his eyes angry. This was a good girl. What else could she have done when that gambler left her? People had talked . . . thought the worst of her long ago.

"Warmin' up, Peg," he said suddenly. "Can I take your coat?"

She looked up, surprise changing to a softness and warmth. "Thank you, Alec," she said. "I was warm."

Koons took the coat into the shadows. He was surprised to feel himself blushing. He had not blushed in years. When he came back to the fire, Gagnon had a faintly knowing smile on his face. Koons felt a sudden murderous fury. *Say something,* he said under his breath. *Make one snide remark and I'll hurt you so badly — !*

The coffee was hot, and Armodel was sitting close beside Scott Roundy. Koons squatted down near Peg Fulton and accepted the cup she handed him. He could hear his mules stomping in the cave. They were eating their oats from the feed bags, and already content. It didn't take much for a mule to be happy . . . or a man either, come to that.

An hour later all were fast asleep except for Alec Koons and Peg. He sat up, tending the fire and she tossed and turned, finally giving in to wakefulness. He smiled at her shyly, wanting to speak but feeling clumsy and tongue-tied. Finally he cleared his throat and, without looking up from the fire, spoke.

"Peg," he said, "four years ago I came nigh to askin' you, but I figured I was too old for you. I'm older now, but . . . well, so are you.

"Will you marry me?" He looked up at her, finally, seeking out her eyes in the firelight. She reached out her hand and took his and held it tightly.

"Of course, Alec. I wanted you to ask me, but I thought you never saw me like that. I'd be proud to marry you."

She fell asleep not a half hour later, comfortably in his arms.

The stage to Willowspring swung into the street at a spanking trot, almost twelve hours late. The wind was down and the sun was out and the little snow was going fast . . . a crowd waited for the stage.

Koons swung his mules up to the stage station and started to get down. Todd Boysee stood off to one side, straight and tall, aloof and lonely in his threadbare black coat.

Koons started to swing down — he wanted to get to Todd first — but something made him look up. The man with the Spencer rifle was sitting unmoved atop the stage. He was half behind Armodel Chase's trunk, and he had his rifle in his hands. He was smiling.

Scott Roundy got down from the stage and handed Armodel to the ground. Roundy felt rather than saw the crowd draw back, and he looked up to see Todd Boysee facing him.

"Roundy!" Boysee's voice was stern. "You huntin' me?"

Scott took a step forward, sensing the old man's feelings. He put up a hand. "No, I — "

Todd Boysee's hand dropped to his gun. Scott distinctly heard his palm slap the walnut butt.

A dull boom slammed against the false-fronted buildings, and Todd Boysee felt the bullet that would kill him. He took a step back — *Scott Roundy had not drawn!*

Boysee felt a sickness in his stomach. Something had hit him hard in the chest, and the boom was heavy in his ears. Then he saw Scott Roundy was shooting, but not at him. Boysee was on the ground, holding his fire. His eyes found focus.

Over the top of a trunk was the muzzle of a Spencer, and behind it and left of the gun a white spot of brow, eye, and a hat. Todd Boysee fired, and there was a spot over the eye and red on the face. Roundy fired again and then the man with the Spencer rifle humped up and rolled over, falling flat and dead into the dust alongside the stage.

Todd Boysee was down and dying. He was no fool. He had shot enough men and seen enough of them shot. "Who . . . who was it?"

"Johnny Cole," a man from the crowd said. "I guess he come to get you for killin' Lew."

"Boysee." Roundy got his arm under the old man's shoulders. "I *was* huntin' you. You're my uncle. My mother was Mary Ryan's sister."

Todd Boysee was feeling better than he had expected. He always figured to die alone. With Mary's nephew here it was different, somehow. There was a girl beside him. . . . Why, she even looked like Mary. A sight like her, in fact.

His eyes shifted to the girl and his hand gripped her wrist. "You love this boy?"

His mind was slipping, he was backing down a dark corridor whose walls he couldn't see. "You stick with him, no matter what. It's all he'll ever have, what you can give him."

Scott Roundy moved back from the walk and stood near Armodel. Todd Boysee had been carried away. The blood was on the boardwalk.

"Where were you goin'?" He turned to look into her eyes.

"Just . . . west."

"Is this far enough?" he asked.

"It has to be . . . He gave me a job to do."

"I was going to ask you," he said, "only — "

"I know," she said quietly, and she did know. She knew what she had read in the eyes of a lonely old man, and what had been in her heart since the night by the fire. There would be times of gladness and times of sorrow, there would be fear, doubt, and worry . . . but no matter what, they would not be alone, not ever again.

# TO HANG ME HIGH

He was a fine-looking man of fifty or so, uncommonly handsome on that tall bay horse. He turned in his saddle like a commanding general, and said, "We will bivouac here, gentlemen. Our man cannot be far and there is no use killing our horses."

It wasn't the first time I had seen Colonel Andrew Metcalf, who was easily the most talked-about man in Willow Springs. He alone did not have to worry about his mount — he had brung one of his hands along, leading a beautiful Tennessee Walker, and twice a day he switched off from one t'other, so as not to tire either of them out. Those horses, I thought, had a better life than some people. Them with a master given to allowin' his horses rest, even on a posse.

My name is Ryan Tyler, a stranger in this country, and by the look of things not apt to live long enough to get acquainted. The colonel had nine men with him and they had just one idea in mind: to ride me down and hang me high.

Only two of them fretted me much. The colonel was a hard-minded man, folks said, with his own notions about right and wrong. The other one who worried me was Shiloh Johnson.

Three weeks ago Shiloh and me had us a run-in out to Wild Horse Camp. He was used to doin' just about whatever he pleased, for the reason that most everyone was scared of him. Only me bein' a stranger an' all, he tackled more than he figured on.

Johnny Mex Palmer seen it, and he said I done wrong. "You should have killed him, Rye. He'll never let it rest now until you're buried deep."

He had seen me beat Shiloh 'til he couldn't stand up, and me never get any more than some skinned knuckles. Well, folks had the saying around that Shiloh was the toughest man in a fight, the fastest on the draw, and the best man on a trail from Willow Springs to the Mesquite Hills.

He set some store by that reputation, Shiloh did, and now he had been beaten by a youngster, and easy-like to boot.

The colonel was a hard-minded man and a driver. Once started after a man, he wouldn't be likely to stop. Shiloh was an Injun on a trail, with his meanness to keep him at it. Up there in those rocks, cold as

311

it was, it didn't look good for me.

The colonel, he swung down like on a parade ground, his fine dark hair almost to his shoulders, those shoulders so square under that blue cavalry overcoat.

They went to building a fire, all but Shiloh. He commenced to hunger around, tryin' to make out my trail. Shiloh smelled coon, he did. He had it in mind that I was close by, and he was like an old hound on the hunt.

Colonel Metcalf, he watched Shiloh, and finally, sort of irritable-like, he said, "Let it go, Johnson. Time enough at daybreak."

"He's close by, Colonel," Shiloh said. "I know he is. That horse of his was about done up."

The colonel's tone was edged a mite. "Let it wait!" He turned then, abruptly, and walking to the fire he put his hands out to the blaze. Shiloh Johnson, he stood there, not liking it much. But Colonel Metcalf ran the biggest brand in the Willow Springs country and when he spoke, you listened. He was no man to cross.

Shiloh was right about my horse. That Injun pony had plenty of heart but not much else. He did all he could for me, and died right up in the rocks not far off the trail. They would find him in the morning, and then they would know how close they had been.

They would know they had come within a few minutes of takin' the man who walked up to Tate Lipman and shot him dead on his own ranch. Shot him dead with half his ranch hands a-standin' by.

Only they never heard what I said to him in that one particular instant before I did it. Only Tate Lipman heard me, which was the way it had to be. It was only that I wanted him to know why he was dyin' that I spoke at all.

In that partic'lar instant, I said to him, "Rosa Killeen is a good girl, Tate. She ain't the kind you called her. An' you ain't going to worry her no more." Then he died there on the hard-packed clay, his blood covering his shirt and the ground. Before his men knew what was happenin' I threw down on them. Then I locked the passel o' them in the bunkhouse and throwed my leg over a saddle.

Me, I ain't much account, I reckon. I'm a driftin' man, a top hand on any man's outfit, but too gun-handy for comfort. Twenty-two years old and six men dead behind me, not any home to my name, nor place to go.

But Rosa Killeen was a good woman, and

nobody knowed it better than me, who was in love with her.

She lived alone in that old red stone house back of the cottonwoods, and she had her a few chickens, a cow or two, and she lived mighty nice.

Once I fetched her cow for her, and she gave me eggs a couple of times, and now or again I'd set my saddle and talk to her, tellin' her about my family back in Texas and the place they had. I come of good stock, but my line played out of both money and folks just when I was passin' ten. Whatever I might have been had my pa lived, I don't know, but I became a lonesome boy who was gun-handed and salty before I stretched sixteen.

Rosa was the best thing in my life, and soon it seemed she set some store by me. Only she had education, and even if she was alone, she lived like a lady.

Folks said she had night visitors . . . an' folks ought to be left to their opinions, but once a subject's been raised a couple of times it goes to bein' a rumor, and when the rumor is about a good girl like Rosa and it's bein' spread intentional-like — well, that tries my temper. That time with Shiloh, he saw that it riled me and so he kept it up. I told him to stop and I told him what kind of yellow dog I thought he was, and he grinned that mean grin of his and put his hand on the butt of that Navy Colt, so I hit him. He was set for a gunfight and it took him by surprise. He went down and I snatched his pistol away and tossed it out where the horses were picketed.

He got up and we fought. I knocked him down 'til he didn't have the wind nor the will to get up. Then I told him there, and the rest of them, too. "She's a lady, an' nobody talks one word again' her. If he does, he better come a-smokin'. You understand that, Shiloh?"

It went against him, standin' there like that with four men lookin' on, four who saw me beat him down, an' him fighting dirty, too. Johnny Mex Palmer was right, I knew he was right . . . I should have got at him with a gun and killed him then and there, but Shiloh was still alive, and now it was his turn.

Not only Shiloh knew Rosa had a night visitor. Me, I knew it, too. One night I had stopped my horse to watch her window light and wish . . . well, things I shouldn't be wishin'. I saw that horse ride up and saw a man with a wide hat go in. He stayed more than two hours and rode away . . . oh, I saw that, all right. But Rosa was a good girl, and nobody could make me feel different.

I asked her about it. Maybe I shouldn't have, it bein' none of my business, but there was a certain way that I felt about her an' I knew if I didn't ask I'd be worryin' and goin' crazy. So I asked but she didn't tell me, least not straight up like I wanted.

"I can't tell you, Rye," she said. "I'm sorry. I promise you it's not . . . a romance." She blushed, an' wouldn't look me in the eye. "You've got to believe me, but that's all I can say." Well, I can't say I was satisfied, but I was surprised how much better I felt. I believed her and I loved her and that's all that mattered.

Only I wasn't the only one who saw. Tate Lipman had seen him, too, and from all I heard, Tate knew who it was. I didn't know, nor did I want to. Me, I was trying to be a trustin' man.

Yet I'll not soon forget the mornin' Johnny rode up to camp and swung down. "Rye," he said, "Rosa asked me to see if you'd come over. She told me to say she was in trouble, and would you come."

That Injun pony was the freshest horse in camp, for we'd been runnin' the wild ones. When I was in the leather, I looked back at them, but mostly at Shiloh.

"See you," I said, but there was a promise in it, too, and I didn't think any of them would make any remarks when I was gone.

She was by the gate when I came riding, and she was pale and scared. "I shouldn't have called you, Rye, but I didn't know what to do, and you told me — "

"Ma'am," I said, "I'm right proud you called. Proud it was me you thought of."

There was nothing but honesty in her eyes when she looked up at me, those dark and lovely eyes that did such things to the inside of me that I couldn't find words to tell. "I think of you a lot, Rye, I really do.

"Rye, Tate Lipman saw the . . . man who comes to see me. Oh, Rye, you know it's not what people think. I can't make them believe, but I hope you do. I'm a good woman, but I'm a good woman with secrets that I have to keep. It would hurt some good folks if I didn't. The man who visits me is a fine man, and I can't let harm come to him."

"All right," I said. Lookin' into her clear blue eyes I could do nothing but believe her.

"Tate Lipman saw him, Rye. And he's heard bad things people are saying about me. Tate rode over today. He . . . he said that no girl like me had a right to choose her man. If one man could have me, then he could, too. If I hadn't had the shotgun he might have — " She put her hand on my sleeve to hold me back. "No, wait, Rye. Let me tell."

"I'll see Tate," I told her. "He won't bother you no more."

"I want to tell you, Rye," she said. "Tate had seen this other man. He said if I refused him he would tell everyone what I was up to and who with. He laughed at me when I tried to tell him it wasn't what he thought, that I hadn't done anything people wouldn't approve of.

"Rye, believe me, if he does it would ruin the reputation of a man and a woman, and I would have to move away from the only people I love. . . . It would hurt me, Rye, and it would ruin a man who has been kind to me."

"I'll talk to Tate."

"Will he listen?" She seemed frightened then. "Rye, I don't want anything to happen to you. Please, I — "

That Injun pony put more miles behind him, and then I was ridin' up to Tate Lipman's place and saw him there before the house. The hands were settin' around by the bunkhouse and they could hear no word.

He was a big, red-faced man, Tate was. He figured he was a big wheel in this country, with a wide spread and ten tough hands to ride it. I'd never liked his kind, and I had heard him say there lived no woman who couldn't be had for a price, and mostly the price was mighty cheap.

What he seen when he seen me wasn't much. I'm a tall man and was a tall boy, mostly on the narrow side with a kind of quiet face. Not much beard yet, although I'm a full twenty-two, two years older than Rosa. My hair was light brown but curly because of the Irish in me, and I was wearin' some old Levi's and a buckskin jacket, much wore.

Well, I spoke my piece quiet and easy, tellin' him what it was I'd come for. His face just turned flat and ugly, and his hand dropped for his gun, and in that minute he was sure he was goin' to shoot me down.

My Colt came up slick an' smooth-like, and there was one stark, clean-cut moment when I saw the shock in his eyes, and when he knew he was goin' to die. And then my bullet dusted him on both sides and he took a short step to his toes and went down on his face, and I turned on them by the bunkhouse.

So that was how it was, and now Rosa

Killeen was behind me, and I believed in what little she'd told me with no thought that it might be otherwise. She'd hoped I could reason with Tate, but he was too big-headed, and that I knew. It was a grave on a windy hill for him and a fast horse for me.

Only the horse wasn't fast. Just a game, tough little pony with twenty miles under him when they first gave chase . . .

The night was cold and the wind bitter. . . . I made myself small among the boulders, with my hands under my arms. I watched the wind bend the fire over, the fire that made coffee for those men down below.

They bedded down, finally, Shiloh mighty reluctant. Hate grows hot and strong in his breed of man, and I knew that Shiloh and me would see each other across a gun barrel, one day.

Night made all things black, and it was like a great tunnel filled with roaring wind, a long wind that bent the trees down and skittered the dry leaves along the hard ground.

They had a rope stretched for my neck down there, a rope they figured to use. Tall Colonel Metcalf and Shiloh. The colonel would order it done like a man orders executions in the army, and he would stand by slapping his leg with his quirt when they set the knot, and Shiloh would look on, smiling that old secret smile of his, knowing the only man who ever beat him was on the end of that hemp.

It took me most of an hour to work my way around to where the horses were picketed, ten of them close together for warmth, but the colonel's blood-bay off to one side, like the aristocrat he was.

Crouched down in the brush, I put my fingers back in my armpits to warm them before moving out to untie that rope. The wind moaned in the long canyon, the rushing leaves swept by, and the dry branches brushed their cold arms together like some skeleton things, hanging up there between me and the black night sky.

Then, when I was inching to the edge of the clearing, a man came out of the trees. It was Colonel Metcalf.

He crossed to the big bay and stroked his neck, feeding him a carrot or something that crunched in the night. I could hear the faint sound below the rush of the wind, so close was I. And then I saw the colonel hang something across the bay's withers, and after a minute he turned and walked back to camp.

Scarcely had he gone when Shiloh moved like an Indian out of the brush, and stood there, looking around. It was too dark to see very well, yet I could picture him in my mind's eye, clear and sharp. Shiloh was a big man with stooped and heavy shoulders and a long face, strong-boned and with eyes deep set. You looked at him, then looked again. You thought something was wrong with his face. The second look showed nothing, but it left you the impression. He was a narrow, mean man, this Shiloh Johnson.

After a minute he followed the colonel, not going to the bay horse at all.

Waiting there in the blackness, I could see faintly the movements of Shiloh as he eased into his bed in the shelter of a log. When the movement under the blankets ceased, I straightened up.

There was a piece of carrot lying where it had fallen and I picked it up. After a minute, the bay took it from me, and then I untied the picket rope and walked him across the pine needles and down into the sand beyond. When I got him to where my saddle was cached, I saddled up, then put the bit between his teeth.

For the first time, I examined the sack that Colonel Metcalf had placed across the bay's shoulders. It was a sack of oats — maybe for a half dozen feedings. A strange thing to leave on a horse's back in the middle of the night.

It was a good horse I rode now, and I treated him like the gentleman he was, let him take his own pace, but held him away into the dark country, toward the high meadows and the long bare ridges. It was a strange land to me, and this worried me some, for Shiloh knew it well, and the colonel almost as well. Along the piñon slopes and into the aspen I rode, down grassy bottoms where the long wind moaned and into the dark pines, and through canyons among the rocks, and stopping at lonely creeks for a drink and then on.

When I had four hours of riding behind me I stopped and walked ahead of my horse, spelling him a might. I made coffee then, from the little a cowhand always has with him, and let the bay crop the rich green grass.

Moving on, I turned at right angles and, climbing ahead of the horse, went right up a steep gravelly ridge. On top, just short of the skyline, I walked him along for half a mile, then picking a saddle, crossed the ridge and went down into the trees.

Sighting a dozen steers feeding, I started

them off and drove them ahead of me for a ways, and then turned and started them back. They bunched for thirty or forty yards, enough to wipe out my horse tracks, and then I turned and rode downstream, keeping to the water until it became knee deep, when I scrambled out. So it went for two days.

Mine was a tough trail, hard to follow even for such a tracker as Shiloh, but he worried me, nonetheless. He knew the country, and when a man doesn't, he may lose a lot of time and distance.

Twice I'd killed rabbits, once a sage hen . . . at dusk I killed another, and in a tiny hollow among the trees and rocks I built a masked fire, built it in a hole and screened it so there'd be no glow on the trees overhead.

Along the way I'd seen some Indian breadroot, and dug a dozen of them. While fixing the sage hen I let these roots roast on the hot stones near the fire. Then I made some desert tea from the ephedra.

When I'd eaten I looked to the bay, moved him to better grass, scouted around, and then returned to my camp. Uneasy as I was, I was dead for sleep, and figured it was safe enough. . . .

When I opened my eyes, Colonel Metcalf

was sitting on a rock with a gun in his hand. "You're Tyler?" he said it, rather than asked, and he seemed to be measuring me, judging me.

Taking it careful, I sat up. There was a gun near my saddle, easy to hand.

"Do you know who I am?"

"Colonel Metcalf," I said. "I reckon ever'body knows you."

He kept his eyes on me. "Do you know who else I am?"

Some puzzled, I shook my head. And then he said sort of quiet-like, "Tyler, I'm the man who should have killed Tate Lipman."

It took awhile for it to sink in, but even then I was not sure. "What does that mean?" I asked him.

"It has been said that the evil that men do lives after them — sometimes, Tyler, it lives with them. You deserve to know what I shall tell you. But only one other person knows. No one else must ever learn of it."

None of this made sense to me, so I sat still. Believe me, I was some worried. If he was here, then Shiloh wouldn't be far behind. And the rest of them, with the rope they carried for me.

He was freshly shaved. His clothes had been brushed. He looked like he always had, like Colonel Andrew Metcalf with his wide ranch and his position in town. His word was law . . . and mostly it was a good law. He was a hard man, but just — or so they said.

My fingers opened, and when his attention shifted an instant, they inched a little toward my gun.

"Tyler," he spoke quietly, "I'm Rosa Killeen's father."

That stopped me . . . it stopped me cold. I sat with my mouth half open, just looking at him.

"Her mother was a good woman . . . a fine woman. We crossed the plains together before the war, and her husband died on the way out. I was a young lieutenant then, riding with the escort, and she was a beautiful woman. . . . She had never loved her husband. He'd been . . . not a bad man but an unthinking one. After his death we were much together. Too much, and we both were young.

"She came of a fine old family, a very proud family. They were Spanish Californians mixed with Irish.

"The Army had orders waiting for me in Santa Fe, and they took me into the East and then to the Confederate War. It was a long time later that I got a letter she had written me. She was dying and there had been a baby girl . . . it was mine.

"I had married during the war. There was nothing I could do but provide for the child in every way I could. But I had to do so secretly . . . to have publicly accepted Rosa as mine would have been disastrous to my marriage, and would have all too plainly pointed the finger of scorn at her mother's family.

"I paid for Rosa's education and, when she grew old enough, kept her near me. It was all I could do, and Rosa understood the situation and accepted it. We did not, neither of us, foresee Tate Lipman."

Why was he telling this to me? If Shiloh and the others came up, not even Metcalf could keep them from putting a rope around my neck. Lipman had two riders in that crowd, two mighty tough men, and Shiloh would never give up this chance to get me where he wanted me.

But I sat still, waiting him out . . . all I knew was that I wanted to live, and to live I had to have that gun. No man at twenty-two is ready to die, and I sure wasn't. Especially for killin' a no-good like Tate Lipman.

"That ain't no business of mine," I told him. "I killed Tate Lipman because he had it comin'. No matter who her father was, Rosa is a fine girl."

"You love her?"

He looked at me sharply when he said that, those cold blue eyes of his direct and clear.

"Yes," I said, and meant it.

He got up. "Then pick up that gun you've been wanting to get your hand on," he said quietly, "and — "

Shiloh stepped out of the trees. "No, you don't," he said. "You touch that gun and I'll cut you down."

There it was . . . the one thing I'd been afraid of — Shiloh gettin' the drop on me, like he had now.

"Shiloh, there's reasons for all of this — " The colonel started to speak, but Johnson shook his head.

"No, you don't," he said again. "I heard all that talk. It don't make no difference to me." I could see the satisfaction in his eyes, the pleasure at having me under his gun. "Tyler murdered Lipman. It was seen. He'll hang for it."

It was there, plain and cold. Nothing the colonel could say was going to stop it now.

"I been suspicious o' you, Metcalf." There was no title used this time, and I could see the colonel heard the change in

Johnson's attitude. "I seen you go to your horse that night, seen you leave that bag. Right then I couldn't figure why. . . . Come daylight, your horse gone, I figured some of it."

He had never once taken his eyes from me, and his gun was rock steady. With some men there might have been a chance. Shiloh was nobody to fool with.

"Only thing," he said it slow, like it tasted good to him, "I can't decide whether to shoot you now or see you hang."

There was silence in the clearing. Far off, I heard the wind in the pine tops, far off and away. It was a lonesome sound.

"I'm holding a gun, too, Shiloh," Metcalf said quietly. "If you shoot, I'll kill you."

No man ever spoke so matter-of-fact. And the colonel's gun covered Shiloh now, not me.

Shiloh was quiet for a long minute, and then he smiled. "You won't shoot me, Metcalf. You wouldn't dare chance it. Some of that crowd is mighty suspicious already, the way you held us back from catchin' him the other night. If I was to die now, along with him, they'd hang you."

Colonel Andrew Metcalf sat very still. Shiloh was smiling, and me, I sat there, wishin' I dared grab for that gun. But first

I had to get my hand on it, make the first grab sure without lookin' toward it, then swing it into line. Time enough for a fast man to fire two, maybe three shots.

Then the colonel stood up. He was smiling a little. "Shiloh," he said quietly, "situations like this have always appealed to me. I've always been curious about what people do when the chips were down . . . well, the chips are down now."

Shiloh Johnson's face was a study. He didn't dare take his eyes from me, and the colonel was to his right and out of his line of vision. He stood there, his boots wide apart, his cruel little eyes locked on mine, his long jaw covered with beard. He wanted to look, but he didn't dare chance it.

"Tyler shouldered my responsibility when he killed Lipman. I'm not going to see him suffer for it. So I'm going to kill you."

Shiloh had it up in him now. He was cornered and he didn't like it. Not even a little.

"You shoot me in the back," he started to say, "and — "

"It won't be in the back," Metcalf said quietly. "I'm going to move right over in front of you. You may get one or even

330

both of us — but one thing is dead certain. We'll get you."

Now I could see what the colonel meant about liking situations, and this was one. I wouldn't want to play poker with him . . . and Shiloh stood there with his face working, his eyes all squinched up, and ready to kill as he was, he wasn't no way ready to die.

It took a lot of cold nerve to do what the colonel said he would do — step over in front of a man ready to kill — but nobody would ever be able to say which of us had killed Shiloh, then.

"Now, look here . . ." Shiloh said. "I — "

"You have one other choice." Colonel Metcalf's voice was hard now, like a commanding general. "Drop your gun belts, get on your horse, and ride clear on out of the country. Otherwise, you die right here."

As he spoke, the colonel began to shift around to get in front of Shiloh. There was panic in Johnson's voice. "All right! All right. . . ."

He holstered his gun, then unbuckled his belts. There was plain, ugly hatred in his face when he looked at me. "But this ain't the end."

He stepped away from his belts and

started toward his horse, which had walked up through the trees from where he had left it ground-hitched when he heard our voices.

Colonel Metcalf watched him go, then turned to me. He held out his hand. I ignored it.

His voice went cold. "Tyler, what's — "

Shiloh Johnson had reached his horse. He put a hand to the pommel, then wheeled, whipping a gun from the saddlebag. It was fast and it was smooth, but I was on my feet with a gun in my hand, and as he turned I shot him through the body. He fired . . . and then I triggered my gun for two quick shots and he folded, his horse springing away as he fell.

"At Wild Horse Camp," I said, "he always carried a spare."

The colonel stood there, very white and stiff. "My boy," his voice was strange and sort of old, like I'd never heard it sound, "I've sent her to Fort Worth. Go to her."

"But — "

"Ride, boy!" The old crack came back into his voice. "They'll have heard the shots!"

He stood there, not moving, and when I was in the saddle he said, "Fort Worth, son. She'll be waiting. Rosa loves you."

As he said it I'll swear there were tears in his eyes, but the bay was running all out and away before I recalled something else. There had been a dark splotch on his shirt front. That one shot — that wild shot Shiloh got off — it had hit him.

He carried it well that day, afraid I'd not leave him if I knew . . . but he carried it well for ten years, and was carrying it on our Texas ranch, when he held his grandchild on his knee.

# AFTERWORD

H ere are the names of the people I would like to contact. If you find your name on the list, I would be very grateful if you would write to me. Some of these people may have known Louis as "Duke" LaMoore or Michael "Micky" Moore, as Louis occasionally used those names. Many of the people on this list may be dead. If you are a family member (or were a very good friend) of anyone on the list who has passed away, I would like to hear from you, too. Some of the names I have marked with an asterisk (*); if there is anyone out there who knows anything at all about these people I would like to hear it. The address to write to is:

Louis L'Amour Biography Project
P.O. Box 41183
Pasadena, CA 91114-9183

Mary Dodge — A violin teacher who lived in Portland; her son's name was Glen.

Louis roomed with them. He knew Mary in the late 1920s.

Mrs. Deslslets — Mary Dodge's sister; lived in Burns, Oregon. Louis corresponded with her in the 1930s.

John Deslslets — Nephew of Mrs. Deslslets

Louise Deslslets — Daughter of Mrs. Deslslets

Marian Payne — Married a man named Duane. Louis said in 1938 that he had known her for five years. She moved to New York for awhile; she may have lived in Wichita at some point.

Chaplain Phillips — Louis first met him at Fort Sill, then again in Paris at the Place de Saint Augustine officers' mess. The first meeting was in 1942, the second in 1945.

Anne Mary Bentley — Friend of Louis's from Oklahoma in the 1930s. Possibly a musician of some sort. Lived in Denver for a time.

Betty Brown — Woman that Louis corresponded with extensively while in Choctaw in the late 1930s. Later she moved to New York.

Maria Antonia "Toni" Cavazos — Louis met her at Edmond, Oklahoma, in the late 1930s but visited her at the Lady of the Lake College in San Antonio while he was on a speaking date. They corresponded for a while. Later she was a teacher in San Diego.

Jacques Chambrun★ — Louis's agent from the late 1930s through the late 1950s.

Des — His first name. Chambrun's assistant in the late 1940s or early 1950s.

Friscia★ — His last name. One of two men that Louis met in jail in Phoenix in the mid-1920s. They joined the Hagenbeck & Wallace Circus together. They rode freights across Texas and spent a couple of nights in the Star of Hope mission in Houston.

Pete Boering★ — Shipmate of Louis's on the *S.S. Steadfast.* Born in the late 1890s. Came from Amsterdam, Holland. His father may have been a ship's captain.

Louis and Pete sailed from Galveston together in the mid-1920s.

Harry "Shorty" Warren★ — Shipmate of Louis's on the *S.S. Steadfast* in the mid-1920s. They sailed from Galveston to England and back. Harry may have been an Australian.

Joe Hollinger★ — Louis met him while with the Hagenbeck & Wallace Circus, where he ran the "privilege car." A couple of months later he shipped out on the *S.S. Steadfast* with Louis. This was in the mid-1920s.

Captain Douglas★ — Captain of a ship in Indonesia that Louis served on. A three-masted auxiliary schooner.

Joe Hildebrand★ — Louis met him on the docks in New Orleans in the mid-1920s, then ran into him later in Indonesia. Joe may have been the first mate and Louis second mate on a schooner operated by Captain Douglas. This would have been in the East Indies in the late 1920s or early 1930s. Joe may have been an aircraft pilot and flown for Pan Am in the early 1930s.

Turk Madden* — Louis knew him in Indonesia in the late 1920s or early 1930s. They may have spent some time around the old Straits Hotel and the Maypole Bar in Singapore. Later on, in the States, Louis traveled around with him putting on boxing exhibitions. Madden worked at an airfield near Denver as a mechanic in the early 1930s. Louis eventually used his name for a fictional character.

"Cockney" Joe Hagen* — Louis knew him in Indonesia in the late 1920s or early 1930s. He may have been part of the Straits Hotel–Maypole Bar crowd in Singapore.

Mason or Milton* — Don't know which was his real name. He was a munitions dealer in Shanghai in the late 1920s or early 1930s. He was killed while Louis was there.

Singapore Charlie* — Louis knew him in Singapore and served with him on Douglas's schooner in the East Indies. Louis was second mate and Charlie was bos'n. He was a stocky man of indeterminate race and if I remember correctly Dad told me he had quite a few tattoos. In the early 1930s Louis helped get him a job on a ship in San Pedro, California, that was owned by a movie studio.

Renee Semich — She was born in Vienna (I think) and was going to a New York art school when Louis met her. This was just before World War II. Her father's family was from Yugoslavia or Italy, her mother from Austria. They lived in New York, where her aunt had an apartment overlooking Central Park. For awhile she worked for a company in Waterbury, Connecticut.

Ann Steeley/Cathy O'Donnell* — A friend of Louis's in Oklahoma in the late 1930s (Ann Steeley was her real name), she later went to Hollywood and had a career in the movies.

Aola Seery — Friend of Louis's from Oklahoma City in the late 1930s. She was a member of the Writer's Club and I think she had both a brother and a sister.

Enoch Lusk — Owner of Lusk Publishing Company in 1939, original publisher of Louis's *Smoke From This Altar*. Also associated with the National Printing Company, Oklahoma City.

Helen Turner\* — Louis knew her in the late 1920s in Los Angeles. Once a show-girl with Jack Fine's Follies.

Frank Moran — Louis met him in Ventura when Louis was a "club second" for fight-ers in the late 1920s. They also may have known each other in Los Angeles or Kingman in the mid-1920s. Louis ran into him again on Hollywood Boulevard late in 1946.

Jud and Red Rasco\* — Brothers, cowboys; Louis met them in Tucumcari, New Mexico. Also saw them in Santa Rosa, New Mexico. This was in the early to mid-1920s.

Olga Santiago — Friend of Louis's from the late 1940s in Los Angeles. Last saw her at a book signing in Thousand Oaks, California.

Jose Craig Berry — A writer friend of Louis's from Oklahoma City in the late 1930s. First person to review *Smoke From This Altar*. She worked for a paper called the *Black Dispatch*.

Evelyn Smith Colt — She knew Louis in

Kingman at one point, probably the late 1920s. Louis saw her again much later at a Paso Robles book signing.

Kathlyn Beucler Hays — Friend from Choctaw, taught school there in the 1930s. Louis saw her much later at a book signing in San Diego.

Floyd Bolton — Came to Choctaw and talked to Louis about doing a movie in the Dutch East Indies. This was in the late 1930s.

Lisa Cohn — Reference librarian in Portland; family owned Cohn Bros. Furniture Store. Louis knew her in the late 1920s or early 1930s.

Mary Claire Collingsworth — Friend and correspondent from Oklahoma in the 1930s.

C.A. Donnell — Rented Louis a typewriter in Oklahoma City in the early 1930s.

Mary Drennen — Friend and correspondent of Louis's during World War II, he saw her or corresponded with her in Des Moines, Cedar Rapids, Dubuque, La

Crosse, Minneapolis, and Chicago.

Duks★ — I think this was his last name, probably a shortened version of the original family name. First mate on the *S.S. Steel Worker* in the mid-1920s. I think he was a U.S. citizen, but he was originally a Russian.

Maudee Harris — My Aunt Chynne's sister.

Parker LaMoore and Chynne Harris LaMoore★ — Louis's eldest brother and his wife. Parker was secretary to the governor of Oklahoma for a while, then he worked for the Scripps-Howard newspaper chain. He also worked with Ambassador Pat Hurley. He died in the early 1950s, and although we know most of the positions he held in his professional life, we have very little information about him personally. Chynne was his wife and she lived longer than he did, but I don't know where she lived after his death.

Haig★ — His last name. Louis described him as a Scotsman, once an officer in the British-Indian army. Louis says he was "an officer in one of the Scottish regiments." Louis knew him in Shanghai in the 1930s, but we don't know how old he would have been at the time. He may have been involved in some kind of intelligence work. For a while, he and Louis shared an apartment that seems to have been located just off Avenue King Edward VII.

Joe Davenport — Louis heard of him in China. In the early to mid-1930s he was to deliver a shipment of guns and ammunition to General Ma but was killed before he could make the connection. He was once a U.S. Marine.

Milligan — A pilot in China in the mid-1930s. A friend of Haig's. We think that he saved Louis's life by getting him out of the country. Born in Texas, once a U.S. Marine.

Lola LaCorne — Along with her sister and mother, was a friend of Louis's in Paris during World War II. She later taught literature at the Sorbonne, and had (hopefully still has) a husband named Christopher.

Dean Kirby — Pal from Oklahoma City in

the late 1930s who seems to have been a copywriter or something of the sort. Might have worked for Lusk Publishing.

Bunny Yeager — Girlfriend of Dean Kirby's from Oklahoma City.

Virginia McElroy — Girl with whom Louis went to school in Jamestown.

Eleanor and Geraldine "Jeri" Medsker — Sisters from Shawnee, Oklahoma. Louis knew them in the late 1930s. Louis last saw Eleanor at a book signing in Thousand Oaks, California.

George Russell — Friend of Louis's from Kingman in the late 1920s, married one of the Von Biela sisters.

Any of the Von Biela sisters — Louis knew them in, you guessed it, Kingman, Arizona.

Arleen Weston Sherman — Friend of Louis's from Jamestown, when he was thirteen or fourteen. I think her family visited the LaMoores in Choctaw in the 1930s. Her older sister's name was Mary;

parents' names were Ralph and Lil; Ralph was a railroad conductor.

Merle Templeton — A man Louis knew from Kingman. He ran a rodeo for Bill Bonelli in Los Angeles. Bonelli was a political figure of some sort.

Harry Bigelow — Louis knew him in Ventura. He had a picture taken with Louis's mother, Emily LaMoore, at a place named Berkeley Springs around 1929. Louis may have known him at the Katherine Mine, near Kingman, Arizona, or in Oregon.

Tommy Pinto — Boxer from Portland; got Louis a job at Portland Manufacturing.

Percy E. "Steve" Stephens — Louis knew him in Kingman; he was married to Alice Von Biela. Louis saw him again at a book signing in Escondido in 1983.

Nancy Carroll* — An actress as of 1933. Louis knew her from the chorus of a show at the Winter Garden in New York and a cabaret in New Jersey where she and her sister danced occasionally, probably during the mid- to late 1920s.

Judith Wood — Actress. Louis knew her in Hollywood in the late 1920s.

Stanley George — The George family relocated from Kingman, Arizona, to Ventura, California, possibly in the late 1920s.

Francis Lederer* — Actor that Louis knew in the late 1920s in Los Angeles. He may have been a Hungarian and was acting in Hollywood as late as 1933.

Anyone familiar with Singapore in the late 1920s, the *old* Straits Hotel and/or the Maypole Bar.

Anyone who is very knowledgeable in the military history and/or politics of western (Shansi, Kansu, and Sinkiang Provinces) China in 1935–37.

Anyone who served on the *S.S. Steel Worker* between 1925 and 1930.

Anyone who served on the lumber schooner *Catherine G. Sudden* between 1925 and 1936.

Anyone who served on the *S.S. Steadfast* between 1924 and 1930.

Anyone who served on the *Annandale* between 1920 and 1926.

Anyone who served on the *Randsberg*, a German freighter, between 1925 and 1937.

Anyone who knows anything about a short-lived magazine published in Oklahoma City in 1935–36 called *Uptown Magazine*. A photocopy of any issue of this magazine would be very interesting to us.

Anyone familiar with the Royal Government Experimental Hospital in Calcutta, India.

The employees of Thorndike Press hope you have enjoyed this Large Print book. All our Large Print titles are designed for easy reading and all our books are made to last. Other Thorndike Large Print books are available at your library, through selected bookstores, or directly from us.

For information about titles, please call:

(800) 223-2336

To share your comments, please write:

Publisher
Thorndike Press
P.O. Box 159
Thorndike
ME 04986